Wise Creatures

KU-175-561

HOT
KEY
BOOKS

ALSO BY DEIRDRE SULLIVAN

Perfectly Preventable Deaths
Precious Catastrophe

Savage Her Reply
Tangleweed and Brine
Needlework

Wise
Creatures

First published in Great Britain in 2023 by
HOT KEY BOOKS
4th Floor, Victoria House
Bloomsbury Square
London WC1B 4DA
Owned by Bonnier Books
Sveavägen 56, Stockholm, Sweden
bonnierbooks.co.uk/HotKeyBooks

Copyright © Deirdre Sullivan, 2023

All rights reserved.
No part of this publication may be reproduced, stored or transmitted
in any form or by any means, electronic, mechanical, photocopying or
otherwise, without the prior written permission of the publisher.

The right of Deirdre Sullivan to be identified as author of this work
has been asserted by them in accordance with the
Copyright, Designs and Patents Act 1988.

This is a work of fiction. Names, places, events and incidents are either the
products of the author's imagination or used fictitiously. Any resemblance
to actual persons, living or dead, is purely coincidental.

A CIP catalogue record for this book is available from the British Library.

ISBN: 978-1-4714-1120-5
Also available as an ebook and in audio

1

This book is typeset using Atomik ePublisher
Printed and bound in Great Britain by Clays Ltd, Elcograf S.p.A.

Hot Key Books is an imprint of Bonnier Books UK
bonnierbooks.co.uk

For Clare Wallace

The girl is looking at you.
Her back is straight.
Chest out.
Her eyes . . .

her eyes are haunted.

things that almost touch you in the night

Sometimes I feel I'm mostly made of spaces. The early parts at least – whole chunks of childhood with these yawning gaps. It's probably a good thing really. Only sometimes, without warning, they grow mouths, attack me. Razor sharp. Images that take my breath away. That leave me reeling.

Shards of broken glass on the surface of a road.

My friends from school, when they tell stories about things that happened back in the day, will say, 'When I was a kid . . .' But I kind of feel like I was never a kid. For as long as I can remember, there's been something very old and tired inside me.

A part of me I keep behind a wall.

That isn't for other people.

That isn't really even for myself.

What I call my childhood in my head is the time before I came to live with Susan and Nina. When I lived with Mam and Dad.

And Them.

a thing that will not die

Nina probably knows the most about me. Definitely more than other people do. And part of it is that we're sort of sisters, or that's what everyone assumes at first. We're actually cousins, which is only complicated because it means they want me to go into how and why and who. Show them the pieces of myself that hurt me most. Mam and Dad. The accident. Separate myself from them with tragedy. And after that, I'll always be the person who was taken in.

An exposed throat.

That doesn't mean I don't care about my other friends – Megan, Conchur, Abigail and Piotr and everyone – or that they don't know me. They know the me that I want people knowing. The me I am now. Not who I was back then. Not the broken, frightened, messed-up parts. Susan says there's no need to share more than I'm comfortable with. That we all come into ourselves in our own time.

I kind of feel like my own time is never.

The people who know you best can hurt you most.

When parts of me that I don't like spill out, Susan says that there is nothing wrong with it, that I'm no different from anyone else, it's just that bad things happened to me when I was young and that changes the way I move through the world. It gives me something to carry, that other people may not have. And sometimes it's a light thing, like a handbag, but other times it's heavy like a rock. It's there, and it is hard. It's not my fault, she says.

She wasn't there.

I let her hug me, and almost believe her.

Until I'm by myself.

Then in it creeps.

Susan is the closest thing I have to a parent. My father's sister. The person who is supposed to take care of me. She never liked my mother, who is dead. Susan thinks it's a good thing my mother is dead. She doesn't put it as bluntly as that, but I have a lot of experience reading in between the lines of people. The pauses between words. Tensions and tilts.

She hated *her.*

Sometimes I think that I should hate her too. But nothing is that simple, is it, ever?

Susan says things like 'It's not your fault' and 'No child should have been put through that.'

Nina says those things as well. It's the story she's always been told.

Neither of them were there, inside my skin
while it was happening.
On the day when everything went.

Tap

Tap

Tap

Tap

Bang

questions you can't answer

I'm watching Nina arguing with air. It's oddly compelling. She's taking a pro-war stance, which isn't very Nina, but you don't get to decide which side you're on in debating. Her hair is wrapped up tightly in a towel, while she goes on about violence being the only language some people will understand. Her face is uncharacteristically vicious, and I snort.

'Daisy?'

'Nina, I once saw you apologise to a flower for picking it. And now you're literally quoting John Rambo. Who isn't even a real person.'

She nods, as though I was giving her constructive feedback.

'I need more pro-war quotes. I normally like to throw a poem in, but all the best ones are anti-war.' Her brow is furrowed as though this is a genuine problem.

'I wonder why.'

'You're not helping,' she says. 'I want to get this right. Last time, we were up against St Columba's and I choked.'

'You didn't choke. Piotr says you were good.'

'Not good enough.' Her face is dark. 'I want to wipe the floor with them the next time.'

'So maybe you are pro-war. Just not the weapony kind.'

'Hmmm. I wonder if I could do something with that. I must ask Mr Q.' She smiles.

I smile back.

'It's kind of nice to see you *out for vengeance*,' I say.

'It's not very on-brand. I will give you that. But this year there's been so much welling up that I just need to let stuff out, you know?'

I nod. I mean, in theory it sounds good, but there are certain things you can't release. Things that need to be housed deep down in the meat of you, away from other people. Behind a big thick wall. I'd never, like, debate the way that Nina does. Even overheard, an argument can make me squirrelly.

'I think you're going to be great,' I say. 'Just get better quotes.'

She nods. 'Will you blow-dry my hair before it?'

'Of course I will. You need armour.'

She grins. 'I fully do. For school as well. Basically I should just be wearing a full suit of armour at all times.'

There's something in her face.

'Was school hard today?' I ask.

'What? No,' she says. 'Well, no harder than normal. I wrote a lot of this at lunchtime.'

'You should just come down and sit with us,' I say.

'I do have friends, Daisy.' She doesn't sound convinced.

'I know you do, Nina. But my friends are kind of better. I hardly ever choose extra-curricular essay writing over them.'

'It's a debate.'

'No, Nina. It's a fact.'

She sighs the sigh of a girl who has to put up with a lot. An accurate sigh. Then she gazes out the window. Her face relaxes and she looks like a still image, or a painting, presumably of a person thinking deep thoughts.

'Daisy?'

'Yeah.'

'The light is really good.' She hands over her phone. 'Would you mind?'

I roll my eyes. For a shy person, she surely loves to take pictures of herself.

I take about five, and she looks through them.

I see her face begin to fall, and fall.

'What? Will I go again?' I ask.

'No.' She holds out her phone. 'It's only this.'

Memories. A photo from a year ago, when there were four of us instead of three.

'It doesn't seem like a year ago,' she says. 'But it's a completely different life as well.'

'Not that different,' I say. 'We're still us.'

She shrugs. 'I suppose so. But I don't know. There's bits of me that are just different now. And it was a small enough thing. I mean, like, no one died.'

She says this to me a lot when she complains. I think she thinks she's checking her privilege, or recognising what I've been through or something. She doesn't understand how complicated it is, to lose someone you're scared of. How it hums through everything. That sense that it was maybe all my fault.

I wanted her to stop.

And then They stopped her.

things that never got the chance to die

After Caroline broke up with Susan, we moved out of her house and into this one. It was a hard time for our family, particularly Susan, who loved Caroline. And Nina, who believed that love endured. When we lived with Caroline, we were in an apartment, but a big, swishy one with art on the walls, two spare rooms and a balcony. It had been two apartments back in the day, and Caroline bought the both of them and turned it into one giant one, long before she met Susan. She didn't have any kids of her own, and wasn't exactly a 'kids' type of person. I liked her but I didn't love her. I could see the writing on the wall. She wanted a different sort of life to the one we had. Susan relied on her too much. You can't do that with people. There was a part of me that was waiting for it to be the three of us again.

We don't fully know what happened between them; we got a whole spiel about growing apart, but by the end they didn't even really want to look at each other, and since the split Caroline has been away for work so much. Well, away for work or just not wanting to see myself or Nina. And it hurts. I do miss Caroline. She could be funny. She made Susan smile.

It wasn't like we were kicked out on the street. Caroline said we could stay as long as we wanted. But in adult-speak that means about six weeks max, apparently. And the house was tense. Not that it wasn't before, when they were almost broken up, but having your home be tense is different to having your home suddenly not be your home at all. In the end Susan found this place, on an estate that was half built and half being developed, outside of town. It smelled of cement and plaster. One other family had lived here before. We don't know who they were. But they had children, because when we moved in first, there were all these cartoon Disney eyes gazing through a coat of off-white paint in my room. Nina wouldn't sleep in there at all.

Susan used to always have time to talk and now she never does. She's working longer hours and she constantly looks like she's in a hurry. When we moved here first, I couldn't sleep, and I got really clumsy in the daytime, like dropping things, or spilling them. And I could feel her getting angrier and angrier each time I did it but that only made me do it more. No one was sleeping properly, and I would hear her walk around at night, or see the coffee cups in the sink the next morning. It was like we were in two separate fish tanks or something, and I was beating at the glass of mine while she was just trying to keep swimming. I do better now, and I try not to bother her with stuff, to do the dishes, hoover the carpets if I see it needs to be done, and she smiles at me and thanks me and ruffles my hair, and it feels a bit like getting back to normal.

At school, myself and Nina just pretend. I mean, I haven't talked about it much with anyone, and I don't think she has either. We don't have friends over now though, either of us. It's not something we talked about, it kind of just happened, and I think it means that we feel the same kind of way about everything. We didn't have to change school, which I suppose is a plus. I mean, if we'd had to move county or hours away that would have been much harder. But Nina doesn't like this house, this life. And I get it – it's a lot of change, a lot of sadness.

When you're unhappy, bad things can creep in.

I get this thing sometimes when I'm asleep but don't know I'm asleep. It feels exactly like I've woken up. Can see the borders of my room, the dim shape of the furniture, just the way it always is. But there is something else there as well. Nothing as definite as a shape, it's like a flicker in the corner of your eye. Only my eyes are all corners. This presence traces the boundaries of my room, and I can feel the shiver of something not unfamiliar pushing against the wall inside myself I've worked to build. Flesh puckers, and sweat beads and I can't move. I cannot make a sound. When I was very small, Dad built a new wall in the garden, and my skin got scraped against it. I remember looking down at broken skin, grey dust, some of it in me, some of me in it. That's how it works when something gets too close. It hurts like that. It doesn't really leave you.

'Sleep paralysis,' Susan says it is, because of what happened. My 'trauma'.

But it doesn't feel like trauma.
It feels like someone's there.
Someone I know well.
Someone who hates me.

I close my eyes and try not to let any of it in. Try to keep it all walled up. Contained. It isn't real, like Susan says. These strange beliefs left behind from what Mam did.

The creatures.

an exposed throat

Nina is sixteen and I am fifteen but people often think I'm older than her because she is tiny and I am very tall. I wasn't always. When I was ten I took a stretch. Before that we could share clothes, and sometimes convince people we were sisters. Proper sisters. I mean, I know there are blood sisters who look nothing alike. But it was more fun lying when the lie felt plausible to us.

When I moved in with them, and Dad was there as well, I used to be so scared. I'd wake and feel like he would be there, looking at me, and I would have to lie there motionless until the danger passed. I thought when he was gone that feeling would go too, but it didn't. Nina said that I'd be safe with her, and even when I wet the bed she would still let me crawl in beside her, damp and stinking. I never woke Susan. She kept telling me I could but I didn't want to get into trouble. Nina would stroke my hair and hum to me and I would fall asleep and wake beside her. I don't know if that's sisterly or motherly but I do know that it made me feel safe in a world that was so dangerous.

Is so dangerous.

Nina showed me that not everyone who loves you is out to get you. She can tell you a hard truth in such a gentle way, it numbs the sting. It's why it makes a weird sort of sense that she'd be good at debating. But I don't know if competition suits her. She takes things to heart. Loss written on her face before she speaks. I can always tell when she is hurting.

This world could carve her up
so easily.

I can be gentle too. I mean, I'm not a monster. I'm guarded though. There is a distance there.

The wall inside me.

I wonder how much of that is because of my training, the way that my mother conditioned me to see people as flawed things to be preyed on. I can be really warm to them, and kind. Make them think I like them, make them trust me. Bit by bit. Of course it isn't real. I remember after a client left, she would put the kettle on and I would have a hot chocolate and she would have a tea and she would talk to me like I was special. Money in her pocket warmed her up, I suppose. And I loved that, but there was another feeling there as well, a sort of fear. That next time would be different. There was never a way to get it right. With her.

With anything.

Mam's fingers were very red, almost purple sometimes. And dry. Her knuckles white as she gripped the cup. And she would look at me with her pale blue eyes and ask me questions. Sometimes she would jot the answers down in her notebook. She had a notebook where she kept details of all the people who visited us. How long. How much. Exactly what I'd told them. Before someone came again, we would prepare for them.

We didn't need to.

There is so much I don't remember though. Nina says that's normal. She only has a flash or two from when she was little as well. But that's different. She has Susan and I have . . . other things. Dad is still here, but he's also not been himself since the accident.

Tap

Tap

Tap

Tap

Bang

a puzzle

Nina gets back early from debating. I see her walk up the driveway, her shoulders high, like halfway up her neck. It must be colder than it looks outside. It takes about five minutes before I hear her key turn in the lock, probably not a good sign. She stomps into the hall, hangs up her coat.

'How did it go?' I ask.

She smiles, but it's a tired sort of smile. Her eyes are sad. 'Oh, fine. You know. The usual way. We said emphatic things. And we were judged.'

'Who were you up against?'

'Some guy named Odhrán. Loved our nation's history, and doing this.' She gesticulates wildly.

'He sounds great. You shall surely marry him.'

'I shall surely shan't.' She crumples on the sofa. 'Teaaaaaaa.' Nina loves tea that other people make her. She claims it tastes better.

'I'll put the kettle on. But only because you have moved me with your compelling argument.' I get up and walk to the kitchen, taking down the mug Susan got her last Christmas, which is shaped like a snowman's head and holds about two and a half regular mugs of tea. I empty half a packet of biscuits into a bowl because she's out this evening and she told me to do something about dinner.

Nina's face is pressed against the arm of the sofa when I come back in.

'Am I interrupting something?' I ask.

'I was having a think,' she tells me. 'Not about the sofa though. About, like, secrets.'

'Yeah?' I curl my legs underneath me on the fattest armchair and stare at my chocolate digestive. It melts a little on my fingertips.

'You know the way you don't talk about all the stuff that happened, with Aunt Therese?'

'Yeah,' I say again, but this time in a very different tone.

'Does it ever, like, well up in you? I mean . . .' She spreads her fingers wide, and closes them again, right into fists.

I put my biscuit down. 'I know what you mean, Nina,' I tell her. 'And no. It doesn't.'

I won't let it.

'But you never feel, like, the need to talk about it? I mean, sometimes keeping things in is just . . . hard, you know?'

I swallow. She doesn't mean to hurt me. This is Nina. I take a breath and count to five, and do that one more time.

'It was so long ago,' I say. 'I barely remember any of it now. And when I try, it's hazy. And I'm grateful for that, Nina. Why would I want to drag that stuff up? It would only make it bigger, and more real. And then bad things would happen.'

Horrid things.

'They wouldn't though.' Nina's voice is soft. 'We wouldn't let them.'

18

'Why take the chance?' I say, and smile at her, like my heart isn't racing, and take a bite of the biscuit. I feel it disintegrating against the roof of my mouth, forming a thick paste. I swallow.

Ivy growing slowly up a wall.

It will cover everything eventually.

when family stops being family

Dad doesn't like it when I visit. I can see it written on his face. The tension in his brow, his jaw, his shoulders. The strain of being civil to his child. Susan says I remind him of a time before. When he was able for more things. That could be it. He does get very jumpy, glaring, shuffling. I can't work out how this man is the Dad that I remember from before. Strong arms holding me up to touch the lampshade in the sitting room. Snuggling into a soft blue scarf around his neck. On a little seat at the back of his bike and my heart in my mouth at the excitement of it. Scrambled eggs. When Mam was away we'd have scrambled eggs on toast for dinner. Cheese on top.

Blood and not my blood on my small hands.

We only visit every second week because more than that would be too draining on the both of us. They sold the house we lived in when I was little to pay for his care. That money's going to run out eventually, and I don't know what will happen then. Susan doesn't talk about that stuff, and part of me is very glad of that. I can see it ticking through her brain now, more and more since we moved out of Caroline's. She plugs everything out before we go to bed, gets angry when we leave lights on. Cuts the toothpaste tube open so we can use up every single bit. There's nothing wrong with any of that stuff, but I don't like the tightness around her mouth. She's trying to look relaxed for Dad right now, but it isn't real. I do the same thing though, around him. Try to smile. To keep the fear at bay.

Susan used to talk about him a lot when I was little. As if he'd died. I think she wanted me to know the person she grew up with and not who he had become since the accident. She would tell me the music he liked (Tom Waits, Van Morrison), the pranks he'd played as a child (he loved putting dead flies in things and offering them to people to eat), what made him laugh (people falling off things, cats that looked like they had facial hair), what food he preferred (mild curries, with naan bread instead of rice, lasagne and potatoes). I wonder if she does the same for him when she visits by herself, telling him who I am. I can't really imagine him wanting to listen though. Is that bad? I'm not picking at him or anything but . . .

You can tell, can't you?
When someone wants you gone.

It's not his fault. He's not able to mask his emotions as well as he used to be.

It's why he doesn't live with us any more.

He would get violent.

I remember him flipping the table.

Nina crying.

Susan yelling at us to get out of the room. Standing between him and the pair of us.

It wasn't Nina he was trying to get to.

He can't help what happened to his brain. Susan can't help that we couldn't both live in the same house. She had a choice to make and she chose me.

I was less work than Dad.

At least at that stage.

He's in a flat now, 'independent living', which is better than the home. Someone comes to check on him most days. A carer. That's good, I suppose. I want him to be happy. Blue scarf against my face and big strong arms. I remember feeling really safe when he held me. Like nothing would dare harm me. Not with Dad there.

Red purple hands around the cup, my throat.

I remember it was my second year of primary school, and I had homework and it was hard to do it because they kept coming to the house, the people. Sometimes I would stay at home to see them. I wasn't allowed to tell my teacher about it. I wasn't allowed to tell my friends. I didn't have any friends though. Not till Nina.

I was scared of what would happen if it slipped out so I stayed very quiet in school. The things that worked with adults didn't work with kids. They didn't want to know the dreadful things I knew. Dying grannies, fathers planning to leave, mothers losing their jobs, houses going to go up in flames thanks to an electrical fault. A sister who would drown in their neighbours' pond when her Auntie Monica was supposed to be looking after her.

All the things my mother must have told me. There is no other way I could have known.

That wall inside.

Susan and my dad grew up on a farm but no one lives there since my granny died. They couldn't sell it. Susan keeps the keys in a little box on the windowsill. She likes to have them near, in case we decide to go, for the weekend. We never do. I don't know why no one wants to buy it. I always really liked it there. Felt safe. I remember I had these little yellow wellies and I would walk over to the hens with Nina and Granny Maude. And they would stare at us with their beady little eyes and bob their heads. I thought that they'd say 'cluck' like it was a word.

Things don't go the way that you'd expect.

They would peck at the ground and at the seed and sometimes at each other. Sometimes they'd peck so hard that they'd draw blood. Granny Maude had baby chicks there too and she had a little sort of oven for them, but not to bake them just to help them live, an incubator, I suppose you'd call it. They looked all neon red and they would step on each other to get to the food she had.

Like people.

There's no point though, is there, in remembering the past. Even when I bring the good things up, the bad stuff comes up too, all entangled, like hair clinging to a plughole, or pondweed wrapped around a rescued artefact. I try to live as though my life began when I was six and a half. As though Susan were my mom, Nina my sister. It's a coping strategy, and I've gotten really good at avoiding reminders and questions. There are some I can't avoid though.

Was it your fault?

Like Dad. I have to visit him, even though we'd both prefer I didn't, I think. It's the right thing to do. Susan says it's the kind thing to do. But I don't think it is. There's a big part of me that would rather have the memory of a safe pair of arms than the reality of a flat that smells of disinfectant, watching him make me a cup of tea slowly and deliberately.

He never turns his back on me.

Not even for a second.

We talk about sport, and I read up on matches and things before we go, so I have something to say to him. I want to say, *I'm sorry*. I want to say, *It isn't fair what happened*. I want to ask if he is happy or if he wishes he had died as well. I think that it must be really terrifying to be in a body that used to be able to know and do things, to control itself, and then have that change. He remembers what it was like before, Susan says. He talks about it sometimes to her. But never to me. We don't talk about before, me and Dad. I think we are alike in that. In wanting to keep away from whatever led to the accident.

When I was little he told me not to look directly at the sun or it would blind me, and I think it's a bit like that. It's there. We can't ignore it. But we can pretend we can. If that makes sense. I know it doesn't really.

When I was a child he used to hug me.

a glimpse of something other than yourself

There's something going on with Nina. A change in her, the past few weeks. An absence.

'You're only picking at your dinner, loveen,' Susan says.

Nina puts a massive chunk of potato on her fork, chews it down.

'Delicious,' she says flatly.

Susan looks at me, a question in her eyes. I shrug. I've no idea. And even if I had, I wouldn't be running to tell her. People need their privacy. Their time. Nina's nails are perfectly manicured. She used to just let the colour chip off flake by flake, but now she's very specific about keeping them perfect. They shine like plastic. I look down at mine. They're just bare nails, cut short.

Nina was like this when we first moved here, but things have been better, so much better. There are dark circles underneath her eyes.

'Did something happen at school?' Susan says.

Nina shakes her head.

Susan tries again. 'Love, you can talk to me. I know I'm stressed, but I'm still your mother.'

'I know that.' Nina smiles. It's not her real one.

Susan squeezes her shoulder. 'Good.'

I rinse my plate and put it in the dishwasher, then start washing the saucepans. Nina gets up to help. Takes the tea towel. Susan goes into the sitting room to watch TV. She's tired as well, I think. I click the kettle on and scrape rice off the bottom of the saucepan.

'Daisy?' Nina says.

'Yeah?'

'You know the ghosts you used to see?'

'Not see, exactly,' I tell her. Feeling the flesh on my arms begin to pucker.

'You had a name for them.'

'Why are you asking me about Them, Nina?' I say, breaking up the congealed chunks of food caught on the plughole.

She knows that I hate talking about this.

Does she want to hurt me?

She bites down on her lip so hard I almost taste the blood.

'I'm sorry. I shouldn't.'

Something in her voice.

I close my eyes. She needs this from me, for some reason. Now. I try to be detached. To just get through it. Her heart is broken. She's not thinking right.

She loves me.

And this isn't about me.

She's hurting me.

I have to try. The water isn't draining. Dirty grey with chunks of scum on top. I get a brush, scrub at the gathered food. I do not look at Nina.

'Daisy, please.' Her voice is very small.

I take a breath.

. . .

'The creatures.'

Shaping Their name furs my tongue with something old and wrong. It's over now. It's done. It wasn't real. I touch the cool metal of the sink. Keep my fingertips on something solid.

'Yeah. I remember visiting you and wanting to see them and being disappointed.' She smiles, and I smile back. It's not my real one either.

I swallow and I try not to lie. Try to think back to the things I've told people before. The gardaí at the time. My social worker.

'It's like Susan says – a mix of things. The way my mother was. And the attention.'

Was it?

'What was it like though, seeing them? You *saw* them.'

I shrug. 'No, not really. It's hard to explain. I just knew They were there. But it was Mam.'

Nina frowns, halfway between sympathy and disapproval. 'I know. But, like, when I was little I had an imaginary friend. Called Peppa.'

I look at her, and shift my weight from one foot to the other.

'I wonder where you got that name from, Neen.'

She grins that helpless grin.

'I know. It wasn't *Peppa* Peppa. She looked a bit like Sita from primary school and always had her hair in two bright bunches with sunflower scrunchies on them. If you believe in something hard enough, you do end up . . .'

'Seeing it,' I say.

27

And I did see Them.
Not often, mind.
But every now and then.
There would be . . . something.

Nina's face is intent and her long dark hair hangs like a curtain down one shoulder. She gets that from her father. He is Spanish. He came to Ireland for college and moved back after he'd finished his postgrad, in spite of Nina. Susan will only say nice things about him, but there's a lot in what she doesn't say. They're not in touch.

I swallow.

'It was . . .'

I reach my brain back there but hit a wall. The dishes are washed now, we're walking up the stairs towards my bedroom. And there is something in her eyes. A question I don't know the answer to.

'. . . I can't remember, Nina. There are parts of it that are very sharp. But the specifics of what They looked like, how They sounded when They told me things. I can't quite reach it.'

My palms against the surface of the wall.
Tracing the rough stone.
Waiting for a little pulse of something.

'But what would they do?' she asks, her fingers combing through her long dark hair, pulling out dead strands and rolling them up into little tumbleweeds that litter the carpet and irk Susan no end.

'They would tell me things about the people who visited and I would feed those things back to the people, who would give my mother envelopes with money in. Sometimes They

28

would be straight in with telling me, like as soon as the person came into the room, or even beforehand, but other times I'd need to hold the person's hand for a while and kind of call Them to me. Like my skin needed to be on their skin. Does that sound creepy?'

Nina nods. 'But interesting too. That's primal. Skin on skin. What did it feel like? The calling?'

I can't.

'I don't remember,' I say.

'Try,' she says, and something in her voice makes me want to answer her. To give her something. I rummage through my nightmares. The ones that keep me pinned against the bed. A butterfly.

'Intense. Like I was willing all the hairs on my skin to stand up. Like my hands were cold but the breath on the back of my neck was roasting hot.'

And her eyes on me always always always.

'Could you still do that?' Nina asks, rolling the hair she's collected between her finger and her thumb. Her nails are the red that people call blood-red, when blood-red is a lot of different colours. The hair has ratted into a small ball. A little spider.

'. . . like, call them?'

. . .

'It wasn't real,' I tell her.

It wasn't real.

'I know. But if you wanted to, could you still be a psychic?' She says it like it's something glamorous, but it wasn't. It was dingy. In the kitchen, sitting down with strangers, trying to

29

filter everything right, worrying in case it wouldn't be good enough to get the little bit of love she had for me.

I don't drink hot chocolate any more. Even the smell of it can make me nervous.

'Like, trick people for a living?' I ask with a smile, but Nina's face is serious.

'I mean like find ways to know things about people without them telling you.'

It didn't feel like I was tricking anyone.
It felt like I was the one being tricked.

I shrug. 'I guess. I mean, there's a lot people say without saying it directly. Like with their behaviour. You know what roads to keep on going down and when to turn back.' It's easier to talk about this part of it. The part that I still use.

She's nodding, as though I've given her something that she wants. I hope I have. I hope that it has helped.

My skin feels itchy.
I hope she doesn't know.
What this has cost me.

And then she asks me if I know Austin Quigley.

a stranger you can hate

Susan drives us to school, and I look at Nina's head in the front seat. Her long dark hair. Her secrets. I am still trying to wrap my head around what she told me about Austin Quigley. I didn't understand who she meant at first. In school, everyone calls him Oz. I feel a bit annoyed she didn't tell me what went on while it was happening. He asked her not to, if it could just be between them until they felt sure of each other.

'It made sense, the way he put it,' she told me. 'Like, when he laid it out, it seemed like being open about it would be stressful, and kind of kill it. And it was kind of fun, to have something that was just ours.' She smiled, her gaze somewhere over my shoulder, remembering.

Neither of us are smiling now. It's manipulative bullshit, how he acted. Is he doing this to other girls? It doesn't really matter. Nina matters. She's not okay, she's hurting, she needs help. I don't know what to do. Last night she said, 'Just be here for me, Daisy. Now you know.'

I scratch my knees through my tights and want to ask her question after question. I used to be able to read her so well. When did it change? When did she start to lie?

She doesn't want Susan to know anything about it.

31

'Mom has enough on without my broken heart.' She was tapping her fingers on my bedspread and I watched them move rhythmically up and down and up and down again. I can't believe all this was going on and I didn't spot it. I wish I had. It seems like Nina needed someone to know. She told me that she wants to cry, like all the time, but it's like her tears are all backed up. They won't come out.

'It's welling up in me, every single minute of the day, and I just can't. And I think it would be good if I could, you know? For the release.' She picked at a little thread sticking out from a button on her sleeve, and I looked at it and thought that it was going to fall off, but didn't say anything, even when it did. She didn't seem to notice. It might still be there, nestled in the carpet.

I nodded at her, as if I knew what she meant. And I do, maybe a little. I keep a lot inside me. But I don't want to let any of it out really.

'You're very quiet, girls,' Susan says, pulling up at the school gates. 'It's refreshing.'

She smiles as though she's told a funny joke, and I smile back. That's what she seems to want. We hop out, and make our way towards the entrance.

'I just have to say –' I say to Nina.

'You have to say nothing.' Her eyes are wide now, fierce. 'Not. A. Word. Don't make me regret telling you.'

'Fine,' I say. 'But just so you know, I have double geography first class and it's going to be very, very stressful. I won't know where to look, like.'

Oz Quigley is my geography teacher's son. He and Nina bonded because he hangs around a lot while his dad works with

32

the debating team. They hooked up, and then it kept kind of happening, and then Nina asked him if they were ever going to tell people, and he asked her for nudes, got them and then ghosted her. A keeper.

'Look at the whiteboard, Daisy. You'll do fine.'

'Easy for you to say.' I glower. I am right. Geography is almost impossible. Mr Q is blathering on about coastal erosion and I'm sitting on my hands because I want to punch him in the face so bad. I mean, not that it's his fault that Oz did that to Nina. Except maybe it kind of is. He could have been fooled though. It's not like people tell their parents everything. And Oz Quigley is good at seeming nice. He's big into the school pride committee, and I had assumed he was gay because he wears rainbow pins, but that apparently was bi-phobic of me. Which is weird because I'm bi myself. Conditioning, I guess.

I wonder if it's bi-phobic of me to call him a massive prick. Or run him over with a car. I can't drive, but I don't think it would be that complicated, if all you wanted to do was really, really hurt someone. It's safe driving you need the licence for. It wouldn't be a hate crime in the bad sense. It would only be a crime I did because I hate him. Mr Q is high-fiving Piotr for remembering what longshore drift is. I look back at my textbook, hoping that he doesn't ask me a question because I have been too busy plotting the murder of his only son to pay anything like my normal level of attention. Mr Q is nothing like his son; he looks a bit like a roadie for a metal band. I haven't met many roadies, but I've seen them in TV shows and there's a bang of techie off him too – like the people who do the lighting and the set stuff for plays and things. Piotr is a little bit like that. He likes gadgets, and explaining them to people. It's not a bad thing.

Lots of people say Mr Q is their favourite teacher, maybe because he talks about his life outside of school a bit. I find it a little cringey. But he organises a good field trip and is more interesting than if he just talked about the GDP of Norway and what grikes are and other geography things, I suppose. He's also big into debating, and he coaches the teams before they go to give out to other schools. Nina calls it competition, but it's basically arguing but where you don't get to pick your opinion. Even the thought of it makes me nervous, arguments are dangerous things to have, but Nina likes it, and Mr Q was kind to her when everything went down with Caroline, she said. Which is more than I can say for Oz. A monster.

How could anybody hurt Nina, who is an angel here on earth? I mean, telling her not to tell anyone, not to post anything about it, and asking her to take down things that didn't even have anything to do with him, just in case someone joined the dots that weren't there. Really horrible controlling behaviour. And Nina did it, because she didn't want to lose him and then he just cut off all contact with her anyway. Blocked her on everything. It's brutal.

'Daisy?'

Fuck.

'Longshore drift!' I exclaim, and everyone laughs. Mr Q smiles at me.

'At least you were half listening,' he says. 'Now, pay attention.'

'I will,' I say. 'Sorry, Mr Q.'

That was pretty nice of him in fairness. It's not his fault his son is basically a monster.

I can't see the two of them together, Oz and Nina like. It doesn't track. I've been mildly (okay, fully) stalking him online to try and get a handle on it. And I can't. I don't even know where they would meet up in school. She said there are places, but she wouldn't give me any more information. She just said *places*, like I'm supposed to believe her that there are all these secret rooms in the school where people can go to clandestinely get with each other before one of them steps all over the other one like she was a piece of trash and not a human being.

He's good-looking. Not hot. Not cute. But good-looking. He's tall and kind of strapping, and he has excellent posture. He sometimes messes with his hair, which is a bit like Nina, I suppose, but not enough to explain this deep connection she says they had. When he realises that's what he's doing, he puts his hands in his pockets. He has the chin of a cartoon policeman, or possibly a lumberjack. He seems to really like stationery. His locker was very tidy when I broke into it first thing to shove a handful of prawns in the back. I got them from the freezer this morning. I think that they were there when we moved in. We're not a big prawn family. I left them in a crumpled bag of Salt and Vinegar Tayto. Salt-and-vinegar is his flavour. It'll probably take a week or so before they really permeate his books.

I'm more of a ready-salted girl myself. But you can't get ready-salted Tayto.

Nina says I'm not allowed to kill him. Or denounce him publicly. But she's in bits. Still off her food, which I don't

35

like. When she got sad before, she didn't eat much either. I don't want her to feel like that again. It frightens me. She does and doesn't like talking about it. The Oz thing. I ask her questions and sometimes she has answers and other times she just starts to cry, and I feel bad for going on about it. There's just something about it. I want to, like, build a big murder wall of how wrong he is, with lots of red string, to make it see it's not her fault. Because she thinks it is. She read me some of his messages, and they are definitely flirty, though in a weird way. He calls her 'an old soul'. Which I don't like, as compliments go. I mean, maybe to a boy who looks like he stepped out of a black-and-white film about healthy fellows that would be appealing, I guess, but still . . .

Old souls can be dangerous things.

'I'm also invisible now, apparently,' she says on the walk home. 'He won't even nod when we pass in the hallway.'

'I know,' I say, and she gives me a confused look so I pretend I only said, 'Oh no,' and haven't observed him blanking her three times in the past few days. I should get a notebook. I mean, she wouldn't like the idea of me having a special stalking notebook, but it's for her own good. Sort of. I don't know. I'm probably going too far. But this has thrown me.

It's not like her at all. I bottle everything, but Nina lets it spill. Another reason why she likes debating. She can always find a feeling, and the words to express it. It's almost insulting to think of her having a secret like this. I don't mean to be weird or needy or any of the things I know I can be, but it makes me question our closeness when she can keep a whole relationship secret. Not that Oz called it a relationship. And of course it's over now. I'm mad at him for hurting her, but I'm also kind of mad at her for hurting me, if that makes sense. And maybe that's unfair, but there it is.

She's still so sad.

We walk in silence side by side until we reach the bus stop. I just want to know what she's not telling me, you know? And that probably makes me some kind of hypocrite, because there are parts of me I just can't talk about at all. Like my mam. It feels like talking about her makes her bigger, stronger. Lights a candle in the window of everything that happened to me. I was too young to remember all of it; it feels like a stained-glass window in a church. An image here, an image there, and thick black lines between the panes. Gaps. Something shattered in me, and now I am just pieces of myself. Bound together by I don't know what. Necessity.

You have to keep on going.

I would touch people. And I would listen. If all that came up was something they wouldn't want to hear, I'd ask Mam if I could have a glass of juice, and she'd get it for me to give us both time to think. Sometimes lights would flicker, or toys would be in the wrong places. But that's from bad electricity or adults tidying up after me, isn't it? None of it was real.

You can't know that.

I look at Nina's hand, hanging limply by her side. I could reach out and take it. Squeeze her arm, and see if something clicked. But that wouldn't be right, even if it worked. It would be a bit like stealing. If I did it.

She meets my eye and does a small brave smile. It starts to rain.

37

an ailment, a complaint

Nina wouldn't go to school today. She told Susan she was sick but she isn't sick, not really. Just sad. I crept into her room last night when I heard her crying, and she just shook and shook like a leaf.

'I just don't understand how he could . . . I wish, I wish he would just talk to me. Just see me, look at me, like really look. Because I know he's not for me. We couldn't. But the abruptness of it. Sharp.'

'A guillotine,' I said to her.

'Yeah, like that. But without warning.' She clutched her stomach. 'It hurts, Daisy. It hurts here, as well as here.'

She touched her heart.

'I didn't expect it to be a physical pain as well as this sadness, you know?'

'I could run him over with Susan's car?' I offer.

'Thanks for continually offering that, Daisy. Remind me to never get on your bad side.'

I rubbed her back.

'We only kissed five times,' she said. 'Isn't it silly? And here I am. In bits. It makes no sense.'

'You are allowed to feel the way you feel,' I tell her, rubbing and rubbing her back, around around, as though she were a dog that needed petting. The way that Susan sometimes does. It wouldn't work for me at all – I'd hate it, but Nina seems to like it, being touched. I close my eyes. My hand brushes the skin between her waistband and her pyjama top.

She's not telling me everything.

It isn't silly to love somebody. I've never been in romantic love. Nina hasn't either. Until now. It looks painful. Why couldn't he just be with her for goodness sake?

She's not his type.

'I'm so cold, Daisy,' Nina tells me. 'So very cold. I wish I could feel warm.'

I know that wish.
I feel it in my bones.

a shadow in the corner

When people are sad, sometimes they just have to be sad, and all we can do is love them and wait for it to lift. This is according to Susan anyway. We're worried about Nina – she hasn't moved from the bed since Monday, even for a shower. Susan took the day off work the first day, and kept asking her if she was okay, if she needed to talk, or go to the doctor. Nina kept on saying she was fine, that she just needed rest. Susan went back to work because she had to, but I could see the worry on her face, just like before. She brings up toast as soon as she gets home. Checks in.

She's worried something will happen.

I go into Nina's room after school, and her voice is thick in her throat.

'How was it?' she asks.

'Fine,' I say. 'It's school.'

There is a pause, and I wonder if that was the right or wrong thing to say.

Nina takes a sip from the smudged-looking glass of water on her bedside locker.

'I didn't see him,' I tell her. 'Oz.'

She picks at the loose threads on the duvet cover.

'I know who you meant.'

I nod. 'Of course you did.'

The air is thick in the room, and I want to open up a window, release whatever's keeping her contained. She scrolls through her phone, and her face looks very drawn and pale all lit up by the screen.

Another person could say the right thing, give her a hug, and tell her it will be okay in a way where she'd believe it.

It will not be okay.

I just ask her if she wants a cup of tea, and take the plates and discarded pyjama tops downstairs with me. I have a lot of homework to do, but I can't start it when she's like this. Her distress would hum at me through walls, be so hard to drown out.

It was a day where everything was off, even in school. The words the teachers said seemed stilted, like I was watching remotely and the signal was bad. I tuned in and out, shook my head and tried to stay awake, alert, present.

It didn't really work. Megan asked if I was okay six or seven times, Abi twice and Conchur and Piotr one time each, so I suppose it was obvious to them that something was up, and there is. It is awful seeing Nina sad, worrying about her sinking into something like despair, wondering what to do. Like, I can't just make Oz like her back again, and even if I could it wouldn't fix this. Also he is the worst person in the world and I can't even tell anyone, because Nina would hate that almost as much as I hate what he's done to her. It's exhausting.

But apart from that, I am okay. It's fine. Nina being sad is big, but also small. In the scheme of things. Piotr was in a horrible mood too, because his little brother had been up all night with teething, and they share a room now his auntie lives with them, so if Alek doesn't sleep, neither does Piotr.

'I wish I could just sedate him, you know?' he sighed.

'Please don't sedate your baby brother, Piotr.' Megan sighed. 'It won't end well.'

They met my eye and looked at me the way they sometimes do, like there's a joke that we both get. A small warm moment. It made me feel the way I wish that hugs did.

'There's just too big an age difference for us to be sharing.' Piotr sighed too. 'I mean, he's my brother, like. Not my son. Fingers crossed Auntie Leona will get a job and be able to move out soon.'

I held up both my hands, with the fingers crossed and curled around each other, and he smiled.

'If I got just one night's sleep, I think it would help.'

Megan rubbed his back. 'It's hard,' they told him.

He smiled at them and nodded. 'Yeah, but it'll be fine. It's a small thing. A small tyrannical insomniac thing.' He bit into his sandwich as if it had done something to him.

I rubbed my eyes and squinted. It felt like too much light was going in. I swallowed it.

Everyone has something.

Sleep or brain or heart.

Susan asks me to set the table and I do, for three. When I go up, Nina is curled underneath the covers again, and I see the bulk of her, and just for a second it seems like something's off.

How do I know it's her?

It could be anyone.

42

something that you almost wouldn't notice

Susan made Nina go in today. She woke up, made herself a coffee, looked at me and said, 'This can't go on. I need her to be supervised. I'm at the end of my tether with the stress.'

I thought about what a tether meant. It's a rope, isn't it? For horses. Like a noose.

A rope around my neck.

Susan's face changed in front of me. Something shut down. Like the way she gets when she has to unblock a drain. She rolled up her sleeves and stomped up the stairs, calling Nina's name.

Nina moaned, 'I'm tired.'

'So. Am. I,' Susan said. 'That doesn't mean that I can just check out. Of work. Of life. And you don't get to either.'

I could hear the exhaustion underneath her words. Since the split, she's constantly on the edge of something. Holding everything together so tightly that sometimes it veers towards a crushing, a squeezing. She dragged Nina out of bed with her hands under her arms like she was a sack of spuds. She said it was what the Americans would call tough love, but I don't think it was her finest hour, parenting-wise. I mean, I wouldn't call it abuse, but it definitely wasn't sound.

Nina called it abuse. 'This is *abuse*,' she said loudly to Susan.

'I look forward to hearing from your solicitor,' Susan snapped, looking for her car keys. They shook out into my bowl when I poured my cereal.

'That's weird,' I said, fishing them out before I added milk.

'How did they even get there?' Susan asked us.

Nina shrugged, scowl still in place. Scowling doesn't suit her. She couldn't even hold it that long. She finished her breakfast in the car, brushing crumbs off her jumper as we made our way through the car park to the big grey building. My year is mainly based in the fancy new extension, but Nina's is in the blocky old bit that hasn't changed in decades, where the chips on the wall expose like five different old paints. It's a bit like a time machine.

I have Mr Q for geography and then Ms Prendergast for double English, so the morning goes by okay. Mr Q told us about an apartment building he investigated back in the day, which had been built in the grounds of an old Magdalene Laundry. There were noises and cold spots, and in the mornings people kept finding things moved around on the counters. Apparently it was mice and one weird neighbour in the end. Mr Q investigates ghosts, but he's not a big believer in them.

'Most of the time there's something else going on, underneath the surface. A source of pain. That said, I wouldn't be arrogant enough to definitively say there's not more to it, sometimes,' he said. 'But you have to look for a mundane explanation before you get the sage out.'

Abigail raised her hand.

'I'm aware of your opinions on sage, Abigail. It was just an expression.'

She put her hand down again, but her face said, *It's not over*.

Poor Mr Q. I mean, Abigail has a point. She always does. She's curious about so many different things, and when she cares, she keeps on caring, like she cannot help it. My stomach gurgled, and I thought of the car keys in my cereal. Probably full of bacteria. Maybe I should have thrown the rest of the box away.

I learned a bit more in Ms Prendergast's class, probably because her son didn't just break my best friend and sort-of sister's heart. We looked at poems, and I thought about Nina, and how many feelings she has welling up and out of her. She writes poems the odd time, and she doesn't show them to anyone but me, but if she did it would not surprise anyone. At break I hang out with Abigail and Piotr and Conchur and Megan, and kind of nod along.

I saw Oz Quigley three times: on the way to PE, when I'm getting my science book from my locker and when I'm waiting for Nina at the gate. He looks at me like I'm strange, and in one way it's understandable, because if someone from the year below me started eyeballing me like I was a French aristocrat and she was a sans-culotte I'd be a bit disturbed. But if it were me it wouldn't be my own fault for toying with the affections of the best person in the world bar none. I make a mental note to do something else to him. Not prawns in the locker again, because the smell is really lingering and our lockers are close by each other. But something that says, *You have a powerful enemy*. In a subtle way.

Nina doesn't go to debate practice today and so we get to go home together. We miss the bus and end up walking home. It takes forever.

'Are you going back to the debate team?' I ask. 'Like, is this a quitting kind of not going or a sad kind of not going?'

'I just think it would be awkward,' Nina says, fiddling with the bottom of her plait.

'He mightn't even be there – he's not on the team,' I offer, smiling hopefully.

'No. But someone put prawns in his locker and now people are joking that he has a stalker, and that's not great.' Her tone is calm, but I can see the anger in her eyes.

'I'm that someone,' I say. 'Happy to take credit. Besides, you're vegan. You'd never hurt a prawn.'

'Did you not think that maybe that wasn't the best way to make me feel better? Like, Daisy, he could accuse you of bullying him if you keep at this.'

'It's not bullying if it's vengeance,' I say. 'Obviously.'

'I don't think Sister Agatha would be big on vengeance.'

'She would. It's in the Bible,' I say.

'Ugh. Stop trying to distract me from being angry.' She does a sweeping gesture with her hands. 'It's childish and stupid and I don't want it and you have to stop. Okay?'

'Okay, Nina,' I say, swallowing back the sting of what she said. 'I lost my temper. I mean, your heart is broken. This is bad.'

'Yes, but it's not publicly bad. Just privately. No one knows about it, and now it's over I kind of want to keep it that way.'

'I do understand that, but have you considered that maybe ALL SHOULD KNOW OF HIS CRUELTY?' I say, doing very emphatic hand gestures.

'I know you mean well, Daisy –' Nina looks down at her feet – 'but I was being foolish, catching feelings. I read too

46

much into something that wasn't even a thing, you know? That didn't mean anything to him. And shouldn't have to me.'

'You care about the people you care about, Nina,' I tell her, 'and that's a good thing. I just . . . It makes me angry, what he did. I feel like he deserves to get hurt too.'

'He really doesn't. And even if he did, that's not up to you.' She reaches out a hand to grab my forearm, which makes me flinch. 'Sorry. Promise me you won't do anything like that again.'

I growl, because I tend to keep my promises.

And then she stares at me until I nod.

Ugh.

'Have you told anyone else?' I ask. 'About what happened?'

She shakes her head. 'There's no one I can tell really. I feel like an idiot. I just keep thinking about the pics I sent him.'

'Were they like *extremely* nudie pictures?' I ask, using the term Susan did when she gave us the talk.

'Not like porn,' she says with a grimace. 'But not ones I'd want anyone seeing.'

'He's probably hanging on to them for his wank bank,' I say, nodding sagely.

'DAISY! You are in no way making me feel any better.' Nina looks annoyed.

'I'm sorry,' I say. But in my head I am thinking about those photos of Nina and how I could get my hands on his phone to delete them off of it. Because it's a bit of a violation, isn't it, to have them once he's started treating her like she doesn't exist? There shouldn't still be pieces of her that he can use.

'What are you thinking?' Nina asks. And I don't want to admit to plotting revenge or phone heists after I'd promised to leave him alone so I told her I was thinking about bears and then we had a conversation about bears and how Abigail wants to get a massive tattoo of a grizzly bear on her back when she's older and not living at home any more.

'Abigail would.' Nina smiles, and I'm not sure if she means that as a good or a bad thing. I think it would look kind of cool to be honest.

'What would you get a tattoo of?' I ask her. 'Probably like some really girly nonsense like a sprinkle of stars or a meaningful garland of flowers.'

She smiles again. 'Exactly! What would you get? A pond skater. Or a saucepan?'

'My special saucepan!' When I came to them first I had a saucepan from the old house and I would sleep with it and carry it everywhere, the way people do with a teddy bear. I still have it, in the top drawer of my bedside table.

We carry weapons with us to feel safe.

Susan isn't home when we get back so we put on the heating, start dinner and our homework. We're really responsible. She's lucky with us, Nina refusing to go to school aside. And that only lasted a few days.

Her fingers digging into Nina's shoulders, her voice shrill.
Anyone you love can turn against you.

nothing you can put your finger on

I dreamed last night that I was back in the house I lived in with Mam and Dad. I came up to my mother's waist, and when she hugged me my face pressed against the warm roughness of her jumper-covered stomach. She smelled the way my mother used to smell. But I had all my memories from now. It hadn't happened yet, but it would happen.

We were in the kitchen and she put me sitting on one of those chairs we had, the hard white ones with padding. I swung my legs. They didn't reach the floor. My throat was dry. I wanted juice but I was scared of spilling.

The door swung open and a man came in – older than Mam maybe – his hair was grey. His face was drawn and he wanted to know about his wife. I closed my eyes and focused on the air around me. They were there, always. They just wanted me to look at Them. To listen. I touched the man's hand and began to speak. I didn't understand the words my mouth was saying. It was my voice but I wasn't using it. It was Them. Not me. They knew so many things I didn't know.

There was a pause, a silence. The man's face twitched, and Mam put a hand on his shoulder and looked at me. I had to say more things. I was so tired. But I tried again, putting my hands flat on the table and screwing up my face. If I scrunched it up really tight I could cling to the inside of my brain and I could hold on to the edges of myself, filter out the bad stuff from the good stuff a bit better. The creatures kept on saying things to me.

In me.

It's in her organs now, I told him. *She will die, and you will live and your son will grow up wishing it was the other way around. You aren't good enough. You never have been. No wonder your own mother hated you.*

I woke up sweating. Any time I dream about Mam I wake up sweating after, and the memory lingers on me all day long. I want to get it off me. I want my mam but never all of her. Just the safe bits. Because there were times I really felt she loved me. In her arms, her hands stroking my head and telling me to *shush it's all right*. The soft wool against my face. The warmth of flesh through it, and that sense of home. Of something right. That, more than any of the other things she did, is what haunts me.

That want.

There is an instinct that you cannot fight. To burrow into someone that you love, and make a home of them. The creatures spoke to me, but not in words that people could understand. It was like another language. One I could translate. Clicks and taps and creaks and squeaks and whistles. Sometimes gentle, sometimes louder, more insistent. There are psychics that have one spirit that's attached to them, a sort of guide. I think I had more of this sense of dread. A heavy presence

50

that knew so many answers people wanted. But the air was heavy when They were in the room. It coated my tongue, my throat, as though there was a stench in the air, but there wasn't, just this sense of something there that hated me and wanted me and loved me.

Tethered to my side for good or ill.

I still don't like people's eyes on me, but in a way I do. I hunger for it, for that sense of validation that I used to get when their gaze widened and their mouth opened and they leaned closer to me, or further away depending on how scared they were. And of course I remember more of it than I let on. But there are things I'll never understand.

The taste of adult things in my child's mouth.

Mam's eyes on me.

The intensity of it.

I had to get it right. Or else.

Or else . . .

And maybe Susan has a point; that it was all her, doing things to me. That what I am remembering is stories that she told me, lies she wove, pressure that I should not have been under. But.

I still find myself sometimes. Wishing for those moments when she loved me.

The girl stands in a bedroom. The duvet cover is purple and the bed is badly made. There are three decorative mirrors on the wall and some prints in frames, line drawings of animals with rich watercolour skyscapes behind them. There are photographs and miscellaneous items stuck around them, coasters and cut-outs and cards. A napkin with a lipstick kiss. A feather. She is cupping an enormous mug of something and her voice is lowered. There

*is an intimacy to the way she speaks, as though she is letting you
in on a secret. Her long dark hair is parted in the centre, tucked
behind her ear on the left side.*

'So. It's been happening again. I feel weird posting this, but I
want someone to see what's going on. This . . .'

She holds up a pen.

'. . . keeps falling off the shelf.'

She puts it on the shelf. It stays on the shelf.

'Well, it's fallen off like five or six times now. I don't . . .'

She takes a deep breath.

'I don't trust things to be normal any more. You know? Every
night there's something different. Last night it was noises, like
a sort of rattling, scratching sound. Like when a cat is stuck in
a cupboard. But we don't have a cat here. I mean it could be
mice, I guess. But I don't think we have those either.

*Anyway, it's cold, even though the heating is on, and my pen
has been repeatedly falling off the shelf, even though it's not doing
it now, which is typi—'*

—

–

-

The pen falls off the shelf.

'Oh. Would you look at that?'

*The girl's face is neutral. Her eyes dart from side to side and
then she speaks again.*

'I don't know how to feel. The shelf isn't slanted or anything.'

*She moves you closer to the shelf. You look at it. It is a normal
shelf, with a pen no longer on it.*

'Huh.'

a girl, just a girl

Screams pierce the night. I startle awake, close my eyes and try to slow my breathing. Are they real, the remnants of a dream? They keep on coming and oh God, it's Nina.

I run out of bed, right to her room. She's sitting up, still screaming. Rhythmically, repetitively. Pausing for a breath between each one. She was shivering all through dinner, went to bed early. Susan said she might be coming down with something, but she said it grudgingly, as though it suited Nina to be sick. She's already in with her. I meet her eye, she looks worried, all resentment gone. She hugs her child, her head curled tight against her shoulder. She murmurs to her, 'You're okay. You're okay, love. I'm here. I'm here. I'm here.'

Nina is still screaming, screaming, screaming. Her breath coming high and fast, so harsh it must be cutting up her throat. I reach a hand towards her. Before my fingers meet her skin they stop and hover awkwardly. I move my hand away, and Nina looks at me, her pupils shrinking to pinpricks, as though I was a flashlight in her face. She looks the way I feel inside, those nights when I am trapped in my own body.

'Daisy.' She gasps. 'Daisy. There is something.' She points to the wardrobe. 'There's . . . something. The door.'

Susan says, 'I've checked. I didn't find . . .'

I look at the door. It's half open. I walk over and close it.

'It opened by itself,' Nina says. 'I saw it happen.'

'It was just a dream, love,' Susan tells her. 'Shhh now. Shh.'

I look down at the carpet. There is a purple sandal on its side. I hold it up.

'It could be this fell out. Maybe they were balanced weirdly or something.'

Nina shakes her head. 'It wasn't that. It wasn't.'

Susan sighs. 'What was it then, Nina? Like a ghost?'

And then I shiver too. I wish she hadn't said that. Nina's screams, they call to other screams. The world before.

Her hands on my shoulders in the bath. The cold, dry skin.

We all have ghosts.

'It could be rats,' I say helpfully.

'Ew, no.' says Nina. 'Definitely not.'

'We do not have rats, Daisy,' Susan snaps. 'After the year I've had they wouldn't dare.'

They both look around the skirting board nervously, their faces mirroring each other. People have a real thing about rats, which I suppose is fair. I'm not a huge fan either. I don't want one biting me, but I kind of wouldn't mind if they were in the house. As opposed to ghosts. Or the idea of ghosts. With rats, you can get someone in to put poison down or something. I see the traps for them all the time in school, especially in winter.

With Them, I was the poison.

And They loved it.

Susan rubs Nina's hands between her own. 'You're cold as ice, love.'

Cold as the grave.

I swallow. Nina's hair is plastered to her face like she is sweating. Something doesn't fit. This isn't right.

'My stomach hurts.' She clutches it. 'Like I'm getting my period. Only I'm not.' She pulls her knees up against her chest and hugs them in. I rub her back, and then go down and make her a hot water bottle and a cup of tea. A hot water bottle and a cup of tea can basically fix anything. It isn't science, but there are things that science can't explain. I really hope this isn't, like, a thing that will keep happening from now on. I don't think I can sustain this level of soundness about being woken up for more than a night or two. I push the air out of the bottle and tighten the cap. I hug it to my chest and climb the stairs, trying not to let the worry in. The gap between the doors of Nina's wardrobe.

It doesn't take that much
to let Them in.

In the bedroom, all the lights are on now. Nina is calmer-looking, and thanks me for the tea. Susan smiles. 'I'm going to take my big baby into my room for the night.' She rolls her eyes. 'I thought those days were over.' But I can see she likes it in a way. Her little smile. The gentle way she rubs Nina's back, she looks just like a mother should. Like comfort. I smile and ask Nina if she's okay now, she nods, and we all say goodnight. It's 4 a.m.

If I opened up my mouth and screamed and screamed and
screamed
I wouldn't stop.

I lie in bed, thinking about the wardrobe in Nina's room. It's not the big, oak-style wardrobe with carvings that you would expect a ghost or a Narnian lad to hop out of. It's that white plasticky sort of wood. It's nothing. Just a fright mixed with a sandal.

It's not nothing.

I stare at the ceiling and look at the cracks in it running one into the other like a map of waterways or blood vessels. If I wake up I don't go back to sleep, my brain's too busy. Everything seeps in.

So many broken hearts under one roof.

softly, slowly, quickly

At breakfast Nina doesn't want to talk about what happened, and we are gentle with her, as though she were a puppy cowering beneath a chair. The cereal boxes are all upside down in the press so when I take one out for my bowl of cornflakes it spills all over the floor and Susan gets pure thick with me, saying:

'There has to be a logical explanation for this.' And glaring at me, as though I am that explanation. When she's annoyed, she gets exceptionally curt and it hits me in the stomach, makes me feel uneasy and unloved. It's like the lack of sleep is now my fault.

Maybe it is.

I find myself being even nicer and more chatty than I usually am to try and make up for what Nina did last night. I put everyone's cups and plates in the dishwasher and set it going.

I put ghosts in her head.

She isn't hurting cause of me though. It's what happened between her and Oz Quigley. The way he acted. It makes sense, if it was someone, for it to be Nina. Her world is all messed up. And when you're in pain, it can't help spilling out of you, one way or another. I don't say anything about that to

58

Susan though, just quietly rearrange and sweep things up. I get the sense that if I put this into words, I will not like what happens next. This low-level hum in my stomach, as though I do not have my homework done. I turned the cornflakes box the right way round, but left the others. I didn't want to make things any worse.

But I always do.

On the way into school, I see Oz Quigley vaping near the bike rack. I'm not surprised. He is a terrible person making terrible decisions. He'll get in trouble for it, maybe even more so because he's a teacher's son. I wonder should I, like, tell on him? I couldn't though. It would feel wrong. I would much rather target him in my own petty way, with stalking and inconvenient prawns. I shouldn't have done that. It was childish. I should have known to keep myself in check. I look him up and down, wondering where he keeps his fucking phone. He raises a hand and glints in my direction a little. I smile back at him, for Nina's sake, my hands fisted in the pocket of my jacket, and try to hide that I know who he is, and what he did.

Her screams.

Her screams.

stories people tell

Piotr asks me if I've seen what Nina has been posting. And I say no and he says that maybe I should look. Takes out his phone. I can see Megan biting their lip and I realise they've had conversations about whether or not to tell me. I look down, and Nina is talking about how cold she is. In the background I can see these little orbs of light, small and delicate as fireflies, wisping around.

The next video is Nina talking about the first video, asking in a frightened voice what those lights in the background are.

'Your sister's having some sort of breakdown,' Conchur says.

Abigail doesn't touch me, but she sits close enough that she could, and I can tell by the look on her face that she'd hug me if I asked. I hate being touched by surprise. I got enough of that when I was younger.

'She's not having a breakdown.' I feel a bit defensive. 'Weird things *are* happening at home. I mean, I haven't seen any lights, but things do keep turning up in random places, and she was really cold last night even though the heating was on and everything.'

'I get really cold even when the heating's on,' Abigail says. 'That doesn't mean I'm haunted.'

'Is that what she's saying she is?' I ask.

'Not directly,' says Piotr, keeping his voice annoyingly reasonable. Part of me would love an excuse to yell right now, but it would do no good. The wrong impulse. 'But other people are saying plenty.'

'Okay,' I say, taking in everybody's faces, and trying to work out exactly what they want from me.

Okay.

The girl is looking right at you.

'Last night,' she says, 'something happened.'

Her mouth is wide but it is not a smile. She lifts a hand and gestures to her wardrobe. Moves you closer.

'This door –' it's a fairly cheap-looking normal wardrobe – 'opened by itself. But it shouldn't open by itself.'

She closes it.

'Like, even if I . . .' she tilts the wardrobe forward, with some effort, 'do this, the door stays closed.'

She puts it back.

'So I don't think like a shoe or a falling jumper could do it. And I can't think what else would. It really scared me. But in the middle of the night everything feels a bit bigger, you know. If any of you have an explanation that's not me being haunted, I would love to hear it!'

She smiles and shrugs, but her expression shifts back to something harder to read. She shows you the wardrobe again. The door is very white but there's a shadow running down the centre. She moves you closer and closer to it until it fills the screen.

stories that need telling

Nina won't admit she's doing anything strange, no matter how much I poke her with my shoe. It's frustrating. We're in the sitting room, watching a show about good dogs, because she needed something 'pure but not romantic'.

'These things are happening, Daisy,' she tells me, pulling it off and sitting on it. 'You need to stop. The other day my mascara flew across the room and hit me in the forehead.' She rubs at an imperceptible bruise. 'And, like, when I do something I do tend to post about it. Like when I learned to do bullet-wound make-up for Halloween. Or when I baked flapjacks. It's not, like, a cry for help.'

'Flapjacks and dress-up are more normal than this though.' I want to get my shoe back, but I sit on my hands instead because she looks at me and sighs so deeply that I can feel it in my bones.

'I know.'

As soon as she got home she changed into her blue pyjamas with the swans on them and a big grey hoodie, which is a sure sign of something being wrong, her needing this whole day to just be over.

'Are you sure about all this?' I ask. 'Because we haven't

talked about it, really. And it's weird people telling me about something that's happening with you that I don't know, you know?'

She meets my gaze. 'It's happening,' she says. 'It's happening. I mean, you've noticed it too, right? The forks in the vase, the cereal boxes, the car keys . . . all these small odd things. They're adding up.'

I swallow, but I nod to acknowledge something in her eyes. I do not say, I think that this is you, you're doing this. I do not say that I do not know why.

When They were here
They lingered like a stench.

'Daisy,' she says, her hand around my wrist, and suddenly I'm part of this as well.

'I think it's getting worse.'

It will.
It will.

The girl is in her room again. This time one of the mirrors is cracked. She looks at it.

'That happened last night. The sound woke me up.'

She runs a finger over one of the cracks, then pulls her finger back.

'I think I cut it!'

She holds it up. Blood wells. She sticks her finger in her mouth.

a spy

Susan asks me if Nina is all right.

'I keep trying to talk to her but she just wants to show me evidence of . . .' She shrugs, and makes a general wavy gesture with one hand.

It's not the kind of thing you can shrug off though. This morning when I came downstairs, all the furniture was upside down. Even the kitchen table. I put it back, as though it never happened. Because I didn't want Susan to be upset, to spend my breakfast wondering if Nina is a liar when I could just eat my toast. Make it not be. When she came down the stairs, she looked at me. Her features didn't flicker. But there was something . . .

'Daisy.' Susan's voice cuts through my thinking. 'Can you see how difficult this might be for us to manage? If this keeps going. If you know something, anything at all, you tell me, right? Or if . . . if there's something you . . . sense?'

My mouth feels dry. My ears are hot. I just . . . I don't know what to say.

Does she think it was real?
Believe in Them?

'Susan.' My voice comes out more hurt than angry. 'I'm not. It wasn't like that.'

You are.

She smells it on you.

She sighs, and I see the guilt on her face. It doesn't quell the panic in my chest.

'I know you're not . . . I don't know why I said it. It's just it's my only other experience of anything close to . . . whatever this is. A mother getting desperate, I suppose . . . It's just . . . I'm worried, Daisy. Nina never gave me a day's trouble before all this, you know?'

I nod, thinking of all the trouble I have sent her way over the years.

When I was with Susan and Nina first, after Dad moved out, I was so careful. I was worried they'd send me back like a cake with hair inside, but it came out. The night terrors, wetting the bed and sometimes I'd feel so scared or angry I'd have to hit out or tear at something. The insides of a pillow, the paper on the walls. Banging my little saucepan on the floor over and over until it got all dented. It was like the me of me went somewhere else and all the things that I had been through just spilled out. I always felt sick after, thinking of Dad being sent away and how that was all my fault, and now I was making life harder for everyone and would Susan do the same to me?

She could.

She would.

She will.

That was my biggest fear. Being sent away.

My second biggest fear.

The girl's hair is wild and her eyes are full of tears.

'I woke up and there were all these THINGS in the room,' she says. 'Can you see them?'

She holds you up and you see little coloured orbs floating through the air. They could be motes of dust. They could be something.

'I just want to be able to sleep,' she says. 'But this keeps happening.'

Behind her, something slowly falls off the shelf that she says things just fall off.

You cannot see her hands.

angry things and sometimes cruel

Nina has three raised red marks burrowed into her skin, meeting at the bottom of her spine.

'I didn't feel anything,' she tells us, 'until the water hit them in the shower.'

Susan looks at me and her face is haunted. I search for what she could have used to do it and find a little pointy tweezers beside her mirror. I don't even know what a pointy tweezers like that would be for, what kind of hair.

It could have made those marks.

Tearing at herself to get the pain out.

But it feels disloyal to think that. Searching her room at all feels disloyal. Like I was trying to catch her in a lie. Like I wanted to find her out, tell on her. And I don't.

But I don't want this, any of this, to be real.

Because if it is, my memories might not be liars either. I saw myself, curled over the surface of her mirror. Found myself afraid to meet my eyes.

Ms Leenane takes my phone off me for searching poltergeists in double Irish.

The Irish for ghost is *taibhse*.

A poltergeist isn't the same as a ghost though. It's not a person.

Or they don't think it is, the investigators online, the ones I've read at least. They call it more of an entity. A presence that was never a person at all, that feeds off our emotions, causes chaos. I scroll and scroll through stories people tell.

A vase flies across the room, barely missing my head. When I look back at Nina she is gazing at me, mouth open.

'Did you see that?' she says. 'Did you see that? It just flew.'

It's not a question. I touch the part of my head it almost hit and rub it just as though there were a mark. I didn't see her though, just the vase. She could have thrown it.

But would she do that, so close it could have hurt me?

People hurt each other all the time.
It's easy, and gets easier.
With practice.

a talisman, a threat

Susan comes home with buckets of white roses. Arranges bunches of them in every room. She has a little bundle of herbs as well. She lights it, wafts the smoke from room to room. It isn't sage.

I watch her do it.

And I don't feel anything.

I've worked hard to leave my ghosts where they belong. That thick stone wall inside me.

Away from anybody They could hurt.

The milk is curdled in the carton when we pour it, even though there's supposed to be three days left. My tea is ruined. I pour it down the sink.

This is all Oz Quigley's fault. I mean, he probably didn't know that being cruel would lead to ghosts, but at the same time he shouldn't have been cruel.

When Nina talks about the stuff she says is happening her face gets this intensity about it, like it does when she is debating.
She wants us to believe.

It pierces through me. And to be honest I want to believe it. I don't want her to have torn up her own skin, or thrown a vase a hair's breadth from my head.

Either I believe in this ghost (which I don't, not really) or I believe that Nina thinks we're all expendable. That her own body is expendable. In service of this creature.

Today he had his shirt unbuttoned way down low and everyone could see his chest hair.

I have a little patch of fur between my breasts. It's not thick, but it's dark. It's like thin ribs of arm hair but all close together. I don't want to shave it because Susan said once we started shaving our legs it would grow back thicker and I didn't believe her but it definitely looks thicker now than when we started shaving.

And maybe a ghost did that too.

Maybe a ghost did everything.

If that's what we're doing as a family.

When I come home one of the bunches of roses is already turning brown.

That's what happens, isn't it? When you bring dead things indoors.

The room smells of herbs and Nina is at swimming, where presumably she'll have a bit of a break from all this being possessed or whatever. I don't go swimming because I hate the sound my brain makes when my head is underwater. Reminding me of something rushing in.

At 3.33 in the morning all of our phones and Susan's alarm clock go off. Nina starts praying and Susan pulls her up to stand, tells her she is going to counselling whether she likes it or not.

'Ghosts aren't real.' Her voice cuts through the air.

I turn to her.
And it's like we both hear it.

Tap
Tap
Tap
Bang

She flinches.
I meet her eye until she looks away.

The girl says 'It's okay if you don't believe me. I wouldn't have believed me either, I think. It's just . . . It's just that it's happening and I don't know what to do or who to tell.'

A banging noise begins, and she jolts to attention.

Her eyes dart around the room, searching for something.

'I mean, is it so strange to think it might be ghosts? I'm not saying it is, I'm just not ruling it out, because I can't think of anything else it could be. I mean . . . a month ago I wouldn't have believed in them. But now. Things are so different. I just. I'd like some answers, you know?'

'Ms Finnerty was out today, we had free Spanish. I made this.'

She removes a piece of paper from a drawer and takes out a coin. She holds up the piece of paper, revealing it to be a makeshift Ouija board.

'I read you can use an old coin as a planchette,' she says. 'There's, like, a reindeer on this one. My uncle gave it to me when I was little – they used to use it back before I was born. When coins had animals on them.'

She holds it up.

'I don't know if it's real silver. I don't know how to tell something like that. I assume it isn't. But if there's a way to ask. How and why. Or who is doing this.'

Her eyes blink very fast.

'I mean, I have to try. I thought about asking Daisy to help me, but I think it would upset her. She hates this kind of stuff. You're not supposed to do this on your own, so it mightn't work.'

She places the coin down and puts her finger on it.

'I'll move it to hello. And kind of wait to see what happens.'

One minute passes by, then two.

'Ugh,' *the girl says.* 'Who are you? If you're even there.'

She moves the coin to goodbye and stands up, turning to leave the room.

Slowly the coin moves back to the hello position.

a victim

You can't kill something that's already dead. But people try things to protect themselves, like burning herbs, or praying. Placing black stones in the corners of a room.

Anointing thresholds with rosemary or chilli flakes. Or salt. They want to feel like they have some control.

Lying to themselves.

Nina says the GP 'didn't know what to do' with her. She gave Susan a list of counsellors, and the phone number of the local priest. 'Helpful, but no help,' was Susan's description. She looked as though she was about to cry.

I'm not surprised. I've scrolled through stuff about this so many times, looking for an actual solution. Something maybe Nina would respond to. And to be honest, it all seems like too little. This is bigger than her being sad. It's like she is a cloud, and everything is cold and fog around her. Susan keeps on trying to get her to go for walks. To exercise, and open up her curtains. She says, 'Just talk to me.' And Nina says, 'I am.' And gets frustrated. I watch them, and sometimes it feels I'm looking through a screen, a world apart as they perform love, and fear and feeling. I want to help. I don't know what to do. I can't do anything.

You can.

You shouldn't.

Susan's been replacing the roses as they rot, but the water they're in seems to smell almost right away. I wonder if there's anything you can put in the vase to make it do that. When I search all that I can find are little tricks to keep them looking like they're still alive.

'I don't believe in ghosts, Daisy,' Susan tells me. 'But, look, they'll do no harm.' She places Mass cards on the windowsills, and every morning they're scattered on the floor. I put them back and sift through smiling faces. Loved one after loved one. Of course my mother isn't there. Susan keeps looking directly at me when she says she doesn't believe in ghosts.

Because she's lying.

Abigail asks me about it, when we're walking to French together.

'How are you holding up?' she says. 'With the whole Nina-being-haunted situation?'

'Oh, you know.' I widen my eyes. 'FINE.'

She grins and fumbles with her locker. It's stuck.

'I think you have to kind of lift the door up,' I tell her. 'Like this.'

It works, and she looks at me. 'How did you know that?'

'Because you do it every other day,' I say. 'I think you're just distracted.'

'Hmm . . .' Abigail's face is wan. 'Yeah, maybe.'

'Everything okay at home?'

'Oh, you know,' she tells me. 'FINE.'

Her shoulder bumps my shoulder, and it startles me a little, even though I know she's being sound. Everyone in the group has taken me aside, basically and told me that they're 'here for me if I need to talk'. But I don't need to talk at all. It isn't practical. I need to think. To work out what Nina is doing. How to sort it.

I see Nina turning a corner ahead of me, beside her friend Yasmin. The two of them are talking and her face looks animated. There's something off about it though, a quality I cannot put my finger on.

Halfway through conjugating irregular verbs, I realise it's that for the past few months, every time I've seen her walking by me, she's been alone. And the weight of that hits me a little. I hadn't thought that Nina could be lonely, but of course she was, especially after everything changed. People haven't been easy for her, not ever, but she likes them anyway. And that's when it starts to make sense, about Oz. About what he did to her. Kind of like something a poltergeist would do. Sense an opening and creep on in.

He used her.

In some ways, maybe I should be grateful that I learned early on how to hide the awkward bits of me, show people a face they can get on with. I write a letter to my fake friend Adeline about the many tourist attractions she could visit here. About the beach. The park. I tell her my hobbies include reading, shopping and looking at films, because those are the things that I know how to say.

times that melt together

I should probably talk to Nina or something, but when I get home I'm so very tired. And how do you even start with, 'I just realised you're probably quite lonely, how's that working out for you?'

I scroll and scroll, looking for a hint of their relationship. Anything. His last few posts are from the time when they were supposed to be together, but there's no hint of anyone, and after that there's nothing at all. As if he disappeared from there as well. From everywhere.

I press the heels of my hands hard against my eyes until I feel like they're about to give and the insides of my eyelids get all twinkly. It's never just one thing. They sense each other. Crowd. *Mam's hands on my shoulders in front of the mirror. Making me repeat.*

I am open. Take me.
I am open. Take me.
I am open. Take me.

And the feeling of a gaze, a head tilt. Of Them.
Getting closer and closer. Until I could feel something against my neck that wasn't breath.

I have tried so hard to be the normal one. To get it right. And all of this is scratching at the wall, begging me to look.

After the accident, They were gone from me. Sometimes if I closed my eyes and focused I'd almost think I heard Them.

Very faintly.

Tired perhaps in the wake of what They had done. And so I stopped closing my eyes and focusing. Brick by brick I built a wall inside my brain. To keep contained the part of me that could damage other people.

I check my phone and a new alarm's been set. I shouldn't leave it alone any more. It isn't safe with her. She's up to something. Why can't I trust the people in my house? It's wrong, it's wrong.

I screwed up my eyes and listened to the beeps of the machines my father was attached to.

And thought,

I am closed. Leave me.
I am closed. Leave me.
I am closed. Leave me.

And the ghost thing. It has to be something to do with me. My past. It has to. She wouldn't have chosen to do this otherwise, would she? And I don't know if ghosts are even real, but the memory of the creatures clings to me, like skin on milk, like mould. They'll never leave me, will They? What she did to me is part of me, and I don't want it to be part of Nina too. I don't want anything to haunt her. Not ghosts, or loneliness, or love, or loss.

Not a scratch on me.
Everyone said it was the strangest thing.

But I knew why.

I wasn't on the menu.

I was the menu.

Everything I touched.

It wasn't safe.

And none of us are safe, here in the world. The people that we love are shinier and sharper than a knife. The things that we will do, for them, to them. Mam loved me and she hurt and hurt me anyway.

Brick by brick I built that fucking wall.

And when it was solidly up there in my brain, I walked away from it.

Only then did I allow myself to think of Susan, Nina.

Dad.

The people I had left.

I breathe in for a count of four, hold it in for four, and breathe out.

I do it again.

And again.

I sit there and I breathe.

I held his hand and looked at his face. The stubble growing.

And I wished so hard for him to stay with us.

Maybe I shouldn't have. I don't know. He doesn't seem happy.

And he's scared of me.

I would be too.

I think.

I know.

I am.

I sit there, breathing, till the sky is dark.

The girl is crying. Her voice is higher than normal, shrill. Grating. Her face is red.

'Nobody will believe me,' she tells you. 'That it happened.'

She holds her hand to her midsection.

'That it's still happening.'

remnants, fragments

Nina and I don't speak on the walk into school today. At breakfast all the mugs on the mug trees were full of stones, those loose chippings like you get on roads. Like . . .

Tap

Tap

Tap

Tap

Bang

And it's not that I'm angry with her. I'm not. I know she's hurting. I wish there was something I could do to make this easier. On her. On all of us. I wish there was no such thing as Oz Quigley, who walks around the school as though everything were normal. As though he didn't ruin her life. And I don't think anyone owes anyone their love. But she's a person. You know, she's a person. Not a nothing.

Numb.

School is strange when home is fraying at the edges. I usually find it comforting. The routine. The being told where to go, what to learn. That structure, like. It takes the pressure off. I don't go around saying that, because I know it's strange. Abigail and Megan and everyone are only dying for college, when they can choose to go or not to go to class, make their own schedules, take their time with work. It doesn't sound that great. I like to feel the boundaries around me. Keeping everything ticking over.

Only it isn't, is it?

But things are different – there's no escape from it – because they're all talking about Nina now, it's like a running joke. The things she sees, her ghosts. I look at Oz Quigley, and I think to myself, You are the ghosts. I hate you.

At lunch I picture his face tilted to Nina's, disappearing, fading into blank.

My fingernails dig into my palms. Abigail asks me if my sister should get help.

'She's obviously troubled.' She shows me a video someone in Nina's year made, showing how you make orbs out of dust motes, how you can make things fly around with wires. 'They're saying she's a liar, Daisy. Is she?'

And something in my gut says no.

She's not a liar.

Even though she is.

I feel like a kid again, breaking adult news to adult people. Mam's eyes on me, sharp. Noticing the bits that I get wrong. I pick at a loose thread on my skirt.

'Are you?' Megan asks. 'Like, are you haunted? Because if Nina is, then you should be too.'

Their voice is gentle but I feel the sting.

As long as they have known me
I've been haunted

Piotr, apparently an expert on ghosts now, says, 'That's not the way it works. With these things they tend to target one person.'

'But the other people in the house, they'd have to feel it,' Megan says, 'just not as intensely. I mean, like in all these horror movies, it might start with one person doing the Ouija board wrong or something, but afterwards there's evil there. It's palpable.'

'Palpable's a great word,' Conchur says. 'Palpable.'

'It hasn't been going on that long,' I tell them. 'But home is different now, and not in a good way.'

'I'm sorry, pal,' says Conchur.

I smile at him and shrug. 'It is what it is.'

We eat our sandwiches. I'm walking to Science when Oz Quigley corners me.

'Can we talk?' he asks.

Abigail looks at me like I have two heads and a whole secret life she doesn't know about. And I suppose I do, a bit. Just not in the way she's thinking with those eyebrows. I nod and he directs me past the lockers to the music room. He leaves the door open, and sits a distance away from me. I look him in the eye, and wish I could tap into the intuition I had when I was small without the worry coming up as well. I'd like to know what he's up to. I feel the anger welling up inside me.

'What is your sister doing?' he asks. 'She needs to stop.'

'What do you mean?' I say, and there is no way I'm going to admit to him I think she's lying. 'Nina didn't do anything wrong.' I glare at him meaningfully. He pales.

'It's not . . .' He's trying to find the words. 'It's not going to help anyone. This ghost stuff.'

'I live with her,' I say. 'I know.'

There is a pause.

I look him in the eye.

I say, 'I *know*.'

He swallows.

'You should have treated her like she was a person, Oz,' I tell him. 'Maybe then this wouldn't all have . . . manifested.'

'Oh,' he says. 'Oh. Okay. Yeah. Yeah, I probably should have been kinder to Nina, Daisy. I'll give her a call and tell her that, if you give me her number.'

I look at him, all wrong-footed.

Something's humming underneath his words.

'You weren't kind at all. And you already have her number, Oz.'

He smiles. 'I actually don't. We were in the DMs.'

'No, you weren't,' I say.

'Oh,' he says. 'I suppose we weren't. I . . . deleted her number. I didn't want to say.'

He is lying.

I stare at him, and it's like he heard that out loud. He startles, puts his hands into his pockets. Scuffs his shoes.

'This should not be happening,' he tells me.

I breathe in for a count of four. Nina probably wouldn't like it if I kicked him directly in the face.

86

'I don't know why you think you can ask me for something and just get it. I don't know you. I don't like you and I'm not giving you her number.'

'Oh,' he says. 'Of course. Of course you wouldn't. Um . . .'

I sigh. 'If you want it you can ask her for it yourself. I don't get why you're talking to me when she's the one you need to have a conversation with.'

'I just . . .' His eyes are wide. His jaw is weirdly strong. He looks like an actor playing a teenager. I can see some chest hair poking up near his throat. I mean, that's just overkill at our age. Conchur has hairy shoulders and backs of his arms but he can't help that, and it's weirdly endearing because he's my friend. Oz Quigley's not my friend.

'I just want all of this to go away,' he finishes.

I look at him.

'Me too.'

But I mean Nina's pain, and he means Nina.

a force you can't control

I sleep in Nina's room and what she calls the ghosts are quiet.
When I check my phone she has posted more pictures of orbs,
and an eyeshadow palette flying through the air.

It's methodical the way she's doing this.

And I don't want to call her a liar.

But she is one.

I tell her about Oz. And what he said.

'He said he wants you to stop doing this.'

'And what did you say to him?'

'I told him to talk to you.'

Nina's lips stretch, but it's not a smile.

'He won't, you know.'

She's doing this because she wants something.

This isn't how They operate.

They don't serve you, you serve Them. And the more
belief there is, the stronger They become. I can feel a stirring
somewhere in me when I think too much about it. An awareness
of the wall I've built.

'I know.'

I rub my scarf down her arm the way she likes. The thin

edge of the fabric going up and down elbow to wrist, elbow to wrist, that soft, soft skin. It calms her. When we were little I would do it with my ragdoll's hair, over and over, and she would make little humming noises, almost like a purr. She doesn't do that now. Because it's weird.

'My head hurts,' she tells me. 'It's heavy all the time and my eyes feel so hot but I can't cry. It's like there are all these tears inside me and I can't cry them, Daisy.'

'Nina,' I say.

'No one would believe me,' she says. 'If I told them.'

'Yes, they would,' I tell her. 'Of course they would. I did.'

She looks at me. Her eyes are very sad.

'I know you did. I just . . . I think maybe they'd think I was overreacting. Or something. But I just can't make sense of it, you know? I don't know how you can be prepared to risk *everything* for someone and then just stop. And treat them like they don't even matter. Like I'm nothing at all. Not even a cold patch on the back of his neck. A scratch across his back.'

'He's not worth it,' I tell her, keeping up the rhythm of the strokes.

'That's not . . .'

Her breath.

'That's not what worries me. It's that I'm not worth it. It's whatever I was worth, I'm not worth now.'

'Nina,' I say to her. 'Nina. Why are you being haunted?'

The wet sound of saliva in her throat.

'I didn't decide to be, you know. I didn't choose this.'

'I believe you,' I tell her. 'I believe you.'

And I'm not sure what I'm talking about, but it's definitely not about the ghosts.

The pain in her is calling to my pain.
To something in me.

a debt

Susan is at the table, scrolling through her banking app and sighing. I don't know if she knows what she believes any more. But ghosts sure do cost money. She's gotten an electrician in, and a plumber. To check the lights that flicker, the pipes that tap. She's getting an engineer in to look at draughts and see if there is something in the house that's causing things to move, the doors to bang while we're asleep at night. I look at Nina, and feel a shiver up my spine, a cold spot. She is so pale, and she has lost more weight.

Something is eating her.
Something is feasting.

When I was little, after the accident, she would let me be Cinderella when we played pretend. She would give me some of her ice cream if I finished mine first. Nina is kind. When she decides to love you, she always looks for ways to love you more.

She listens to Susan telling her there's nothing wrong with the house, and says, 'I knew that though. You should believe me.'

'Nina.' Susan rubs her eyes with her hands, and then raises her head to meet her gaze directly. 'There's no such thing as ghosts. And none of those people found anything. You have to be doing this.' She gestures to me. 'Daisy surely isn't.'

'No,' Nina tells her. 'No.'

Susan's face is stoic; she gets like that before she's going to cry though, but if you didn't know her, you'd think that's cold. 'Nina,' she says, 'I don't know what I did to make you like this. Is it because of what happened with Caroline? The move?'

'No. Look, it's not your fault . . . It wasn't anything . . . .' Nina starts. Then tears come to her eyes. 'Sometimes bad things just happen, Mom. Bad things are happening. To me. To us. I wish you could believe that.'

'I do believe that. Look at where we are. And what we've been through,' Susan says. 'But that doesn't mean we stop trying.'

'I am trying.' Nina gets a square of kitchen roll and dabs her eyes with it.

Susan sighs. 'I've looked up some of the counsellors on the list – there's one I think you'll like. I could make an appointment?'

And Nina rolls her eyes. 'You think counselling sorts everything. How about you just parent me? How about you just fix this? If it's all in my head –'

Susan's voice sends shivers down my spine. The desperation in it. Her hands tap on the surface of the wood. Once. Twice. Three times.

'Nina. I. Am. Trying. Too.'

I make a sound and the two of them look at me as though I'd walked into a home that wasn't mine. As though I was intruding. Which I suppose I am in some ways. I mean, Susan's not my mam, Nina's not my sister.

Except that Susan is and Nina is.

I don't have other people.

I need this family to be okay.

Since everything, I've never wanted to be able to read between the lines of people the way I used to. To know the things that they don't even know about themselves. But in this moment I wish I could read minds, contact something that could tell me why all this is happening. It would make things so much easier. I've thought about telling Susan about Oz. But I can't. I can't do it to Nina. Not with her so taut. Stretched tight and twisted up.

'Try harder, Mom,' she says.

And Susan reaches out and holds her hand. 'Okay. Okay, my darling. I believe you.' Her voice is kind, but there's a flatness too.

Nina starts to cry. I slink away.

the pressure of her hands on my shoulders

We're visiting Dad. He's helping out at the garden centre twenty hours a week, and everything seems to be going well for him. Which is nice. He has been through enough.

So have I.
And he won't look at me.
My fault.
My fault.

The cup of tea in my hand is almost boiling. He barely puts a drop of milk in. That's how Mam took it apparently. So hot it's dangerous. It's cold in the room though, so I'm grateful for the warmth of it. I thank him.

He grunts. Eyes flit to Susan, asking how I'm getting on at school. He's making an effort.

Not for me, for her.

I smile at him, tell him it's going fine, it's all small talk. No one mentions ghosts.

He asks where Nina is, we say she's with a friend.

She's still in bed. She didn't sleep much last night.

'You'd think,' Susan said to me in the car, 'that she'd only be dying to get out of the house, if it's so haunted.'

I didn't know what to say to that. Beyond, 'I'm not sure it's the house.'

There was salt in the sugar bowl this morning. Cheerios stacked in little vertical piles on the floor. When I touched them with my finger, the structure collapsed right away.

Seaweed in the plughole when I showered.

It's escalating.

But still, none of it scares me.

It isn't them.

I ask Dad about work.

He asks where Nina is again.

His voice changes and he meets my eye.

'Have you done something to her?'

Susan tells him to *Calm down, Fiachra,* but he won't be calm and I can hear all of the hate that he was holding back spilling out.

'There's something going on and you won't tell me.' He holds his head and closes his eyes tight and shouts:

'You. You leave her ALONE. You've done enough.'

I know that he means me. My stomach curls up inside my body.

Susan looks at me and I see a flash of something – sorrow, blame? I keep my mouth shut tight. I sip the tea. It burns my tongue and I feel the loose skin on it against the roof of my mouth the whole drive home and after.

The girl's make-up is running. She pulls off an eyelash and rubs her eyes, making it much worse.

'They left me alone in the house.'

A banging from the wall.

'It targets me the most when I'm alone.'

A blur as something flies across the room and hits the side of her head.

She rubs it.

'OW. Okay, let's see what that was. Great. My nicest eyeshadow. And it's all fallen on the carpet and everything.'

She grimaces.

'Better get the hoover, I guess. That's something they don't tell you about ghosts. All the cleaning up you have to do.'

The girl shrugs. She is wearing a slouchy black top and you can see the strap of her bra. It is burgundy-coloured and matches her lipstick.

She runs a hand through her hair and rubs the side of her head where the eyeshadow hit.

hate and who you come from

The visit with Dad unsettles me for the rest of the evening. I can't focus, and I keep . . . I just keep wondering why the thing he clings to is hatred for me, anger.

What I deserve.

Nina sits on the sofa, barefoot, like nothing has happened. Susan watches her like a hawk. I scroll through ghosts. Sometimes they're just recordings. Residual hauntings, it's called. Like, you'll be walking in a historic location and see a woman running down a hall, or hear the wheels of a carriage rolling by. Or footsteps.

Someone might walk past you through a wall, and then you find out there used to be a door there. Those ghosts don't really have anything to do with anyone. They're just like memories that are so intense or something that they outlast the time in which they happened.

I read something once about how you only really die when the last person who remembers you dies. And it sickened me. I want there to be an ending. For it to be over when it's over. The idea of lingering makes me very uncomfortable. The threads that connect us to each other are so strong, and of course you don't want the people you love to be gone entirely, but you don't want them not to be either. And we don't get to choose what's left behind. This thing of Nina's, whether it's real or a hoax or imagined, it's angry. Small handprints on the shower door this evening when Susan was in there.

'I don't see how she could be doing that, Daisy,' she tells me.

I thought of the yellow fly swatter we have shaped like a slapping hand. Or even paper cut-outs, somehow, maybe. It wouldn't be that hard. None of it would. But if it is her, doing this all by herself, that's not much better. Pain, and sorrow.

Rage.

'Like, there's some of it that she could do on her own, but other things . . . I'm not sure any more. And I thought that if we got those people in, the engineer and everyone, that there might be a reason for it all. Some explanation. Carbon monoxide. Mould. I mean, it's good the house isn't damaged or anything, I suppose, but . . .'

I make Susan a cup of tea and she sits at the kitchen table with her head in her hands. When I place it in front of her she reaches up and gives me a little hug.

'We'll get through this,' Susan says.

I nod.

We won't.

She takes a sip of tea and motions me to sit beside her. Plonks her tea back down on the table. Some of it spills. She makes a little face and gets a cloth. I think of her arms around Nina that night that she was screaming. She doesn't touch me that way. She's learned not to. 'Laura, Conchur's mother, told me,' Susan says, 'that one of the teachers is a paranormal investigator.'

'Who, Mr Quigley?' I ask, my voice rising at the ridiculousness of becoming one of the stories he tells in class to make himself seem important or interesting or whatever it is he wants from thirty kids.

'The debate guy?' Her voice is rising, grasping for some hope. 'Would we be mad to ask him to come in?'

Oz's dad, I think.

I start to wonder.

the smell of her

Susan held a sort of family meeting with us this evening, about calling Mr Quigley. It was oddly formal. I could see her scanning Nina's face the whole time, trying to read between the lines, to see if this was the right thing to do. I looked between them both, the tension tight in my stomach, waiting for something awful to happen. It felt too calm. Nina politely telling her it was a good idea, her voice so even, as though she had prepared for this. There were biscuits but no one ate them. There was moss inside the cutlery drawer, under the forks. This couldn't all be just for Oz. To get him to the house. To, what, confront him?

Teachers coming into students' homes to hunt ghosts doesn't feel like the sort of thing the school should allow. Or that Susan should go for. It feels blurry. I know intellectually that teachers are people, but I don't think they should be the sort of people who intersect with our personal lives. I hate the thought of him going through our stuff. This house where we're all broken in different ways and can't seem to fit together the way we did before. But apparently I'm the only one who sees how weird this is, because when I said it to Susan, she pointed out that half of them do grinds outside school anyway.

'That's different,' I said. 'It's still teaching. This is something else.'

Susan said, 'At least we know who he is. I'd rather not have a complete stranger in the house. Coming in here, poking through our things.'

Our pain.

Our grief.

Our secrets.

'But of course he's your teacher, and if you don't feel comfortable . . .'

I wanted to say something, but Nina put her hand on my wrist, and even though her skin was warm, a coldness filtered through me. She knew, she knows, I don't like being touched.

She doesn't mean it.

She just needs my help.

She needs this.

'No,' I say. 'It's fine. I mean, better the devil you know, right?'

Susan smiles at me, and so does Nina.

'Laura said he helped a friend of hers. With something similar.'

I resist the urge to roll my eyes. Conchur's mom is one of these people who always has some bit of advice for you. When she gives me lifts, I get this vibe like she is being extra nice to me and I absolutely loathe it. I didn't think that Susan and her got on that well.

None of Susan's friends have been over recently, I realise. She might not want to have them in this weird space where anything can happen. Scratches long as fingers, stark against Nina's skin, and missiles through the air. I've yet to see one

101

fly all by itself though. It's always just out of the corner of my eye. And what must it be like for Susan? I mean, I'm worried about Nina, but she's her mother. And she can't protect her from whatever this is.

Nina woke last night screaming and sweating, and saying she could hear a scratching in the pipes.

'Something took my headphones.'

Nina listens to music going to sleep, and Susan's always giving out to her about it. She thinks we look at our phones too much, but I think she's projecting, she looks at her phone way more than we do and actually drives home if she forgets it, which she says is 'in case something happens' to one of us, but I think it's like a security blanket for her.

Susan was not best pleased to be woken up.

'Jesus Christ. They probably fell under the bed or got tangled somewhere, Nina.'

You'd think at this stage she'd be used to it, but no. I shrugged and started searching.

'Something *took* them.' Nina's face looked pale and drained of everything but sadness.

'Mom, can I sleep in with you?'

'Again?'

'*Please.*'

Susan sighed, and off they went to bed. I padded back to my room. I've never slept beside Susan. She's like a mother to me, but she's not my mother. And sometimes there are little differences, things we do not share, that kind of slap me in the face or something.

I lie in bed, waiting for the shrill of Nina's voice, the pad of her feet going downstairs to rearrange whatever it is 'the ghost' will have done in the morning. There's a sort of sick anticipation. And if it is her, all her, she's hurting herself, and hurting us . . . and hurting in general, I suppose.

And I don't understand why.

I mean, I've never had my heart broken.

Romantically.

But it doesn't seem like enough, you know? For this much pain.

But then, it's hard to gauge what people feel.

wise creatures

Sometimes I almost wish I could remember more about my life before Nina and Susan. Maybe it would help. With Dad. With now.

It's like my memory is a braid of hair and one strand is the stories I've been told, and one strand is the impact of what happened.

And the third strand is cobbled together from memories, from dreams where I can't move, from something in me that I can't let out.

I don't even know if there was more than one of Them. Of it. When you're dealing with something amorphous, that can shift and alter, it's hard to know. I used to tell people I heard Them, but it wasn't like hearing with your ears, if that makes sense.

What They told me just appeared in me.

Because that was Their base.

In me.

They were bigger and hungrier than I was but They could still fit right inside my brain, my body.

Take root.

I say I can't remember, even to myself, but the truth is that I don't want to. Why would I want to think about those two red hands. The mirror. The adults that I spoke to day after day. When I started school I worked so hard to fit in, because I hadn't been around other children much. I didn't go to playschool, Montessori. It was just me and Mam at home. The visitors.

And Them.

Hot chocolate burning my tongue, and her eyes on me, asking what else I knew, jotting little notes down. Rubbing my back and giving me a bath. Telling me I was her precious girl. It wasn't all bad. There were moments when we were a family. It's not one thing or another. You can't always tell, with people. What it would take, to turn from good to bad. And it's in all of us, that capability, but with Mam there was something about me that made it easier for her to follow her worst impulses. I wish I knew exactly what it was that called out to that side of her.

To Them.

Skin prickling at the thought. It's dangerous to even bring Them up inside myself. Like someone or something running long, thin fingers right across that wall. Forcing me to grasp at the fragments left behind. When They were there, I could sense Them, feel Them, but I could never get a handle on what exactly They had been before They were this presence in my life.

Maybe a ghost too old and too cold to remember being human. Maybe They never were alive at all, in the way we think about it. Anyway, it doesn't matter now.

I think she would have kept me home forever if she could have. Close beside her, close enough to touch. And I am glad she didn't get the chance. Once I started going into the world I noticed more and more my differences, the bits that weren't right.

I don't know why she didn't just homeschool me. Maybe Dad said something. He always liked me to have friends my own age. He'd take me over to Susan's, or to houses where his friends had kids, and I would watch them playing and try my best to join in where I could. I remember usually an adult would have to tell me that it was okay, because I was so used to waiting for permission.

Of course, now I know the creatures were just a sort of tool, a way to get me through what my mother did to me.

Like an imaginary friend.

But not my friend.

When people hear my mother is dead, they always feel sorry for me. And sometimes I feel sorry for myself. I mean, she was my mam after all. And maybe if we could have sorted out the creature thing, this thing she called my gift but really was just her need for me to make her money, things could have gone a different way entirely. We could have gotten on. I never went beside her into bed though, when I was scared. Because she was a big part of what scared me.

Looking at a woman's face and not wanting to say the things I saw.

She loved me though. She'd tell me that she was doing this because she loved me. And I loved her. I wanted her to smile and say *good job* and take me in her arms and stroke my hair.

My head under the cold tap in the sink, so cold it burned the back of my scalp the nape of my neck, promising that next time I'd do better.

There was a comfort in it, and she could be nice. She was so nice to my dad. We both did our best to keep him happy. And by the time he got home from work, it was dinner, cartoons, bed. He visited our world but he wasn't immersed in it. He could get out whenever he wanted.

Her hands.

Her hands on me.

Ghosts are easier than other monsters.

'I don't know why I'm still doing this,' the girl says. 'I mean, it's not like anybody cares. Not really.'

She drums her fingers on the desk and looks up at the ceiling.

More orbs float around her, this time pale green and orange in colour.

She places her hands flat on the table and breathes.

'I get more nervous now posting,' she says. 'At first I didn't think anyone would even notice, really. But now I know you do. And I do understand that it's a hard thing to believe.'

Her fingers worry at the side of her neck and the pale skin turns an angry shade of red.

'Why would I make it up though? Anything would be better than the way I'm feeling now.'

each one unique

Here we are. In hell. Watching my geography teacher and his son move around our house for the purposes of ghost investigation. I send Megan a sneaky picture of the two of them, staring grimly out the sliding door towards the garden shed.

> what has your life become

> I know
> It feels like wrong that it's the weekend too

> it is wrong

> Deeply Wrong

> Thought & Prayers

I smile. Megan's good at knowing what to say to me. Nina is over the other side of the room, fingers wrapped around a massive mug of coffee. She hasn't been sleeping well, and Susan has been letting it slide when she makes herself americanos the size of her head. Before all this, Susan was big on monitoring our 'caffeine intake', and pushing tea instead of what I call 'the devil's petrol' to make Nina laugh. Or it used to make her laugh, before she got haunted.

It is really disconcerting to see a teacher outside of their natural habitat. I've heard tell of it happening before, Conchur having seen Ms Murph buying pregnancy vitamins in Boots and telling the world and its mother before she ever started to show. Megan drawling at him, 'You'd swear you were the father, Conchur.' Before taking a long drag of their juice box. Megan likes to drink from juice boxes even though we're not little kids any more. But in their hands, a juice box has the cool of a well-placed cigarette in a 1950s French movie. I scratch my elbow and wish I had a big mug of something myself, just to have something to do with my hands and mouth. The pauses in conversation feel incredibly drawn out and I might need a holiday to recover from the horror of Mr Quigley's weekend attire. A studded belt, God help us, and a silver ring in the shape of a bird's skull. His hair in a little ponytail, paired with his usual dark jeans, black T-shirt and cardigan. His beard is impressively shiny. He might have oiled it, if that is something that bearded people do. He's wearing black Converse and his whole vibe is very 'I might be a teacher, but it's the weekend now. All bets are off.'

Oz Quigley walks from the sitting room into the kitchen, looking as if he wants the floor to swallow him up. He is dressed much better than his father, in a soft-looking sweatshirt, grey jeans and battered runners with bits of leopard print on them. He's here because *a paranormal investigator never goes into a premises alone*, according to Mr Quigley. And apparently there were no other paranormal investigators available to him apart from his own son. Maybe he alienated them by demanding they examine Ordnance Survey maps and answer a series of questions about the landscape. I mean, obviously Nina knew that Oz would be here. That's the point of this, I think. Though I can't be sure. She hasn't really spoken to them much. She keeps looking at her hands, or out the window.

I'm finding it amazing how much of a teacher Mr Q still is, with his voice and hand gestures, even while being a ghost hunter or what have you. I wonder was he always like this, explaining things until he'd make you sick. His anecdotes in class made it sound a bit cooler than it was, to be honest. From where I'm standing, paranormal investigators have rules that sound a lot like the rules of being a teenage girl. Always have a friend to check up on you when you're out, and bring equipment. His big duffle bag of paranormal tech probably cost more than my little purse of tampons and painkillers, but it's definitely not as useful . One time I gave a tampon to Abigail and she nearly cried with relief. Her periods are like that gif where all the blood comes out of the elevator, and she has next to no warning about them. Sometimes three weeks, sometimes six, always *intense*. Mine aren't as bad as that, but I don't look forward to them. On a scale of one to THE GEOGRAPHY TEACHER WILL BE ROAMING AROUND YOUR BEDROOM NOW, WITH BEEPING ITEMS, they're about a three and a half.

'We approach this very scientifically,' says Mr Q. Oz looks like he wants to murder his father and run away to New Mexico. I smile politely at him, but if the smile had subtitles they would read *I hate you*, and we both know it. He strokes his weirdly square chin. He definitely didn't get that from his dad. It wouldn't fit under the beard.

Nina rinses her cup and puts it in the dishwasher. She's made an effort – her make-up is impeccable and her hair is loose. She runs her fingers through it and sits beside me, wrapping her legs around each other twice. Susan offers Mr Quigley another cup of tea and he accepts.

Oz Quigley raises a hand with index finger extended.

'Hi, Nina.'

'Hi,' she says, her voice low. 'Thank you for coming.'

'Your mother filled me in on the phone,' Mr Quigley says. He reaches his hands out for the new cup of tea.

'Thank you, Susan.' He says it like she works for him.

'So, now that you're all here and we've had a little walk-through of the place, I'd like to talk about how my part in this will work. I've already gotten some details from Susan, but I'm going to interview you all separately, to establish what's been going on for the individual members of the family and get a clearer picture of what this might be. All going well, myself and Austin Junior will take a walk around the property and examine it. Susan, you've had several professionals out to look at the plumbing, electricity, etc., I presume.'

She nods.

'And the carbon monoxide.' He smiles. 'It can so often be something like that. Black mould as well is often a culprit.'

'We don't have mould,' I tell him.

Just all the rot inside me.

He smiles again and nods. His teeth are very clean and even

112

but there's a sort of yellow sheen to them. My hands worry at the cushiony part of the chair.

'Of course, Daisy. I just said that to communicate that sometimes there can be unexpected but perfectly reasonable explanations for the sort of things you're going through. Once myself and Austin Junior . . .'

Oz flinches.

'. . . here have established that everything is normal, as it were, we'll ask you to leave the premises so we can observe the house ourselves, and see what we can see. If we notice anything you need to know about, we'll share the footage with you once we've reviewed it and we can decide how to proceed from there. Does that make sense?'

All three of us nod.

'Do you have any questions?' he asks, sounding like he's covering an essential portion of the geography paper.

Nina asks how long this will take, more or less.

'Hard to say.'

'And can you make it go away?' Her voice trembles but she looks up, meets his eyes.

He sighs, reaches out a hand, stops himself. His voice is oddly gentle. 'If, and it's a very big if, there is some preternatural activity taking place, we need more information before we can make any promises.'

Nina nods, sharply, sadly.

'We'll do our best though.'

Oz Quigley looks at the floor, mortified.

I mean, I would be too. His father is ghostbusting all over his secret ex-girlfriend. It's not a good situation.

'So,' Mr Quigley says, 'myself and Austin Junior here –' a flinch again – 'will grab a bite to eat and we might reconvene here at say three o' clock.'

'I can make you something if –' Susan offers.

He cuts her off. 'No. I promised him we'd go to some ridiculous vegan-chicken place to make up for a weekend on sidekick duty.' He smiles. 'And you'll need your space. We'll be back at three. This room will do for the interviews, and if the other members of the family can be out of earshot while we do them, that would be great. They will obviously be recorded.'

Susan nods.

Mr Quigley rises to his feet. 'We don't have to do them all today, though it would be good to get as much as possible out of the way, so we can proceed with the investigation. I'm also going to contact a local historian and a friend on the force to confirm that there haven't been any events here that would leave a . . . mark.'

I look at Oz. Stifle a smirk.

'It's a fairly new build,' Susan says. 'One family was in here before us. And they seemed fine.'

'Yes,' Mr Quigley says. 'We had a new build in Tipperary a few years back, and it turned out to have been built on a famine grave. I can't discuss the details, but it was an intense experience.' He gazes into the middle distance, moodily. I never really thought of him as being ridiculous before, but there's something about the confidence of him that feels like a mask with something else behind it, and it's unsettling me.

I look down at my hands, and startle. They're red and chapped with longer fingers, deeper nail beds than mine.

Her hands.

I shudder and jump up.

Nina turns to me, her eyes wide, curious. 'What did you see?'

I meet her gaze. She wants me to back her up. But I don't have the words to say what happened. If it was a cold spot, an item moved, then of course I could.

But this . . .

'Nothing,' I tell her firmly. 'I saw nothing.'

not child's dreams

When I arrived at Susan's house first, I was scared of the dark. But I suppose what I was really scared of was sleep. Night-time, the darkness, meant sleep. And while I could gird myself, guard myself during the day, at night my brain was free of those limitations and it could start playing with me.

Tap
Tap

I remember I would dream of my mother looking for me. I would be hiding and she would be looking and she would be so angry, but when she found me, and she always did, she always found me, I would see her face, the blood vessels around her eyes. She would reach out a hand to grab me and I would wake up having wet myself.

Susan would hold me sometimes and say, 'She's gone. She cannot get you any more.'
And it was a terrible thing to say about my mother.
But it was exactly what I needed to hear in that moment.

I don't know what would have happened if she'd got me.
If my body hadn't kept me safe.
She was my mother and she was not my mother.
Just like when she was in the world.

Mr Quigley and Oz messaged around four. Something came up. I felt myself relax. I hadn't been aware that I was even tense, sometimes it's like that.

'Very unprofessional,' said Susan, aggressively putting cutlery away.

Nina made a little humming noise and I just kept my head down and said nothing. But I felt this hotness in my stomach.

'The cheek of them.' The sound of stainless steel clashing together.

I rub my temples. Need to leave the room. I want to throw things.

They do not want to be here.

They're coming back tomorrow to ask questions and do a walk-through of our house. Looking for ghosts, or reasons to doubt Nina, who is in her room but live on the internet, talking about cold spots and orbs and showing off the scratches that keep appearing on her legs, her back. The blankets apparently got pulled off her bed last night. She has a video of it, and I don't even know how she managed it, but it has to be staged because it's clearly filmed on her phone and she couldn't have it charging and film her bed from that angle.

She doesn't tell me what she's going to post or when she posts it. Half the things that she describes, I haven't seen at all. And there's a huge part of me that thinks if it were real, then she would tell me. But she didn't tell me about Oz until after it happened. And she's off-kilter. When she heard they weren't coming she exhaled, as though she were relieved, but isn't this what she wanted? To have him see how miserable she is? I mean, she hasn't said that. I pick long dark strands of hair from my pillow, and wrap them round my finger like a tourniquet.

I'm guessing, always guessing. What she's doing. What she wants. What this is. And it's exhausting. I just . . . I wish she'd be honest with me. I mean, if anyone knows what it is to be haunted, I do.

We watched three episodes of a show about bears and gemstones before Susan went up to bed, and I turned to her and said, 'Is this helping at all, do you think?'

She shrugged. 'What do you think?' Her face was hard to read.

'I think that I kind of expected you to try to get him on his own. Confront him.'

She stood up, picked up her cup. 'That's not what this is about, Daisy. I thought you were here for me.'

'I am,' I say. 'I am. But this is hard, you know?' My voice came out much harsher than I meant it, and I looked at the curtains as though they were a window, tried to breathe.

'It feels like you think I'm stalking him. That all of this is lies. You call yourself my sister, but you're not acting like it. You've seen me waking screaming in the night. Is it so hard to believe that I am haunted?'

'No,' I say. 'I do believe you, Nina.'

Because she needs me to.

And she is haunted.

I think of the pattern on the curtains, that kind of blue swirl round and round. It doesn't make a discernible shape. I want to pull them down. To scream and scream. But if I let it out, I'd never stop.

By me as well.
As much as any ghost.

She sits down again and curls in on herself. Normally she notices when I start to come apart, but I don't think she's even speaking to me, not really. Both of us are somewhere else. Around and around the blue against the cream. That's how rot gets in, not all at once, but in these little curls, bit by bit. And then it's everywhere. I push the heels of my hands into my eyes and think about disappearing, swirling up and out of where I am.

'I wish that I could cry, you know? Maybe if there was a way to let it out. But it's building up and up, and everything is awful.'

'Not everything,' I tell her. 'There are biscuits, and I could get you one.'

'There's no biscuit big enough to fix this,' she says. 'But please, Daisy, tomorrow. Don't tell him that you think that I'm a liar. Because that would break me, and I'm already in bits.'

I take a deep breath and I count to ten.

Her hands.
My hands.
The curtains.
She doesn't understand
what she is doing.

'I don't think that you're a liar, Nina,' I say, and realise it's true. I don't. 'It's like I have this sense I should believe you, but I'm not sure about what.' I rub my eyes. 'That didn't make sense. I'm sorry.'

'No, I get it,' she says. 'Maybe you're still a little psychic.'

Red hands around my throat.

'Don't say that.'

Red hands wrapping tightly around Nina's neck.
And squeezing, squeezing
my hands her hands together,
hers and mine.

'What?' she smiles. 'Don't look like that. It wouldn't be a bad thing. You could help me, if things get really bad.'

I try to laugh, but it comes out pure awkward. I can't remember the proper things that other people do when they're not frightened. I try to make my face look the way that Nina wants my face to look.

'Yeah, I could, I guess.'

You could of course.
But should you?

lies you tell to strangers

Lots of people do it, try to read the future, or the present. Tell you things you don't already know. Even at school, folding paper into little paper oracles, Saoirse Twomey with her tarot cards. It sends a shiver up my spine. Even though I know it isn't real. I do not want any of that stuff around me. Any link to anything beyond. I try to remember what Susan told me time and time again, when I was little. That it's all made up. That the things she told me weren't true. That I did not deserve them. That she loves me. From the top of my head to the tips of my toes. Creatures and all, and did I want a hug? And I would nod. Susan was the only person I would let touch me, for ages. She doesn't ask as much any more if I want to be held. I think it's because I'm older and maybe because I look like Mam as well. She loved me so much when we were little. I used to get worried that I was too much work when the badness in me spilled over into their world. She used to say, 'You are not a burden. You're a joy. We're glad you're home with us, where you belong.' And not always, but sometimes, I would not let the past or the future or any of it bother me, but breathe her in and feel as though I had a proper home in her and Nina.

The world would always find a way to remind me of what had happened though. Who I was.

Or maybe who I am.

I don't know how I knew the things that I remember knowing. I've looked it up, the tricks. The different techniques that people use, to convince others, to make the things they say feel true. Cold reading. Fishing with various blanket statements and then getting more detailed piece by piece. The typical 'Does anyone know someone whose name begins with J – it could be . . . Jack? No, John. I'm getting John.' The type of stuff you see mediums do on YouTube clips of American TV shows.

I don't remember ever doing that, but there is so much that I don't remember. Images and knives inside my brain. I reach out and they hurt me, over, over. She must have fed me the specific stuff. She could have got it out of them. People put a lot of trust in psychics. I was a child. I liked the taste of play dough. No one should ever have been using me for anything. But part of me, now, wishes there was a way to use what I used to be able to do to help Nina. Not to scare anyone. But to give her what she's looking for. Or just to glimpse what that might be. Because while I don't believe in this, I know that she is haunted. You only have to look. Her face. Her eyes.

I see myself in her.

'Susan,' I said last night, 'I don't know if it's a good idea to have them here. I mean . . .' My voice trailed off. 'They aren't of their word, you know?'

She nodded. 'I don't know what else to do, Daisy. Something has to change, and nothing will if I don't try – do something . . .'

I looked at her and swallowed down my frustration.

This will not help.

It only makes things worse.

Night came and went, I didn't sleep a wink, and now Oz Quigley is leaning against the shed at the back of the garden, and his father is setting up recording equipment in the kitchen.

They're going to interview Susan first, then me, then Nina. If I had to do it, I'd do it the other way around. Get Nina's story first to establish a backbone and then examine the details more closely from a more sceptical point of view. But I'm not a geography teacher with a sideline in paranormal investigation, so what would I know. He has, like, three suitcases of equipment, but apparently all he's going to do is talk to us. The secret big-boy ghost stuff has to be earned, apparently. He's on his third cup of tea, and I needed to get out of the house before I smacked him. There's more than enough going on without me losing control.

The garden is one bit of the house I really like. We took the big blue pots of rosemary and lavender with us from the old place, and there's honeysuckle winding up the trellis on the shed, and lots of dandelions in the grass. I smile at Oz Quigley, because I should at least pretend to be polite, but keep my eyes all distant, grim and dead. I want him to know that this is all his fault. He isn't welcome.

He smiles back. With no hate. Which is almost rude. I mean, he knows we're enemies. Make an effort. He has a little gap between his two front teeth, about as thick as a five-cent coin. It is distracting.

'Daisy.'

'Austin.'

'Ugh,' he says. 'Don't call me that.' He stands up straight and brushes invisible dirt off his sweatpants.

'Do you not like your name?' I ask, surprising myself with the lack of anger in my voice.

He shakes his head. 'It never felt like mine. I'm named for him, so . . .' He jerks his head in the direction of the sliding doors, where Mr Q is plugging something in. His jeans are slung dangerously low.

'Oh. Okay,' I say. I can see why that would be a strange thing for him. I look at my feet. 'I don't think I'm named for anyone. And Nina's name is just the Spanish for child.'

He barks a laugh, and I feel guilty for saying anything to him that's not 'Get out of here', but also kind of stuck, because there are things I want to know that Nina hasn't told me, and maybe he's the only other person who could. It's stressful.

'Do you do this sort of thing often, like, be your dad's ghost-buddy?' I ask, barely keeping the contempt out of my voice.

He shrugs. 'Fairly often. He fell out with some of the other investigators.'

'Was it because he kept telling them how much better his tech was than theirs?' I ask.

He crooks a smile. 'Something like that.'

It wasn't though.

'I kept watching your face in the sitting room,' he says, 'and I feel like you also can see how ridiculous this is.'

'Are you calling her a liar?' I ask, my eyebrows knitting together.

124

'Look,' he says, 'I don't know your sister well enough to judge that, either way. I do know that she's hurting, but if she's being haunted, I don't know what my dad, the enthusiastic geography teacher, is going to do to un-haunt her.'

'Apart from not show up when he says he will?' I ask.

'That was my fault,' he said. 'Something came up.'

'Was the something not wanting to be around Nina and this house?'

He makes an awkward face. 'It wasn't *not* that . . .'

I roll my eyes.

His voice is low.

'I mean, it doesn't feel right. I don't get it.' His face looks miserable, and if Nina is doing this to punish him, she is doing a splendid job. But I don't think it's that.

I tilt my face towards a patch of sun, away from Oz. 'I think Susan – who is, in fairness to her, exhausted and post-break-up – thinks it will show we're taking Nina seriously,' I say. 'Give a bit of . . . I don't know . . . weight to what she's going through. Because she is going through a lot, Oz.' I'm talking to him like he's a person and not a villain, I realise. I'd want to watch that, and maybe he sees some of that written on my face because his falls a little.

'I know that, Daisy. And believe me, I do feel for her.'

'Do you think you'll be less of a dick the next time that you're with someone?' I ask him. 'Not to be confrontational, but, like, I feel that heartbreak in this instance has directly led to ghosts.'

'I was afraid of that,' he says. 'And yes, I'd hope to be kinder to the next person I'm with than what Nina experienced.'

'Are you going to apologise?' I ask.

'I don't know if she'd hear it,' he says. 'I mean, it is my fault. The way things ended. And that can't have been easy for her. But also, it's the way it had to be, you know? She's better off without whatever it was.' He makes a nebulous gesture with his hand, as though their relationship was a concept and not a cruelty.

He feels for her.

He rubs a hand on his chin, as though it's itchy. 'I suppose we better go back inside and, like, "interview" you all.'

I narrow my eyes. 'You say interview like what we say doesn't matter.'

'Well,' he says, 'Dad likes to be right as often as he can, and I get the sense that he's already made up his mind.'

'Oh,' I say. It's weird. Talking to him makes him harder to hate. And there is something. Humming underneath his words. I can't quite make it out. It's like there are subtitles but they're fuzzy.

They don't have to be.

a question

Mr Quigley and Oz are sitting on one side of our kitchen table. It's a yellowy pine sort of table with a red-and-white checked tablecloth on it. The tablecloth was initially bought for a slightly smaller table so it doesn't exactly fit, but I resist the urge to adjust it. Susan has gone for a walk to 'decompress' after her interview. I think she feels like it's fine to leave us here with Mr Q because he's a teacher, but it doesn't feel fine. Something is off with Susan at the moment. She used to have this ability to do all of the stuff and make it look like nothing, but now it's like it's hard for her to move through the day at all, and since she's less able to take care of us, she's decided we're more independent, not being home for dinner, or checking if our lunch is in our bag. In little ways like that, it's fine. It's just . . . when it's big things. Like this. This is too big for us to be alone with. I don't think that it's safe.

It isn't safe.

Nina's in her room. She hasn't even really spoken to Oz or looked at him this whole time, directing all her questions at his dad. If this was about getting his attention . . . I don't know. Maybe there isn't even a point to it. Sometimes things are simply truly pointless.

Like this whole interaction.

I sigh.

They look at me.

I look at them, like, Let's get this out of the way.

Mr Quigley's eyebrows do a thing and he begins to speak, slowly and with authority.

'I will be recording this on my Dictaphone and my mobile. It is important to back up these things. You'd be surprised how often there can be interference with electronics. In these cases.'

He pauses, as if he is expecting me to ask him what he means. I keep my face unmoving until he presses the button, with a little cough.

'So, how long ago did this start?' His voice is neutral, but he is my teacher so it still feels like an exam.

'It's hard to say. It was all little things until it escalated. Um . . .' I try to think of an exact timeline. Without directly saying, *When your son fucked up.*

Mr Quigley looks annoyed.

'About two months ago,' I offer, thinking of the night Nina showed me the texts. Because that was the start of it really. Her broken heart.

Something passes between him and Oz. I feel it, like a shiver up my spine.

'And how did it manifest at first?' He tilts his head to one side and for a second he reminds me of a basset hound.

Every dog has teeth.

'Little things. Items being in the wrong place. Car keys in the cereal box. Furniture being awry. All things that could just have happened anyway, if somebody did them.'

I look down at my hands. They're still my hands.

'But nobody was doing them.' He looks at me. His eyes are bloodshot.

The scratches on her belly and her thighs.

'No,' I say. 'Nobody was doing them. I didn't really register it as paranormal though, until I saw what Nina was posting.'

'This would be the footage of the alleged preternatural activity she was experiencing,' Mr Quigley says into the Dictaphone.

'Yes,' I say. 'A friend at school made me aware.'

'Why do you think she didn't tell you about it?' Mr Quigley asks.

I swallow. 'I don't know. We've always been close, but maybe she was trying to figure it out for herself. It's not . . . usual . . . what has been happening. It's difficult to put into words, perhaps.'

'Maybe she didn't want to remind you of your own past,' he says.

I gasp. Well, I don't actually gasp. But I feel as though I do, inside myself. My stomach clenches.

'Susan informed us of your particular history,' he carries on. 'In case it was pertinent.'

She betrayed me.

How could Susan do that?

'I don't see how it would be,' I say, trying to keep it together. Is this my fault now? I've tried my best to be good. I really have. I can't help . . .

But I can.
It would be so easy to
help
Nina.

Oz looks at me, like he's apologising for his dad.

I look down at my feet. Okay. I can do this. Autopilot. Click.

'What would you like to know?' I ask him coolly.

'You were a psychic child.'

'I was a child who did what she was told,' I say. 'My mother managed me, and earned money through it. There was a lot of . . . coaching.'

'Children are more open to the supernatural,' Mr Quigley tells me. 'It wouldn't be unusual for a child to see a ghost. Oz, for example, had an imaginary friend named Marcus. My brother Marcus died when he was twelve. Oz never knew him.'

Oz looks like he wants to throttle his father. I don't really know how to respond, so I do a little 'mmm' noise to be polite. I really don't want this to impact my geography results. He carries on, oblivious to everyone's discomfort. I continue to be checked out. I'm good at this, just saying the lines that I'm supposed to say until it is all over.

Like she taught me.

Mr Quigley's voice is a low hum, and it's all a bit 'longshore drift' right now.

'Do you sense the same sort of energy here as was in your home when you were a practising psychic?'

He makes it sound like I was a grizzled fifty-year-old with a crystal ball and a cigarette permanently dangling out one side of my mouth.

What did Susan say to them, exactly?

'I was six,' I say. 'When I moved in with Susan and Nina. It was a long time ago.'

'Even so. You must remember something.'

I close my eyes.

Her hands.
My shoulders.
I am open.
Take me.

'Daisy.'

'Daisy?'

The screech of a kettle on the boil.
A rabbit in a snare.

'Daisy?'

Sometimes animals will chew off their own feet to get out of a
trap.

'Daisy?'

Champ through sinew and bone, blood between their teeth and
down their throat.

'It was a long time ago,' I say again. 'I barely think about it any more.'

'But do you sense the same sort of thing?' he asks again.

I shake my head. 'This is different,' I tell him. 'This is real. I believe her. Nina wouldn't lie.'

It doesn't feel like I am lying to him.
Her face.
Her voice.
There's something in this house.
Something is happening.

'Are you sure about that?' he says. 'Sometimes girls will. To get attention. Make a point.'

I glare at him.

'Not just girls. And certainly not Nina.'

We go through a few of the different instances, the things flying through the air seem to be what interest him the most. And I tell him the truth. Or a version of the truth where I don't think Nina's lying.

And as I do, it feels like the whole truth, because, even after everything, I don't think Nina would lie. I think it's more a form of self-harm.

Red lines on her skin.

Pain in her voice.

There has to be something to this. Something more.

When I leave the kitchen, she is sitting outside, face wan. Before she goes through the door she meets my eyes and asks how it all went.

'Okay,' I say. 'Okay.'

She clasps my hand.

Her palm is sweaty, and I can see the panic in her eyes.

Without a foot, a rabbit negotiates the world differently.

They're slower now.

They smell of fear, of blood.

And some things like that.

an answer

I press my ear to the door and listen for the hum of their voices. I can't make out everything, but the tone is different somehow with Nina. Maybe because he knows her from debate. It feels a little like debate at first; he states, she counters, but there's a question underneath her voice, a vulnerability.

He wants to catch her out.

They go back and forth and I can hear the challenge in Mr Q's voice, but Nina's is fading, harder and harder to make out. He asks her to stop mumbling, to speak up, repeat herself, and it feels like a cross-examination scene.

He is going to hurt her.

I think of when we used to go to the farm as kids, the lake behind it. There were these little bugs called pond skaters. They'd balance on the surface with their legs splayed out, just balancing and never falling in. Looking at them made me feel really peaceful, and kind of frightened at the same time. Because they were doing okay, but underneath them was this murky deep that we'd been warned about so many times.

And then,

Three scratches down her back.

It bursts out of him. Harsher than I've ever heard before.

'Why won't you admit that you're a liar?'

Her voice is panicked. 'What?'

I picture his face reddening, eyes bulging.

'I mean, you're wasting my time, your mother's time, you've traumatised your poor cousin, bringing all this stuff up from her past, and for what? What did you think would happen when we came here, Nina?'

There is a pause, and I can barely make out her reply.

'I don't . . . I don't know.'

Her breath is coming fast and high.

Ensnared.

She's having a panic attack and still trying to answer questions through it.

I hear the tap running. A glass of water plonking in front of her.

Mr Q's voice:

'You're acting like a child. A silly child.'

Should I go in there? Instead of listening at the door. Is that what she would want?

'I . . .

'I . . .'

'You . . . You . . . You what, Nina? You what?'

She needs help.

Oz's voice cuts through. 'Dad, stop.'

'She has to learn that actions have consequences. She can't just play havoc with other people's lives. And that's what you were doing Nina, isn't it? Playing.'

Her voice again. It's broken.

'I don't know.'

'You don't know,' he says, mirroring her tone. 'Well, I don't know either. You can go now.'

She comes out. Wringing her cardigan out like it's a wet towel. I go to her and can see the tears about to come. I should go in and tell them what they did is unacceptable. That they should leave. She sees it in my eyes. Hand on my elbow.

'Don't,' she whispers.

I nod, but there is fury in my gut.

She isn't playing.

This is born of pain.

I hear raised voices coming from the kitchen.

'Let's go upstairs,' I say. 'Don't let them see you cry.'

'I can't,' she says. 'I can't. They won't believe me. Why won't they believe me?'

But maybe I can help her.

Help her show them.

She isn't lying.

They should be afraid.

'You can,' I say. 'You can. And we can make them. You and me. Together.'

a noise

The year that everything changed and I came to live with Susan and Nina, I moved schools. I don't remember being worried about it, when I look back on that weird time, between one life and another; it's a little like I'm watching a recording of myself or something. I don't know why. Things were getting better, my class was welcoming. I was making a huge effort to fit in, and be friendly and no trouble. I remember studying the games they played in the yard and getting Nina to go over them with me at home, so when I went back in I'd be able to join in seamlessly. I didn't want to give anyone any more reason to hate me. And they didn't.

Dad was still living with us at the time, but he was a different version of himself. He wasn't gentle. Once he tried to push me down the stairs, but I was too quick for him and he stumbled down a couple of steps himself and then turned to me with an expression on his face I still remember. It wasn't the dad I knew, but more like Mam. Sometimes I would spy on him and Susan talking just to see his face relaxed, the way he had been. I didn't understand what I'd done wrong, and I would bring home pictures I had done to show him, or try to tell him about a cool dog I had seen on the way home from school or something that had happened with my friends, but it never went right and eventually Susan started getting between us at times like this, sticking my art on the fridge, or pouring me a juice and listening to me while Dad went to another room with a cup of tea. I kept trying though, and maybe if I hadn't he'd still be living with us. If I had learned to give him space and time.

Nina was the kind of kid who liked imagination games when everyone else wanted to play chasing, hide-and-seek. She wanted the same things I wanted for Christmas even though I was a year and a half younger. I loved her for it. We would play together, but in school that kind of thing can open you to a world of hurt. I love her, but she's never been as good at making friends as I am. She wants to be, but something doesn't work. I think it's how much she cares how people see her. While I don't really want anyone to see me at all. Not all of me. The bad bits. I learned early how dangerous it is to be open. She's just herself, while I am something else, made up of the parts of me I think they'll like the best. The safer ones.

Take me.

What happened to Nina was small stuff, but small stuff is big when you're little. There were these girls she used to be friends with and then they stopped treating her like their friend. They scribbled on her copybook, ripped up a picture she had done, opened up the yoghurt from her lunchbox and poured it on the rest of her lunch so she had nothing to eat until the teacher gave her some carrot sticks and hummus, which must have been from her own lunch, thinking about it now. It wasn't a spare food kind of school. Nina would find me in the yard and play with me and the kids in my class, and it was nice to have her with us, but I was aware that it was weird as well. I was good at tuning in to normality because I wanted it, the same way that other kids want to be special. I had been special, and it was bad and terrible. I just wanted to be like everybody else. Nina was the cousin who minded me at night, when I cried, and never complained about me keeping her up when it must have been annoying.

And then one of them – this girl Sharon Mannion – called her a loser in front of me and I punched her in the face. There was no reasoning behind it, when she shaped the word it was like something in me snapped and I became all instinct. Her nose bled, because I had a mean left hook for a six-year-old, and she fell in the dirt. I told her Nina was my best friend and she needed to be a nicer person. That's also what I told the teacher when she gave out to me, and Susan when she came to pick us up and pop in for a 'quick chat'. And Susan told me that she understood exactly why I did it, but I couldn't ever do it again. Not that way. With punching. I remember bursting into tears when she said that, because I wasn't expecting her to understand, and I had been so worried that I would have to go somewhere like Dad did.

After Sharon, I looked out for Nina. I asked some people from her class and found out more and more of what happened. I went looking for her at lunchtimes, so she wouldn't have to come find me if she wanted someone to play with. I had been getting through day by day, humming somewhere between fear and numbness, and helping Nina gave me something to focus on, and it wasn't hard. To keep her close. To mind her.

Little by little, school got easier. But Nina never really had a group, the way I do with Abigail, Conchur, Megan and Piotr. Maybe she was scared that it would happen again. And maybe she was right. It could. Things do. Or maybe it was just that there was no one in particular she clicked with. And it's not that I'm a nicer person than Nina, it's just luck. It's not like she's entirely alone, she just doesn't have anyone that's as close to her as my friends are to me. She's kind of at the edge of the gang, rather than in it in it, if that makes sense. And I think that's why there's this humming around school about her. That this, this haunted thing, makes her weird and mockable, while with someone else it could be fascinating.

There are memes going around about her. Screenshots from videos she's posted with mean comments underneath them. Piotr sent me some, and Abigail too. Megan says they've seen them but didn't want to worry me, because 'What can you do?' and Conchur just looks angry about it. I mean, they don't get it. They care, but Nina's one degree removed from me. I'm their friend. And she is just my sister.

Not even a sister.

I think of her face, frozen at the most awkward angle, making her look like she had no neck at all, and underneath in all caps.

LIAR.

FUCKED A GHOST.

EVEN MY IMAGINARY FRIENDS HATE ME.

Then a gif of a Ouija board, spelling 'SEEN'.

I think of Sharon calling her a loser. But I can't punch everyone. Much and all as Mr Q could use a slap. And even if I could, it wouldn't fix this. I glance down at my hands. They

139

look like mine. And I get the full-length mirror from the hall and bring it into my room. It's heavy and there's a coating of dust on the topmost edge of it. I place it against the wall at the foot of my bed.

Mam's hands on my shoulders.
Her voice.

I close my eyes.
I want to help.
I can't.

You can.

They went quite quickly after the interview. I think Mr Quigley knew he'd gone too far. He started packing up pretty sharply, shuffling papers and unopened boxes full of stupid tech. When Susan came back from her walk, she looked like she'd been crying. I tried to tell Susan about what had happened, but Nina stopped me, told me to 'leave it alone'. She was quiet all evening after that. They both were and I could see the worry in their eyes, the same expression painted on two faces. They are the same, and I am not what they are.

I need to fix this. I wonder what it might mean, if he decides she's lying. The impact of it. Would everything go away? Or get much worse? I feel like it might break her, to be shamed like that. In front of Oz. I keep thinking of Mr Quigley's face in school, and the tone I heard on the other side of the door. And it would be hard to reconcile them if I didn't know how many faces a person can have. Can hide.

I get under the covers, but the glint of the mirror and everything else keep playing and replaying over and over in my head.

Just look at the surface of it, baby.

It's me.

It's you.

But it isn't you.

It's your reflection.

Just stare at yourself until you look like a stranger.

Not me?

No. Someone else. When that happens I want you to nod your head, okay?

Okay.

I get out of bed, take my fleecy dressing gown from the hook behind the door and hang it over the mirror. It doesn't help at all.

I cannot sleep.

tap

Nina is sitting on the floor, her hands around her knees, making herself as small as possible. She's always been good at that, when we were little, playing hide-and-seek. The only problem was that she'd start giggling. That's how you'd find her, following delight. No trace of that today.

'He's gearing up to tell everyone I'm a liar, Daisy,' she says to me, and there are two red spots on her cheeks. 'And I'm not one. Or I am. I don't know. I don't *know*.'

She looks at me like she is waiting for me to lash out, hurt her.

In so much pain.

I sigh.

'You're not a liar, Nina,' I tell her. 'This feels like a different kind of thing.'

'It's not the truth though,' she says, and her voice is small. 'It's not the truth. I wanted . . . I just wanted him to have to look at me. You know. To see what he had done.'

Her face is miserable.

'So fucking stupid.' The venom in her voice.

She needs your help.

We're sitting on my bed, waiting for Mr Q and Oz to call over and share their 'findings'.

'He's going to say I made everything up and there's no point in investigating and it'll get out and everyone will laugh. They'll laugh at me.'

They are already laughing.

I look at the mirror, covered up with a dressing gown. And I swallow. The thing about what Mam did to me is, once she'd done it we became a team. Two of us together, with this secret.

And Them as well.

The creatures.

Me and Nina are a team too. We have been since I came to live with them.

Sharon Mannion's voice.

She's not a loser.

And she isn't lying.

'No one's going to laugh at you, Nina,' I say. 'We'll work this out. Together.'

'What do you mean?' she asks. Her face is open, curious.

I swallow down my anger. Try to channel it towards a plan. It's not much of a one. It's all I have though. My voice comes out all sing-song like a child's.

'We can make it true. Together. The way Mam did to me, back in the day.'

'But . . . that wasn't real,' she says.

'Real can be a murky sort of thing,' I tell her. 'And any way at all that I can help . . . you know I'll do it, Neen. You know I would do anything for you.'

She breathes relief. 'Oh, Daisy.'

I bite down on my lip and taste the blood.

She reaches out for me, but doesn't touch me.

She is hurting. Hurting.

It's too much.

I hear her voice, but it's from far away, like underwater. 'Daisy, you don't have to do this. I mean, I got myself into this situation, you know. And I can take it. Everything that comes at me.' Her lower lip wobbles.

On the edge.

'You're my family, Nina,' I say. 'I don't want you to be hurt any more.'

I want to know what you're not telling me.

'If we . . .' she says, 'what do you think will happen?'

I look at her. I think of the wall inside my head. And for the first time in years and years, I strain to see if I can hear what's on the other side.

'Probably nothing,' I tell her. 'But, you won't be alone in this. I'll be beside you. With you.'

Nina swallows. 'Okay,' she says. 'Okay. How do we do this?'

She rises from the bed and her voice is bright, like we're putting a decal on a wall or making a new recipe.

She has no idea
what will happen,
what you're doing.

I swallow down the doubts. I count to ten, and stand in front of her, facing the mirror.

'Put your hands on my shoulders,' I say. 'I'm going to focus on my reflection until it feels like I'm looking at a stranger, and then I can say the words.'

Stop it.

Stop it.

Stop it.

I feel a jolt in my gut, and I'm not sure if it's nerves or something pushing.

'What do I do?' she asks.

'You make me not back out,' I say, biting my lip. 'It's not . . . it's not a good memory, this. She wasn't . . .'

Nina squeezes my shoulder. I do not shudder. Jut my jaw so hard it hurts my chin.

'I know,' she says.

'You know,' I say, 'but you don't feel it.' I stab my hand into my stomach. 'Here.'

'Oh, Daisy.'

Nina's hands on my shoulder are so different to the ones that I remember. They settle instead of dig. I look at my features until they stop being a face and become shapes instead. The space between my eyes, my mouth. My nose. My eyes forget what a face is and how to read one. It's just a collection of features. An alien thing.

I want to blink but I'm worried if I do that I will lose it.

Run.

And I'm gone beyond the right thing or the wrong thing. Here, in front of the mirror, this feels like the only thing to do.

And so I say it.

'I am open. Take me.

'I am open. Take me.

'I am open. Take me.

'I am open –'

Take me.

'What?' Nina says. 'You jolted there.'
I swallow, and I tell her it was nothing.
But it wasn't.

something you can't put your finger on

Mr Quigley is sitting on our nicest armchair, like he owns the place. Susan is perched on the couch and there's a pot of tea on the table. Oz Quigley is there too. He looks furious. His chin is even squarer, if that's possible.

In front of the mirror.
Nothing happened really.
I don't hear anything different.
I don't feel any different.
But . . . there was this sense of something reaching out and touching me.
Inside my head. And maybe it's just sense memory, hands on shoulders, making me uncomfortable. Stories that Mam told me to get me to do what she wanted me to do. It's hard to look at things that hurt us, scare us. That doesn't mean they can't still do that.

I look down at my hands. They're still my hands.
Nina squeezes her shoulder against mine and shrinks into the back of the sofa, like she wants it to eat her. She's put on lipstick, and covered up the big spot on her chin with concealer.

I don't know where she even got the time.

I was standing in front of the mirror.

And now we're here.

He strokes his beard like it's a beloved puppy dog.

'Having interviewed you, and done an initial assessment of the house . . .' he says. And his voice is the voice a teacher has right before you have to go to the principal's office.

'. . . we both feel that there is insufficient evidence to justify continuing the investigation.'

Susan looks at Nina. 'Nina, love . . .' She reaches out a hand.

'You think I'm lying,' Nina says.

And Oz begins to say, 'No –' but his father cuts him off.

'Junior – don't. It's kinder in the long run.' And he sighs. 'Yes. I think you're lying, Nina. The instances you've posted can all be disproved. The evidence all points to things that could be done by human hands quite easily. And we have to take that into account . . .'

Her voice cracks. 'It happened, Austin,' she says. 'It happened. It was real.'

Austin.

I glare at Oz, he's looking past us, at the curtain rail. Susan turns to us. Her eyes ask questions. What will we do next?

Just wait.

Just wait.

'We have concluded otherwise,' he says. 'Which is what happens in ninety-nine per cent of these cases. I'm sorry we couldn't be of more help.'

His voice becomes gentler. 'These things can be psychiatric

148

in nature. There's no shame in it. It's much more common than encountering a presence actually. I could give you a list of other investigators, most of whom are based in other counties, but I don't think it would be fair of me to refer you on to anyone. The help you need isn't the kind of help we can provide.'

He nods briskly.

'Wait,' I say. 'So, the scratches. The things flying through the air. The things that moved around. The noises. The orbs. The seaweed. Everything. You think it was all Nina.'

He nods again. 'We don't need to rehash it. I understand it's a painful subject and still ongoing, but all we can do is make measured assessments based on what we've observed.'

He stands. 'It's probably for the best. You must be sick of us two hanging around the place by now.'

He waggles his eyebrows in what I think he thinks is a jovial manner.

'Come on now, son, let's get this show on the road.'

Oz Quigley looks at his father like he hates him.

He does hate him.

He turns to us. To Nina.

'I'm sorry,' he says. 'I'm so sorry, Nina. I wish we could have been more help to you. But . . .'

She smiles. 'It's okay, Oz. It is what it is.'

'Yeah.'

'Well,' Susan says, a little brusquely, 'thank you both so much for your help. I think the rest is something we will look at as a family.'

She stands up. 'Thanks again.'

149

I look at Nina, pushed against the back of the sofa like it could swallow her up. I look at her, like.

We tried.

And we did try. Mr Quigley shakes Susan's hand, and goes to move.

Nina stands up, suddenly blocking his path. She holds her hand out to him. He flinches before taking it.

It isn't rudeness though.

It's something else.

Oz looks at the two of them. Like he despises everything about himself, this moment.

And I . . .

Jaws unhinge.
And something in my gut.

a fright

We decided to walk to school this morning. The air is crisp, and we need to talk without Susan. She offered to drop us, but Nina told her the movement would be good for her, and she's always telling us that there's a great cure in exercise, so she couldn't really argue.

'She keeps trying to have heart-to-hearts with me,' Nina said. 'Like coming into my room and asking how I am, while gently holding leaflets about counsellors.'

'Subtle,' I say.

'I know.' Nina rolls her eyes. 'It's hideous. I'm trying my best not to stab her. And it's not her fault, I know.'

'Having them in was a bad idea,' I say. 'Mr Q –'

'Having them in was what I wanted, Daisy.' Nina's face is hard to read. 'Like, it would have kept on going and going because I had this weird idea in my head that it would somehow fix things, and I don't know why because it makes no sense.'

'I understand,' I say. 'Remember when I tried to help you out by re-enacting painful childhood memories? Thank God that didn't work.'

'Sometimes it is ridiculous how sisters we are,' Nina says.
I nod.

Nina adjusts her school bag on her shoulder.

'What do you think will happen now?' I ask.

'I've no idea. I mean, people were already being horrible, you know? So they can't be more horrible.'

People can always be more horrible.

'If you need company for lunch or anything, I'm here,' I tell her.

'Thanks, Daisy,' she says, but I know she's not going to take me up on it. 'I think, if I'm quiet about it, and Oz is quiet about it too, then maybe it might just die down a little. And no one has sent me any awful messages for a few days, so that's always lovely.'

'Oh, Neen,' I say. 'I'm sorry.'

'I'm used to it,' she says. 'Kind of. And you're here.'

'Have you been sleeping?' I ask 'Since . . . ?'

Her face brightens. 'Actually, yeah,' she tells me. 'I mean, I didn't get what I wanted from it, but I kind of realised that I didn't want him back, you know? That maybe the way he acted was a kind of blessing or something. And I can just kind of . . . pretend it didn't happen and move on with things.'

Build a wall.

'Sounds good to me.'

It doesn't work that way.
You know that, Daisy.

words

No one has sent me any hateful stuff about Nina for a few days. I asked Abigail, Conchur and everyone to keep forwarding it on to me so I can keep track. Like, if there's any sort of bullying thing and Susan has to get the school involved, I think it would be good to have some evidence.

Piotr, Abigail, Conchur and Megan are gentle with me, though they did ask a lot of questions about Mr Q and Oz. I told them all about his boringness and studded belt and glossed over the way he spoke to Nina. I don't want to discredit her, even though he deserves to pay for what he did. No teacher should act like that to one of their students. Part of me wishes I'd recorded it on my phone instead of just in my brain. If we tried to complain to Sister Agatha, he could just deny it. And Oz would back him up, or just stay silent. Not that Nina even wants to say anything. Even to Susan. She thinks it's over now. And that's enough.

Megan asked me if he found anything, and I said, 'Sure they barely did anything, just talked to us and fucked off, they were no help at all.'

Which isn't necessarily true, but how could I tell them more when I don't have the words for it exactly, this heavy sense of fear, surrender, loss?

Susan was kind of annoyed about the whole thing.

'He didn't even put his cups in the sink,' she said, as if this was the hallmark of a master criminal. 'And I didn't like his tone when he talked about you, Nina.'

'It was not a great tone,' I said. 'Geography class is going to be so weird and awkward now.'

Nina bit her lip and looked out the window, so I felt bad and tried to soften things.

'Which might have been the ghost's plan all along.'

Susan's voice. 'That isn't funny, Daisy.'

Nina tilted her head, her lips curved upward.

'It is a bit, and Daisy has a point, Mom. Ghosts famously hate geography . . . but . . . I mean . . . I just have this feeling like . . . maybe we can draw a line under it now, and whatever it was might just be . . . gone.'

Her voice was very low, we almost had to strain to hear. Susan looked over at me, and there was such hope in her eyes it almost made me cry. I feel it too. Normal is such a little thing to want, but when it's missing it becomes enormous. But maybe . . . all this bad stuff coming to the surface, this confronting . . . it mightn't be the worst thing in the world.

It's Megan's birthday on Saturday, and they're having a thing, which is nice; it's just myself and Abigail sleeping over, Conchur and Piotr have to go home, which is ridiculous because what do their parents think, that we'd all have a big orgy if we slept in the one room together? I mean, Susan's the same, which doesn't even make sense, as you would think she'd realise that people who aren't boys can also fool around with each other. I suppose the odds are it's safer or something. I'm looking forward

154

to it though. I bought Megan a top they wanted, with a cat on it. Like a sort of abstract art demonic-looking cat. Susan has these coasters she got in Australia of something called the Dreamtime and the art on the T-shirt looks a bit like that, all dots and colours. It's really nice, but I'd never wear it, if that makes sense. I like that Megan sees the world a different way to me. Fewer rules, more joy. I got them a sketchbook as well. I don't know what it is, but I want to make them smile, particularly since they've stepped into themself. I need to keep that side of things in check though. For their sake. Getting close to me – I don't know if it would be good for anyone.

an unexpected jolt

I get a notification.

It's Oz Quigley. I feel a bit taken aback. He shouldn't be messaging me. Nina wouldn't like it. We're not friends.

How are you holding up, friend?

JESUS CHRIST. I swallow.

We're not friends. Not after what you did to Nina.

Okay pal.

It was not okay.

I know, buddy.

Is this how you wooed her?
By persistently ignoring her express wishes? SO SEXY.

I'm not great at wooing, to be honest.

Am I supposed to feel sorry for you?

A friend would. So no.

Thank you for listening

How is Nina?

I think of the dark circles underneath her eyes.

Okay
She's eating more
And sleeping
Which is good

Food and sleep are important

They are

What are you going to do next?
I mean if it keeps happening.

Don't know
It's been quiet for a few days now though which
is something

I see that he's typing but nothing else comes up, even when I check it later on.

Nina sees. 'Who are you messaging?' she asks. 'Is it MEGAN?'

'No,' I say. 'Oz Quigley. He messaged to ask how you are.' I hold out the phone to her but she doesn't take it.

'That was very . . . human of him,' she says, and her expression is hard to read.

'Yeah,' I say, 'I suppose it was. It was also the fucking least he could do.'

'I don't know,' Nina says. 'I think the least he could do is never contact me or my family again. I mean, they were no help.'

'Less than none,' I say. 'The way he spoke to you. That man. It wasn't right. He, like, got off on making you feel small.'

She doesn't say anything.

'Nina?'

The smallest twitch at the base of her throat.

'Maybe he had a point.' She looks away from me, towards the window. 'I mean, I was carrying around all this fear, Daisy, and it had to spill out some way and maybe that's what the ghost was. Or is. And it wasn't Oz's fault. What happened. In a way, he had nothing to do with it. All me. My energy or whatever. They tend to glom on to teenage girls, don't they, ghosts? Bit by bit until all of a sudden you're haunted and your life has changed completely.' She smiles ruefully.

'Do you think it will come back?' I ask. 'The ghost, or poltergeist, or whatever it is?'

> *It's not just her.*
> *It's something.*
> *Something bigger.*

> *What was that?*

I shake myself. She needs me. She is speaking.

'No. Not at this stage. I mean, it's been a week. A week is a long time in ghost world.'

I smile. It will be nice to not come home wondering how haunted it will be.

'I've deleted loads of apps off my phone too. In case I get tempted to post.'

'That's good,' I say. 'People aren't nice.'

'Yeah. I've seen. My friends sent me loads of them. *Just so I'd know.*'

'Yeah, everyone was sending them to me as well out of *concern.*' I roll my eyes. 'But you kind of wonder how people kept on receiving them?'

Nina stares out the window. 'They either joined in, or didn't say anything,' she tells me. 'That's what people are like.'

'Is that not a bit harsh?' I ask.

'I think it's accurate. You know the way after the break-up with Caroline, Susan kept on saying, "People can surprise you," about things like Gemma and Owen helping us move?'

'Yeah?' I'm not sure where she is going with this.

'Well, people can surprise you in other ways too.'

'Nina, what actually happened?'

She turns her head and looks at me with her big, dark eyes. 'I'll tell you, Daisy, someday. But not now. Okay?'

'Okay,' I say. 'As long as you know I'm here for you.'

'Sure, I've always known that.'

My phone buzzes again. I think of Oz's face. He looks like a colourised black-and-white photo. Not good-looking exactly. But classic. I flip my phone onto its front so I can ignore it.

You can't ignore it though.

'Are you going to Megan's thing tomorrow?' Nina is smiling.

'Yeah,' I say. 'Do you want to come?'

'No, no,' she says. 'It would be weird.'

'They'd be fine with it,' I say, though to be honest I'm not sure they would be.

She rubs at the back of her neck.

'You okay?'

'Yeah.' She smiles at me. 'It's just a draught or something.'

a weight on your chest

Susan drops me outside Megan's house. Her hair is really shiny. She looks nice, all dressed up to have dinner with Tricia and Gemma and them. It's been ages since she went out, with everything going on. She seems almost happy this evening. As though a cloud has lifted. I suppose that makes sense.

I'm half an hour early, which is an annoying amount of early to be. I almost wish Nina had come with me for the company, I don't like the thought of her being on her own. I debate walking the block but I have my bag with present, pyjamas, sleeping bag, etc., in, and it feels like too much effort. I didn't get a lot of sleep last night. I think we might have mice. I could hear one scuttling around the floor of my room, and the thought of it creeping all over my things with its little animatronic-looking mouse feet is deeply unpleasant. I feel like we should be pest-free for the next fifteen years, after the nonsense we've had.

It's wild how quickly it seems to have died down. It's a huge relief, but I look at Nina and I worry that whatever it was that caused the haunting is still there, lurking inside her.

Megan's house is nice. A bit like ours, but not as new, or as cold, and with an extra room for their brother David, who is nine, to play in. Their mother, Etta, answers the door.

'Hi, Daisy. How are you keeping? Megan's just getting ready, they'll be a few minutes. Come on into the sitting room.'

She looks at me, her smile a little strained. I don't know if I'm still supposed to tell her how I'm keeping, so I just say thanks and smile. The sitting room is nice. There's a big TV and a squishy sofa. Megan's shoved the beanbag from their room in there, it's a massive yellow one with a corduroy cover and I kind of want to flop down on that, but it feels rude, so I sort of perch on the sofa, and say, 'This looks nice.' It does look nice. We're getting pizza, but there's all sweets and crisps and things laid out in little bowls and bottles of Diet Coke and 7 Up and some cupcakes.

'You've gone all out,' I say, smiling. 'There's enough here to feed our whole year.'

'Megan bought it all today in Tesco.' She smiles proudly. 'They saved the money up from their cleaning job.'

Megan works as a cleaner on the weekends for a couple of houses in their estate. They prefer it to babysitting because they can just put in their headphones and scrub. I prefer babysitting myself. Snacks and cartoons trump toilets every time. I check my phone. No new messages.

Good, I think, turning off my data. Let it stay that way.

Megan comes in, cradling their cat, Simon. Simon is a one-eyed tuxedo cat and Megan's nickname for him is My Actual Child.

'Happy birthday,' I say. 'How is the baby?'

'My furry son is my heart's delight. Aren't you, Simon?'

Simon makes a noise halfway between a purr and a cry for help while Megan snuggles his furry tummy.

162

'Mom and me just had a chat about pronouns.' Megan smiles angrily, rolling the curtains and perching on the piano stool beside the television. 'Typical birthday high jinks.'

'I'm sorry, pal,' I say.

'I know it's an adjustment.' They widen their eyes. 'But when I correct her, it's like she takes it as me saying she's a terrible mother who goes around doing hate crimes all day long. And I suppose it's good that she feels bad and wants to try, but it's just. Exhausting. And it's my birthday. I feel like my birthday shouldn't be all about her, you know?'

I nod. 'I mean, I don't know. My mother is . . . kind of . . . dead, and Susan's different.'

Megan makes a face like they don't know what to say.

'But it's your actual birthday, Megan. Like, fifteen years of you in the world. And I'm sorry you had to have a hard conversation with your mom.'

'It's fine.'

'It isn't fine. Like, it doesn't have to be blatant intolerance to be emotionally draining.'

Megan swallows. 'She told me how many hours she was in labour with me. Again. And literally all I wanted was an "excuse me I forgot I will try harder".' They push their face into Simon's fur.

'Like, she acts sometimes like me being non-binary is this test for *her*. Like who I am is difficult.'

'Oh, Meg,' I say. 'That's bullshit. Can I offer you a hug or some cake? I could also spill something on her good sofa, if that would help?'

'Thanks, Daisy. I'll take the hug, please. But it will be an

163

angry hug.' They rise from the stool and move towards me. I stand up.

'Like how Vikings used to hug when they needed a hug mid-battle.'

I wrap my arms around them, and Megan rests their head on my shoulder. I can see the soft point of hair at the back of their neck, that piece that they crop closer. I don't mind hugs like this. When I have offered.

Simon, who Megan is still somehow cuddling, in spite of our hug, lets out a very put-upon chirping sound.

'Your son is a bird,' I tell Megan.

'He surely is. Lil chirpy sparrow, hopping around asking for crumbs, flapping his little sparrow wings. My angel child.'

'How long do cats live?' I wonder.

'Why would you ask that?' Megan gasps. 'A HUNDRED YEARS. They live A HUNDRED YEARS.'

'Fair,' I say. 'What movie are we watching?'

'I haven't decided. I have, like, a shortlist of five, and thought we could take a vote.'

'Piotr will end up deciding.'

They nod. 'Probably. But it is my birthday, so maybe not? Like, I know he likes to be the boss of films, but perhaps I could be the boss of things, on this, the anniversary of the day I burst forth into the world after seventy-two hours of labour.' They roll their eyes.

I nod.

The doorbell goes, and Megan heads to answer it. Simon snuggles into me, and I rub his head. He's a really friendly cat, like even people who aren't cat people tend to love him.

164

Mainly because Megan insists we do, for fear of damaging his fragile feline self-esteem.

'He'll never get into a good college if you don't all believe in him,' is the kind of thing they say about him.

Piotr and Conchur arrive together, both wearing slightly different stripy jumpers. They tell us that it wasn't on purpose.

'I mean, of course it wasn't,' Megan says. 'Nobody would dress that way on purpose.'

'It's too coordinated not to be noticeable, but not coordinated enough to look, like, good with it,' I add.

'Thanks, Daisy,' Conchur snaps. 'This is what I get for wearing more than one colour.'

Conchur is a big fan of black, grey, navy blue. Like the colours your eye kind of drifts over. It's quite a soothing way to dress actually.

Abigail arrives an hour late, full of apologies.

'Dad forgot to pick me up from French grinds. And it was a WHOLE kerfuffle,' she says, plonking her overnight bag beside mine in the hall. 'He's still getting to grips with my schedule. And Mom is kind of letting him.'

Abigail's parents separated last year, and her dad moved out for a while. He moved back in a month ago, and is trying to do more of the stuff Abigail's mom usually does, like lifts, but he is also always stressed about work, so he forgets her a lot.

'Are you okay? 'I ask.

She rolls her eyes up and flaps a hand at her face like she's trying not to cry. 'Yeah. I am. But it's like –' she swallows – 'it's like before I could get angry at Dad, or give out about him. But now, when I do that, I worry that it'll, like, break up the

165

family again or something, so there's all this tension in my stomach all the time. And I just want to SCREAM.'

'You can scream,' Megan says. 'Let it out. We don't mind.'

'Really?' Abigail brightens. 'You won't mind?'

'No,' Megan says. 'We're your friends. It's what we're here for.'

Abigail releases an ear-splitting howl.

We all look at each other.

'I kind of meant like metaphorically,' Megan says, their face bemused.

Etta pops her head in. 'Is anyone being murdered?'

'No, Mom,' Megan says.

'Grand so, saves me calling the guards. I'll be in the kitchen if you need me. Having a glass of wine the size of my head.'

Megan looks at me, and raises an eyebrow. I smile.

'Thanks, Mom. Bye.'

It's a really calm evening. Like on Abigail's birthday we went drinking, but Megan didn't want any of that, so we watch a movie with absolutely no ghosts in it and talk all the way through. I'm curled up on the sofa beside Abigail and Conchur, trying not to look at Megan too much in case it gets annoying. Everyone is wearing shoes but me and them. I hope it isn't rude, that I'm in socks.

Conchur tilts his head towards me. 'You look worried. Everything okay?'

'Yeah,' I say. 'I was just thinking about shoes.'

'That really sounds like a lie,' Abigail says. 'I mean, you don't really do lies so I know it's not, but you looked way

166

more anxious there than you did when your house was haunted.'

'I think it could have been mice,' I say. 'I heard them in my room last night. Like some of the scuffling and things moved about was probably absolutely mice.'

'Well, it certainly wasn't ghosts,' says Piotr with a snort.

'I don't know,' I say. 'I don't think I can speak for Nina, and I don't think I know everything about the world.'

'But ghosts though?' he says.

'If this were a horror film,' Conchur tells him, 'your scepticism would get you a gory yet satisfying death.'

'Oh my God, yes,' says Megan. 'He'd be, like, squished by a garage door, hand in a blender, repeatedly stabbed on camera all over his face and body.'

'By ghosts?' I ask.

They nod. 'Of course by ghosts.'

'Sceptics never get the death where it's like one beautiful trickle of blood down the side of the head,' Abigail says. 'That's how Nina would go. She's totally the main character's hot best friend. That hair. You can just see it wrapped around a serial killer's hands, like.'

'See, Nina probably needs a compliment right now,' I say, 'but this is not one that I will be sharing with her.'

'It isn't real, Daisy.' Abigail's voice is offended. 'Like, I wouldn't wish anything bad on her. Not really.'

'It's not a movie or a story though,' I say, and I know I should just stop and not keep going, but it spills out of me despite myself. 'It's me not sleeping through the night. It's cuts on her skin and hollows under her eyes. It's fear, Abigail. All day long.

Worry about if something will happen and what it will be and what it could mean, about Nina or about the way I perceive the world. It's all the screenshots you guys sent me about someone I love, because you thought I should know, but I don't know if you thought through what knowing that would feel like for me. Or if I had to know about every single one of them.'

I'm curled up in a ball, looking down at my knees.

Megan's voice is gentle. 'Daisy.'

I keep on going though. It's been welling up. 'Like, I wondered why you kept on getting them sent to you. Was it that sending them to me made you feel better about not sticking up for my family when we were going through something really hard? Like, you were bullied, Conchur, in primary school. And so was Nina, and now it's happening to her all over again, and I can't stop it.'

'But she posted –'

'Oh, she was *asking* for it, was she? With her public fear and pain?' I put my head in my hands and try to stop myself from saying more things.

'She wanted people to see it, Daisy,' Piotr says. 'And people are largely horrible.'

'I know,' I say. 'But I thought . . .'

'We're sorry, Daisy,' Abigail said. 'None of us have been in this situation before. A haunting, like.'

Conchur doesn't say anything.

'Are you going to say something, Conchur?' Megan asks.

'Are you?' he says.

'Yeah.' They turn to me. 'I'm sorry if it didn't seem like I cared, because I do. And I did stick up for Nina. Not as much

168

as I should have though. Like, it was gentle protest, not actual giving out.'

Conchur sighs. 'It did bring up stuff for me, thanks so much for the reminder, Daisy. And I mainly got my brother to send me stuff, because I genuinely thought you knowing would mean you'd know, and you could tell her what would be good for her to know. Like, some of the people sharing that stuff were supposed to be her good friends. I'm fairly sure it's what I would have wanted . . .'

He messes with his hair. We don't make eye contact.

'Look,' I say, 'I'm sorry for getting ranty. And I know you were all trying to help. It's just been a lot to deal with.'

'We get it,' says Abigail. 'Or we don't, really. But we're here for you.'

I smile.

'I know.'

'My mom is at the bottom of the road.' Conchur gets up. 'Are you coming, Piotr?'

'Yeah.' Piotr grabs his jacket. 'Happy birthday, Megan, see ye Monday.'

'Bye.'

The door clinks shut. I sigh.

That wasn't way too awkward, was it?

'So. Piotr was looking at you a *lot*,' Abigail says, smiling at Megan. 'Do you think he still . . . ?'

Megan nods. 'I don't know. He did get me a sketchbook and a pin with a cat on it.'

Abigail smiles more. 'Sketchbooks are his love language.' She waggles her eyebrows.

I GOT THEM A SKETCHBOOK TOO.

They smile at me. 'I thought it was really sweet.'

'It was sweet,' Abigail tells them.

I smile. 'Really sweet.'

My jaws hurt. Megan has this small little smile. Like a quirk of the mouth, with just a hint of teeth. It warms you up, that smile.

I look down at my hands. They're still my hands. It's over. These are good, normal problems to have.

We change into our pyjamas, but basically stay up talking and eating and watching two more movies, one set in New York, where Megan wants to live someday. Not forever, but for a year or two, and one about a very handsome and successful cat, because they want Simon to have good role models.

Abigail and Megan are asleep, and I can see the street lights dimming, the grey light of the morning filtering through. I check my phone. Four messages from Nina.

> Hey, why'd you come back from the party?
> Is everything okay?
> Call me when you get this?
> Where'd you go?

I reply.

> I'm still at the party, Nina
> Party being a very strong word
> It was basically just five people eating a lot and watching films

Three people now

She's typing.

. . .
. . .
. . .
. . .
. . .

Who was in my room, watching me sleep?

a trace

When Abigail's dad dropped me home, Nina had gone for a walk, and she didn't come back for an hour and a half. I was humming with anxiety by the time she bounced in.

'Nina.'

'Daisy?'

'What were those messages?'

'I don't know. It must have been a dream. I woke up and my wardrobe was open a crack, which I thought was funny because I have that thing about keeping it closed.'

'Yeah,' I say. My hands are shaking a little, so I sit on them, look up at her.

'And I went back to sleep, but just before I did, you were in the room looking at me; you were wearing a quilted dressing gown with little daisies, like the one you had when you first came to live with us.' Her voice is strange – it's like I'm listening to a recording. I suddenly feel very far away.

'I don't still have that.' My voice comes out a whine. 'Even if I did, it wouldn't fit.'

> It wasn't me.
> She needs to know that.
> Does she?

172

'I know,' Nina says. 'That's what convinced me it must be a dream. You were there in your dressing gown smiling but it wasn't the same smile you normally have, It was more like . . . I don't know. It felt like a pretend smile, if you get me. Like your mouth was a top that didn't fit right. But I was so tired, and I was glad that you were there because I get a bit frightened since everything, and you're a really calming presence.'

I bark a laugh.

'Well, for me you are. So I was happy you were there and I drifted back off, but when I woke up you were gone, and my wardrobe door was shut again, so I went looking for you, and that's when I messaged . . .'

'It could be sleep paralysis,' I say. 'Like what I get sometimes.'

'Yeah,' she says. 'It felt so real though.'

'It can,' I say. 'Sometimes it feels like you're there for ages, like. And there can be things there too, bad things, that feel so real.'

She nods. 'Maybe so . . . But, Daisy, I could move.'

'If I show up in your room again, Nina . . .' I say. 'If I show up and I don't seem like I'm me, could you do me a favour?'

'Okay.'

'Don't look at me or talk to me. Just pretend I'm not there.'

'Do you think . . . ?' she asks.

'I don't think anything,' I tell her. 'I just. I just think we need to be a bit careful with dreams like that. That don't feel like they're dreams.'

'What do you see when you get dreams like that?'

'Shadows, mainly. Nothing to write home about.'

She nods again. 'Thanks, Daisy.'

I go into the bathroom and wash my face, and push the rough fibres of the towel against it until I feel like they have marked my skin. They haven't though.

I trace my hands over my forehead, cheeks.

I can't see anything. There is no difference.

images that flicker

Nina is on the laptop. I can hear the clicking of the keys. Her room is dark and when I knocked she said that she was busy. And what can you do, if someone will not let you in? You leave, you find another thing to do. You worry.

I have been thinking about what watched her sleep.

I sit on my bed and I look at the mirror. Waiting to feel something on the nape of my neck. I should put it back in the hall. It might help me to feel like I'm alone. I used to keep a packet of biscuits in my room for studying, but with the mice I've started putting them in the kitchen, which means they get eaten. Nina and Susan both get snacky when they're stressed, while I'd forget to eat. I like to have a biscuit while I'm focusing on something though. A small ritual, stolen by the mice.

I am open.

Take me.

I said the words.

And now . . .

I reach my two hands out and lift up the mirror. It's taller than I am, and really good if you're trying to see an outfit from head to toe. I carry it out to the hall, to the place it used to be. There's a hook there for it, and I won't miss it from the foot of my bed, I should have put it back ages ago, but for some reason I didn't. It was like I didn't want to touch it, which is ridiculous because it's not dirty or anything, it's just a mirror. Glass and metal and a wooden frame.

I am open.

Take me.

I hoist it up onto the nail poking out of the plaster of the wall and release it. There is a sound from Nina's room, something between a cough and a laugh. I call to her.

'Is everything okay?'

'It is. Stop worrying.'

I turn back to adjust the mirror.

And meet my gaze. Eyes narrow, intent on getting it straight. I straighten my hair, wisps escaping from my scrunchie. Smooth it down.

Look at myself. And wonder.

What will happen?

A wide white smile opens my face. I squint, and put a hand up to my mouth.

It's closed. Relaxed.

I am not smiling.

I continue staring at my reflection as it catches itself, adjusts its expression back to meet my own.

And winks at me.

I am transfixed. I don't know what to do. I look at me.

Slowly my reflection turns and walks into Nina's room. Shuts the door.

I try to move.

I can't.

The mirror's empty.

'Nina,' I say. And then a little louder. 'Nina. Nina?'

Daisy.

Her hands.
My shoulders.
Listen to them, pet.
You need to listen.

a scar

I stood there at the top of the stairs for hours until Nina left her room. When she did, it was like I'd been given permission to move. My shoulders slumped and I traced one finger over the breath-fog on the mirror, keeping my eyes open to see if I'd come back. I blinked, and there I was. But this time it was just my own reflection. It was doing what I was doing. Just standing there, stock-still, my mind reeling.

What have I done?

good at hiding

It's been quiet.
But the mice.

They are not really mice.

The sounds they make.

hard to see

I'm trying to ignore what happened with the mirror. I mean, what I think I saw. It was probably my imagination playing tricks, and maybe if I keep a level head, it might not happen again. Like Susan used to say to Nina about the bullies. *Ignore them, they'll get tired soon enough.*

It didn't work though.

I don't want to make things more difficult than they have to be.

I wrap a thick green scarf around my neck to mask the chill, if it comes, and pull the sleeves of my jumper over my hands. I want to wrap myself in layers and layers of cloth today, until I'm all protected from the world.

'You look like you're about to drop down dead,' Susan says very matter-of-factly. 'Have an egg.'

Susan made fried eggs for breakfast. She had a craving apparently. I spread butter and ketchup on toast and make a sandwich with the egg inside, brown lace around the edges and runny yolk, like butter-blood. My teeth meet each other and I chew and chew until it is a paste, and then I swallow.

'Good, eh?' Susan smiles. She's in much better form these

days. Smiling, humming, making surprise eggs. Having no ghosts agrees with her. How could I ruin that?

Nina covers her toast with peanut butter and begins slicing a banana. Nina doesn't like the idea of hurting animals. I used to forward her plant facts every now and then, about how plants mind each other in the forest. About this botanist who claimed that trees scream as they are chopped down. But then she genuinely started getting upset about vegetables so I stopped.

'Would you ever go back on meat?' Susan asks, not for the first time.

'No.'

'Or even the odd egg?'

'Absolutely not.' Nina's eyebrows draw closer together, I can see her take a deep breath in.

'Hmm. We should bring you to the GP. Check your iron levels. It could have contributed to all this stuff.' Susan's brow is furrowed.

Nina scoffs. 'Ugh. Look, my iron levels are always fine. I'm tired. And you're tired too . . .'

'I'm not that tired.' Susan's smiling though.

'And Daisy is fully over there being tired while eating an egg. My diet is probably better for me than yours is for you.' Nina smiles. 'But I don't want to judge.'

'No, never,' Susan says. 'But I still think we could give it a go. Would you do it for me? The blood test?'

Nina smiles. 'You know I think I don't need to.'

'I do.'

'You know I'm never going to eat meat again.'

Susan smiles. 'I know you think you won't.'

'I won't. Ugh, Mom.' Nina rises from the table and starts packing her lunch. She is wearing a long-sleeved shirt and the cuffs are tightly buttoned.

I look at her face, scanning for signs of . . . what?

Of something.

a dull surprise

Last night I dreamed I got my period, and I was trying to wash blood off my sheets. Scrubbing and scrubbing but there it was. I couldn't get the bloom of it to fade. And down between my legs, the blood kept coming.

an ellipsis

Nina finds me and pulls me into the girls' bathroom with the yellowed walls. When Susan was in school, they used to smoke in there. She told us that once on parent-teacher night. She doesn't smoke any more, though sometimes when we were younger I remember her and Caroline out on one of the little balconies, passing a cigarette from one to the other. I asked her once what it was like back then.

'Harder in some ways, softer in others,' she said, running one hand through the front of her hair, so awkwardly that I could almost see the girl she'd been. Her mouth turned down at the corners. Sealed. She likes to tell me happy things, I get it. The strange weight of deciding what to share. Then and now, she's always had her secrets. She never really talks to Nina about her dad. Not the whole story. It must be hard to keep so much inside.

Exhausting.

Since that night, the mirror, I haven't reached out for Them. Whatever They are. But I feel the gooseflesh rising, not just when I'm at home, though mostly there. There is this constant low hum somewhere between traffic speeding past and a fridge door left open. It gets louder, quieter. Never stops.

I am open.
Take me.

I've been so stupid.

'I've been so stupid,' Nina says. 'And you're probably going to hate me for this.'

The linoleum feels strange under my feet, as though the floor beneath was giving way. I shake my head and try to ground myself. 'I'll never hate you, Nina.'

'Good.'

'It is good. You're WONDERFUL.' I smile at her and she smiles back in spite of herself.

'So,' she says, and the so is like a five-page history essay.

I widen my eyes.

'So . . .' she says again.

I trace my hand over some of the writing on the doors. 'Some of it's really old,' I say. 'Lot of history.'

'Yeah,' Nina says. 'You could do, like, a whole museum just on school bathrooms, probably. Susan used to meet her first girlfriend in a particular stall. In secret.'

Her voice when she says 'secret' sounds so sad.

'Who, Joan?' I ask. Joan had long red hair and played badminton. Susan told me about her when I told her I was bi. Joan lives in Colorado now, married to a dentist called Leona. She showed me the pictures on her timeline. I remember smiling at her and saying, 'They look so happy,' And she smiled back and said she thought so too, she hoped they were.

'Yeah.' She said it to me. 'I think she was trying to get me to open up to her.'

185

'Yeah, she used Joan for that on me too, back in the day . . .
Did it work?'

Nina rolls her eyes. 'Of course not.' She sighs.

'So what was your *so* about?' I ask.

A first year comes in, takes one look at us and leaves again.
Nina smiles at me, mouths, 'Boo!' I touch her sleeve, and watch
her features twist. Her voice is small.

She doesn't want to tell you.

'So. You know the way things kind of died down, apart from
that dream?'

I nod.

'Well . . .'

She unbuttons her cuffs.

'. . . I woke up with this.'

There are raised red marks all the way up her arm.

I wince.

Her pain, her pain.

She swallows.

'There was . . . there was a lot to what happened before,
Daisy, but this . . . This wasn't me. This wasn't my ghost.'

I reach my hand out to her arm. 'Can I?'

She nods. I haltingly trace my hand down the length of her
forearm, investigating, soothing –

– My fingers almost mirror the marks. Four thick runnels.

My fault my fault

They don't look like ordinary scrapes. The others were
thinner, the work of fingernails, a razor blade perhaps.

I feel the flesh on my forearms begin to pucker.

'Nina,' I say. 'This looks like . . .'

186

She nods. 'I know.'

Her voice is very small. It's almost nothing. 'It's like . . .' she says. 'It's like something is inside me. Trying to get out.'

I close my eyes.

> *I have been pushing Them away.*
> *And They have hurt her.*

a power

Nina wanted us to do the Ouija board tonight. She said that leaving Them alone wouldn't work. That anything had to be better than nothing. I told her there was no point. They are already here. It's just a waiting game now. To see what They will do. The things They want. Her hands moved in the air, her eyes were flashing.

'That's what I mean. We could just ask them, Daisy. And then we'd know.'

I do not want to know.

I remember more and more each day.

Things I couldn't – didn't want to – touch.

Looking at a colleague of Mam's. Her face sceptical, indulgent.
Thinking that I was a fraud, a child.
Childhood makes fraud more palatable.

I look her up and down and tell her the things They tell me
about her.
A litany.
A list.
Her crumpled face.

188

Mostly it was comforting for people. But every now and then an evisceration would be necessary. And the hum of satisfaction underneath the words they were giving me was like when Dad and I were walking down by the woodland path behind our estate and we saw a cat and thought it was asleep, and Dad prodded it with a branch and all of a sudden there were maggots everywhere. Teeming. It was not alive. Just full of life. That writhing mass of hunger. That intensity.

Maggots cannot but be maggots.

The creatures are like that.

And They know things.

A voice in my head couldn't hurt my Nina on her arms.

So it must be real.

But how much of it.

Am I breaking down?

Or was I already broken?

Something awful spilling out of me.

And onto her.

a favour

I got given out to today. Miss Dunphy basically went for me in front of everyone. It was humiliating; you'd think she'd know that the reason I've been missing out on homework, falling behind, is because I'm wrecked from all of this. Whatever this is. Humming in my head, and all this tension. Constant tuning in and tuning out. I don't know what they want from me. Before, I never thought about what they wanted. It was what *she* wanted. It was her.

Not only her.

My legs are really itchy underneath my tights, but I resist the urge to scratch and scratch them. It's not the kind of thing you can do in school. There's always an audience. I just feel really nervous and jumpy and off. Like something's watching, close enough to touch me.

Megan comes up to me.

'Hey.' They've changed their earrings to little hoops with small beads on them. I make my face do a smile.

The mirror smile.

I don't quite disguise what courses through me.

'Hey.'

'You okay?'

I might start to cry with the gentleness in their voice.

'I just need to have a minute or something,' I say, tucking my hair behind my ears, and then putting it back again.

A curtain.

Swirls of blue.

Their arm on my elbow, steering me in between two stacks of lockers. We're supposed to be in class. But nothing is what it's supposed to be.

Megan's not okay.

I catch my breath.

Cracks in the wall and something winding through them.

Ask what happened.

There is it again.

That isn't me.

'Megan, are you okay? Why aren't you with everyone?' I keep my voice steady, try to breathe through everything I'm feeling.

'I wanted to find you.'

They're in their uniform trousers, and their shirt is buttoned right up to the chin. There's always something about the way Megan wears clothes that makes them sing.

'Well, you've found me,' I say. 'Let's go to geography.'

'Do we have to?'

Piotr.

'What did Piotr do?' I ask, in a rush.

Their face goes pale.

'How did you . . . ?'

I shrug.

191

'I got a feeling.'

Not a feeling.

Them.

'Okay,' they say. 'We both for sure need to not be here.'

They reach out their hand to take mine, but it's not an order, it's a question. Our jumpers rub together. Static shock. We sneak up beyond the meditation space (a former principal's office with a seagull poster on the wall), and through one of the older classrooms. Megan pulls me through an old science lab and out onto a little fire escape.

'This door's alarm doesn't work,' they say. 'So you can just open it and step out. I like it for that. And also, because if the lab's not getting used, you can crouch behind the benches and no one will see you.'

'Do you skip class a lot?' I ask.

They do.

'More, recently.'

Short stubby little fingers with bright blue nails drum on the railing.

The paint is flaking a little and there are weeds growing on the metal floor.

'Um, Piotr kind of likes me, I suppose. And he's been messaging a lot. A lot a lot.'

Screen lighting up.

The middle of the night.

'Okay,' I say. 'And was there anything?'

'He just made it clear that he'd like us to be more than friends. And . . .'

Their face is hard to read. A sort of blankness.

192

'And how do you feel about that? You did hook up that time,' I say, trying to inject some enthusiasm into my tone.

'We did . . . but that was almost a year ago. And lots has changed since then. Has opened up.'

'Okay . . .' I say.

'We've both needed time. To process –' they gesture to themself – '. . . me being me.'

'Okay,' I say again.

The way he smells, he tastes.
They can't just turn it off.

'I can't put my finger on it exactly. And it's not that he's said it flat out. But I feel like he wants me to be the . . . girl he liked back then. Or the version of me that didn't correct people when they called me that. I don't mean he'd ask me to, like, change my pronouns back or anything. He knows me better than to say stuff like that. But in his eyes, I would be . . . and I can't.'

'How do you feel about that?'

Horrible.
So horrible.

They sigh. 'Like my skin is too tight for my body. Or something.'

I nod.

'I like him so much, Daisy. But I like being who I am more. And if it's a choice, which it appears to be, I will choose Megan.'

'I'd choose Megan too,' I say. 'I mean, what you're feeling – it makes sense.'

They press the fleshy part of their palms against their cheekbones.

193

Trying not to cry.

'I don't want to hurt him. By being who I am.' The crack in their voice.

The gaping space between the wardrobe door.
Swirls on the curtain.

'He's hurt you by being who he is though.'

'Yeah. But he doesn't even register that really.'

Their leg is jigging up and down. I feel the motion of it through the floor.

I take a breath. 'Do you want to be with him?'

They close their eyes and open them again, the way they do when they're trying to answer a hard exam question.

'I don't know. I mean, it's not just him. It's everyone, or most people. It's hard to understand. But I can't let him kiss me and touch me if he doesn't even see me. And it isn't fair. It isn't fucking fair.'

'No, friend,' I say. 'It's not. And you're allowed be angry. Or sad. Or anything.'

'I don't feel like I am though. And I just wish that I could jump forward a little bit and know that things would be okay. That I'd survive this. Not just him. But everything.'

They drag their sleeve across their face, and grimace.

I close my eyes, and reach my hand to touch their wrist. I want to . . . I don't know. To offer comfort.

Bad idea.

A little red-brick house with a back garden and a cat named Walter.
A hula hoop is hanging on the wall.
Megan is happy.

194

'You won't live here,' I tell them. 'You'll be somewhere else. And you'll feel safe, and more than safe. Fulfilled.'

'Ha,' they say. 'I'd almost believe you.'

'You should believe me,' I say. 'Did I ever tell you I used to be a child psychic?'

'What?' They smile, but take a step away.

I do a little flourish with my hands, like 'Surprise!'

'Before I lived with Susan and Nina.'

'So you were, like, really young . . .' Their voice has changed, concerned. I do not like it.

There is danger here.

'Yeah,' I say. 'But that's not the point. The point is that when I have feelings, really strong feelings about someone, they usually check out.'

'Hmm.' Something flattens in their face.

> *To shut you out.*
> *To ward you off.*
> *Keep safe.*

'What?' I ask. There's more they want to say. I sense that too.

'Is it not a bit . . . intimate, reading someone's future?' They sound annoyed. I don't know what to say.

'Should I have asked first?'

There are some saplings in front of us, leafless in the cold. They look like cocktail-stick trees poking out of plasticine. I feel my face turn red. I was trying to help.

Megan's voice is low. 'Maybe. I think maybe.'

'It was good though.'

'Yeah, but the future is just a story, Daisy. Until it's lived, it's just a hope we tell ourselves or something.'

This will happen.

'I'm sorry, Megan,' I say. 'I didn't mean . . .'

Their face is hard to read, arms slung over the railings.

'I know. I know you didn't. Maybe I'm overthinking everything.'

'What are you going to do, about Piotr?' I ask.

Megan shrugs. 'I suppose be friends with him still. I mean, I've been honest, and if he doesn't like that, it doesn't mean I have to change my behaviour.'

'And if it gets weird?'

'Well, I suppose the group dynamic will change a bit, but it wouldn't be on me.'

'Of course it wouldn't,' I say, feeling a sort of weight in my stomach at the awkwardness of it.

A long exhale. 'Why is nothing ever simple?'

'I do not know,' I say. 'The ghosts are back.'

'Oh, for fuck's sake.'

I widen my eyes at them. 'I know, right? There's always something.'

'There is. Daisy, I've been meaning to say to you . . .'

'Yeah?'

'You know Oz Quigley?'

'Yeah?'

'I think he likes you.'

I snort. 'What makes you think that?'

A small crook of their mouth. 'He has eyes, doesn't he? And he's always using them to stare at you.'

I blush.

'I don't know.' They pull their jumper down towards their hips. 'I just have a feeling.'

I picture Oz, draped against the side of the shed. The way his face twisted when he felt ashamed. I don't . . .

I cannot touch that.

'Nina wants me to do the Ouija board with her,' I say, a subject change so both of us can breathe.

'DOOO IT!' Megan's voice is suddenly highly enthusiastic. 'Use it to get to the bottom of stuff. Have you psychicked her?'

'I don't think psychic is a verb.'

'Anything can be a verb, Daisy, if you COMMIT.'

We smile at each other and it's like we're sharing one smile that passes back and forth. It's so warm. I am glad they want to be my friend after whatever passed between us there. Whatever scared them.

'No, seriously, I saw this article about Ouija boards, and there's this thing called the ideomotor effect, and it's kind of about reflexes you're not aware you have. Like, you could be pushing the planchette but think it was something else doing it. But really it's your subconscious or what have you.'

'Oh,' I say. 'Okay. I'll look that up.'

'But, like, if you did it with her, it might be a way to get to why she'd be doing this, you know? If it was her and not a ghost.'

A big long pause.

They look at me.

'Like, maybe she wants to tell you stuff but can't. And this could be a way to do that, maybe.'

'Megan,' I say, 'every horror movie I have ever seen has told me that using a Ouija board is a terrible idea.'

'Sometimes we have to question the stories we are told, to work stuff out, you know? Trust your instincts.'

197

'I don't know. My instincts are terrible. Remember those leggings I wore the first non-uniform day in first year?'

'Ha,' they say. 'Those were not great. Trust my instincts on this so – it couldn't hurt.'

The bell goes. I sigh. Smooth my hair a little.

'Better get ready.'

'This was nice,' Megan says, with a little crooked smile. I can see the point of one of their canines poking out between their lips.

'Yeah, it's a good spot.' I rub my hands along the rough railing. 'Thanks for sharing it with me.'

'Not a bother.' They stretch their arms out wide. 'It's nice to be outdoors, you know. Like, at least in primary school there was yard time. Here, it's like, eat a roll and fuck off.'

I snort, and we walk back through the old lab.

'Labs are intrinsically creepy,' Megan says. 'I think it's the dissection.'

'I think my threshold for creepy is higher than yours, because of the haunting,' I tell them.

'Fair.'

We're at the door, when they touch my shoulder.

'Daisy?'

'Yeah.'

'You know that thing with your hand you did for me?'

'Yes.'

'Do you ever do it for yourself?'

'No,' I say.

We part ways and I watch them move away from me. I think of the hard bones beneath their skin, the way their voice sounded when they said 'intimate'. I shouldn't have reached out for something that was theirs and not my own. And I said no. But that wasn't the full story.

Of course I have done that.

Of course I've tried.

It's just . . . for me, there's never been a future there to find.

The girl is joined by another girl.

'Do we have to record this terrible idea?' the other girl asks. 'I mean . . .'

'You never know,' says the girl. 'What if we get, like, proof or something?'

'No matter what happens, people are going to think it's faked.'

'Not everyone.'

The brown-haired girl sighs. 'Can you just not post this?'

The other one smiles. 'Okay. Okay. I won't . . . unless something really good happens.'

She holds up the board, but there is no planchette.

'This time I thought we could use a shot glass.'

She holds it up, turns it around. It is blue, with 'Ibiza España' and an outline of a map with a man and a woman standing on it.

'Where's that from?'

'Back of Mom's drinking press. I think someone must have brought it back for her from Ibiza. I don't remember her ever going.'

'She could have got it in a charity shop. Things like that end up in charity shops all the time.'

'She does like a rummage.' The girl sighs. 'Okay. Let's get on with it. I'm nervous. Are you nervous?'

There's no reply.

They sit on the floor. The angle makes it hard to see what's happening.

'Okay,' says the girl. 'Hello.'

A phone vibrates. They both jerk in surprise.

an unexplained chill

Listening to . . . I don't want to say ghosts, but that's kind of the closest word for it, really, is a particular kind of thing. They don't talk in voices, more just appear in my head and you'd almost think you're making it up, like they're your thoughts but they aren't. They winnow their way into the part of you that's you, the core that's with you all day every day, and they assimilate, but there are things they know you couldn't know.

It's hard to work out which bits of me are them right now. When I was little I didn't second-guess myself as much.

I didn't know how bad it could get.

What they were capable of.

Until I did.

The board is just a prop, right, like the mirror. Nina's face is intent, her eyes are closed. Her fingers are on the shot glass and I can't read exactly what she's thinking but I reach out for it anyway.

She doesn't want you knowing.

Isn't ready.

I know I think I know. But I need answers.

I close my eyes and I try to tune them in.

My phone buzzes.

It's Oz Quigley.

He just says:

> hey

And maybe that's all I need to do.

I take a breath.

And clear my thoughts, my head.

And just think:

> *hey*
>
> *hey, creatures*

When I open my eyes, Nina's face is stern. Like Susan's when I have done something wrong. She puts her phone down, moves towards me.

'Why is he still messaging you?' she asks, and her voice is decidedly neutral.

I shrug. 'I don't know, Nina. Checking in on you, I suppose. That's normally what it is, when he contacts me.'

'Can I look at your phone?' she asks. 'I want to see.'

'Nina, that's not fair,' I say. 'Why can't you just believe me?' She holds out her hand.

'Nina, you're being ridiculous.'

'I don't like it, Daisy. You know how I feel about them.'

'Them?'

'Him and his dad. The way they acted when we had the ghost.'

There was no ghost.

I hand her my phone, and put my pointer finger back on the little shot glass.

202

'Do we have to move it to goodbye?' I ask, idly pushing it around a bit, from one letter to another.

D.A.I.S.Y.

She's scrolling through.

'It doesn't fucking work anyways. It's all made up.'

I can feel how frustrated she is by Oz messaging me, encroaching on her space, and I feel guilty. I should block him.

I try to push the glass towards the goodbye, but it won't budge.

'Nina.

'Nina.

'Nina!

'It won't move.'

She rolls her eyes. 'You're just trying to distract me. Seems like you guys message a lot.'

'Not a lot a lot,' I say. 'A bit.'

'But, like, a lot, for people who aren't friends.'

'Yeah, maybe,' I say. I try to lift my finger off the glass but it's held in place. 'Can you put down my phone and just, like, help me?'

She sighs, and puts down my phone.

Her hand on top of my hand.

The planchette jerks to Q to W to H to A to T. I try my best to push it to GOODBYE.

NO

NO

A

R

E

‘What are you . . . ?’
Nina's face is pale.

Slowly, as though watching a motion capture of a bud unfurling, cracks appear in the sides of the shot glass and it splinters into tiny little pieces beneath our fingertips, making mincemeat of the tops of mine.

different things to different people

We sit with antiseptic, kitchen roll and bandages between us.
The shards of glass wrapped up in a Penneys bag in the bin.
The carpet scrubbed of blood. What flecks are left, you'd have
to know that they were there to spot them.

Her hands on my shoulders digging in.

Nina's eyes dart to the mirror, and then away as quickly.
Like a bird pecking at a crumb, sensing a threat.

I sigh.

She smiles.

'So . . . are you going to reply to him?'

I bark a laugh. 'Oh yeah. Absolutely. BEST FRIENDS.' I
shrug. 'Nina, I'm sorry. If you don't want me to talk to him,
I won't.'

She blinks a bit too much.

'No. no. It's grand. It's not his fault I'm mental.'

'You're not mental.'

'Daisy. I'm fairly sure I am. I make up ghosts.'

I look at her. Hear her take a deep breath in.

'Even before all this, I mean . . . I just can't cope like other
people do.'

'I wouldn't say that's you being, like, difficult; more the

world being difficult for you.' I move beside her, put my head on her shoulder. 'And I think . . . it's going to get worse.'

She pokes me in the ribs. 'You always think things are going to get worse. Maybe they're nice ghosts this time, you know? Who'll put things back in presses. Do the hoovering.'

'I'm so sorry for this, Nina,' I say, and there's a little crack inside my voice.

Thick marks up her arms.

Blood in the grooves of fingertips.

'At least we have each other,' she says. 'Like, we're not facing this alone. Myself and Mom are here. And we have got you.'

I nod, but she just doesn't understand.

What the creatures are.

The things that They can do. Inside me, and outside me.

'I mean, how bad can it be?'

And I think.

You helped me call Them,

but I brought this on us.

It's tied to me.

And it will be my fault

if something happens.

'I'm frightened too, Daisy,' Nina says. 'That glass. It felt . . . deliberate. Brutal. Kind of slow and fast at the same time.'

'How are your fingers now?' I say.

'You got the worst of it,' she says with a smile. 'They'll heal . . . Isn't it weird, how little scratches can be more annoying than the big ones?'

And I say, 'Mmmmmm,' but the blood is rushing to my head, around my body. I suppose it always is, but I don't think

206

of it. My heart, my lungs, my brain, they all go on without me really noticing. Until they don't.

Tap
Tap
Tap
Tap
Bang

'It will be okay,' I tell my sister.
She smiles, cos I don't lie.
But I am lying.

secrets

Susan wakes us in the night. Her face is the way it was the night she told us Caroline and her were breaking up. The lines under her eyes have gotten darker and darker since then. Right now they look like someone drew them on. She pulls her robe around her, squares her shoulders.

Always worried she won't be enough
all by herself.

'There's something in the walls, girls,' she says, and I can hear her trying to keep her voice even, to communicate to us that she is calm. Of course she isn't calm. She woke us up because she didn't want to be alone. I stand closer to her and try to channel a more rational and capable version of Susan. One who thinks more clearly about things. Douses our apple slices in saltwater so they won't go brown by lunchtime. That sort of energy. That sort of comfort.

She won't keep you safe.

'Could it be mice?' I ask. 'They do come into houses, looking for warmth.'

Nina rolls her eyes. 'Good luck to them. It's freezing.' She casts a long lingering look towards her bedroom door, only dying to go back to bed. Susan doesn't really seem to notice.

It's almost like she's talking to herself.

'No, not mice. It's like damp. Or black mould, but more navy blue than black.'

The colour of a road.

Tap

Tap

Daisy.

'I probably shouldn't be waking you,' she says.

'No, you shouldn't,' says Nina. 'How dare you.' She's kind of joking, but I wave my hand to shush her.

'Nina, you do this all the time, let Susan show us her wall-mould.'

Everything will

rot

will fall

apart.

Susan smiles. 'It sounds ridiculous when you put it that way. And I'm sorry, but . . .' she is looking somewhere far away, 'I just want you to look at it. To see it.'

She feels like

there is something

looking back.

She opens the door to her room. I rarely go in here. Nina generally barges in, but I always knock and wait. I don't remember being taught to do that, maybe it's something I picked up by myself. A reminder that I am not always welcome.

Her daughter

not her daughter

all at once.

Susan's room is neat, with folded laundry on the chair beside her dresser. Her bed is the one she and Caroline shared, it's kind of old-fashioned looking with a wrought-iron frame. It's always been her bed since we were small. A floral patchwork throw over her duvet. The sheets are rumpled. The bedroom walls in our old house had wallpaper, here they're painted. Susan says that she'll get them done when she has time. She always leaves stuff like that for as long as possible though. She hates having strangers in the house, it puts her on edge, it always has. I remember staring at a plumber with her when I only came up to her belly button, and the sense that if we looked away he would do something awful pouring off her. Caroline handled that sort of thing once we moved in with her, but maybe Susan is better about it now, considering all of the people we've had in and out with Nina.

Not your mother.

The paint is rippling up and out from the wall in a thick curve, round and dimpled as a baby's leg. I reach my hand out to touch it.

Awful.

'Don't,' says Susan, but I press it anyway, and navy stuff spills out from the cracks, like a spot that has been squeezed. It's got a thick grainy consistency, like warm tarmacadam. A shudder of revulsion goes right up my wrist bone into my chest. It leaves a sort of coal-dust film on my hand and I don't want to wipe it on my pyjama bottoms so I go into Susan's en suite and scrub away. It sticks and sticks. I can see flecks of it between my nails and I have the strongest urge to get a knife and saw and saw and saw my arm off to get it gone away, away, away.

Tap

Tap

Tap

Tap

Bang

'DAISY!' Susan shouts, and I turn to her.

'I can hear you.

"I've been calling you for ages, love,' she says. 'Where were you? Your eyes went like this.' She rolls hers back in her head, and reaches out her arms. 'You're shivering. Would it help to hold you, love?'

Nonononononononono.

I shake my head. My skin feels too hot and cold at the same time, and I'm trapped. I'm trapped. I cannot function. As I scrabble to get them away from me, away from whatever this is, I move back towards the blanket box at the foot of the bed and trip. I see the distortion of the wall for what it really is.

Veins on a hand.

Say I am open, take me.

Say it.

Say it.

I go towards her mirror, and I can see what I hope is myself. When I reach my hand to touch the surface it is clouding up, damp with something that's not condensation. My hand towards my nose. It's sweat. Susan and Nina are staying where they are, staring at me. I cannot read their faces but I will them to know me well enough to not come closer. I lose my balance, cannot touch the wall to right myself. I wrap my hands around my legs and try to go away, to leave my body.

I am open.
Take me.

Susan looks at me, and I can see her putting adulthood back on, like an ill-fitting suit. She swallows, and her voice when she speaks sounds the way it does on important work phone calls. Curt and to the point.

'I blame you for this, Nina,' she says. 'You started it with the ghosts. Go down and get poor Daisy a cup of tea. I'm taking your bed tonight, and we'll deal with whatever this stuff is tomorrow. You can sleep beside me or take the couch. I'll see about this in the morning. There's probably a rational explanation.'

Nina nods and heads out the door, giving me a worried little glance on the way out. A smile like, *Are you okay?* I smile back like *yeah*.

Obviously not.
When am I ever?

Susan hunches down on floor, next to me. 'Daisy, love, this was a lot for you? What do you need?'

I look at her face. If I asked, she'd let me sleep in with the two of them. I could bring the blankets in, make a little nest on Nina's floor.

She doesn't want that.
She is too tired for this.
Too tired for you.

I let the panic hum away in the background of me and I tell her that I am okay now. That it was scary but we've been through worse. That I just need to sleep. All the things I think she wants to hear. And if my voice is a little flat, my eyes a little dull, she doesn't seem to notice. She moves beside me, our shoulders an inch apart, and we stay there, breathing together, until we are in something like a rhythm.

'Can I hold your hand, love?' Susan asks.

I nod.

She takes it. I can feel her fingers and her thumb against my finger-webs.

I also can't feel anything at all.

After a while, Nina comes up with the cup of tea, and I take it to my room and sip it slowly, staring at the space between the curtains until the sky pales and the morning comes.

dead decaying things

The smell of coffee permeates the house. Susan's face is bright. She has put more make-up on than usual. It suits her.

'How did you sleep?' she asks.

I smile. 'I didn't.'

She takes a sip from her espresso cup. 'Fair enough.'

I went into her room first thing this morning. Looked at the wall. The mould is still there, and the paint is warping with it, crinkling up like skin that has been burned. The air upstairs is thick. It smells familiar.

Welcome home,
Daisy.

I put my fingers tight against my temples, drawing circles, trying to drown Them out. This. The absence of this is how I knew the haunting wasn't real. I didn't feel a stranger in myself. I sit down gingerly, as far away from them as I can manage.

It's in me.
Or it wants to be.

I feel the urge to carve at myself rise in me. If I could cut Them out, this sense of rot. In geography we learned about algal bloom, this rapid growth of something that was always there before but now it's stronger, more. It poisons other life, it blocks the sun. What's inside the water cannot breathe. The world is dangerous now.

A place with teeth.

I stare at Susan. A small amount of spittle has collected on the outside of her lip. She hasn't noticed. Her lips are red pulsing water creatures, and I have to push to focus on her words.

They're here.
They're here.

'I miss when all the ghosts did was throw the odd thing and annoy Nina,' she says. 'I mean, this is probably going to cost thousands to rectify.' Her smile is getting wider as she speaks. Wider and tighter, puckering her skin.

Her face is lying.

'Will I make you another coffee?' I ask, going over to the kettle. Pressing click and waiting for the hum.

'Thanks, Daisy,' she says, popping four slices of bread into the toaster. As if we weren't rotting from the inside. As if we were still safe.

Nina walks in, quiet as a mouse. I turn towards her.

It smiled at me.
It went in Nina's room.
And there it stayed.
The other me,
the me who is the creatures.

'Want one, Neen?'

Nina shakes her head.

'No.' Her voice is low. Last night was a lot. For all of us.

215

I decide to make the coffee anyway. They'll want it when they see it. My hands need some sort of task to focus on. I spoon it carefully into the coffee-pot and add the water.

It takes a while for things to bind to you.

To grow in strength.

'So, has anything else happened since the investigation?' Susan asks, her tone going for light but coming out sharper than she means, I think. 'Anything I need to know about? Because neither of you seemed all that surprised by my walls.'

She butters the toast, and plonks it on the table.

I shrug, and try to keep my voice as calm and level as I can. 'I've been hearing bits and pieces at night. Like I said, I thought it could be mice.'

Nina is untangling the ends of her hair and smoothing it down. A knot comes out in her hand and she leaves it there, beside her untouched toast.

'Nina.' Susan is exasperated. She scoops it up and puts it in the bin. 'We're eating, pet.'

'Sorry. I wasn't thinking.'

'Well, we all need to be thinking. Because whatever this is, it's not mice.'

'If we . . .' Nina says, '*were* all thinking, you wouldn't have buttered my toast, would you?' She tosses one slice each on each of our plates.

'For fuck's sake,' Susan says. 'Can we focus on the haunting for a second?'

'We . . .' Nina rises, grabs two slices of bread and puts them in the toaster. 'We did the Ouija board the last day and the glass shattered. Is that the kind of thing you mean?'

216

She's standing with her back to Susan. Her hands are on the counter, and they're shaking.

'It is.' Susan's voice is terse. 'Why didn't you tell me?'

I look at Nina. It hadn't even occurred to us to tell Susan. There wasn't like a conversation or anything, it's just the way it goes. The raised marks on her arm. The creatures in the mirror, in my brain. The hunger in Them. I chomp down on my toast.

It tastes of salt and fat.
Of something animal.

Nina smiles blandly. 'Because we didn't want to worry you?'

'Worry me?' Susan's voice is shrill. 'Why would I be worried by the both of you literally summoning spirits a wet week after we've had the paranormal investigators in? When precisely did this happen?'

Nina turns to me as though I have the answers. What is she up to? Is she actively trying to make Susan lose the plot?

'Um . . . like two nights ago?'

Susan is aghast. I can see her reaching for the words before she speaks, and faltering. 'So, you did this thing that every horror movie ever made warns people against, and the very next night, my room goes all . . . I don't even know how to describe that stuff. But I take it I can lay the blame at your feet.'

She gets up, scrapes her toast into the bin and runs the plate under the tap before putting it in the dishwasher with barely suppressed rage.

'We didn't even do that much,' Nina tells her. 'Daisy got a text, so it only moved a bit and then the glass broke.'

I hold up my hand.

'Oh. That looks sore,' Susan says.

I push down the French press. 'It is a bit.'

I pour a cup for Susan and a cup for me, and fill them up with normal milk for Susan and oat milk for me.

Susan takes a sip. 'So . . . what exactly happened with the Ouija board?'

'It just kept spelling nonsense,' Nina says.

> *WHAT*
> *ARE*
> *YOU*
> *DOING*
> *TO*
> *ME,*
> *NINA?*
> *GOODBYE.*

I turn towards her.

> *It wasn't nonsense.*
> *Ask what really happened.*

I say, 'And then it cracked.'

A small look passes between us. There's a loneliness to this, the knowledge that's been growing in me since this all began. That there's something big she isn't sharing. I remember the night of my first kiss, I was trying to work out how I felt about it and it was all really complicated, not the kiss itself but the feelings it brought up, that sense of danger, and I was saying nothing and she just sat there, minding me, and asked the right things till it all spilled out. I think she knows I'm here, and that I want to help.

But I don't want to force anyone open. That isn't who I am.

Head under the cold tap and the harsh surprise of it.
Her palm against your neck.
You weren't supposed to struggle but you did.

Susan lets out an exasperated sound and squeaks her chair across the floor. She says, 'I was really expecting more of you girls.'

She means you, Daisy.

Nina gets up, starts quietly tidying away the breakfast things. I look at her. If I wanted to, I could find out what happened. She wouldn't even know. I could just ask.

It's not even as difficult as asking. It's more a tuning in.

But I won't do that.

The way Megan reacted when I told them.
My skin on theirs.
As though I'd stolen something.

I don't want to invade her privacy.

And I don't want to owe them anything.

I feel the hairs on the back of my neck move.

Just enough.

friendly

Geography class has become unacceptable since Mr Q spent time in our house. It's not that he's acting differently or anything. It's the same as it always was, only now I look at him and hear the way he was with Nina, the anger and contempt in his voice, and the hatred wells up and makes it hard to concentrate on grikes or how great he is or what have you. It makes my skin itch.

I want to hurt him.

So, I'm finding it a bit difficult to get my head around what Susan said last night. She thinks the mould constitutes proof of an actual haunting. She must have been convinced by all his talk about equipment and scientific methods seeing as she's decided that the smart right thing to do in this situation is to invite him back. I don't agree. Because of sense and facts.

It's wrong, it's wrong.

'I don't think it's a good idea,' Nina said. 'He wasn't much help the last time.' She pushed her hair behind her ears and pulled her knees right up against her chest.

'He was,' I said, 'in fact a bag of dicks.'

'DAISY!' Susan was appalled. 'What an image.'

Nina snickered. 'A whole bag of them?'

I nodded. 'Packed so tight you'd have to work at it to do the zip. An awful, awful person.'

We were in the sitting room, and I stared at the swirl of the curtains and thought of the mould on Susan's wall. Tried not to think about Them.

Hello, Daisy.

'I don't know.' Susan shrugged. 'At least he tried to help. Most people didn't.'

I looked at Nina, and she looked back like: *No.*

Like: *Don't say anything*, and so I didn't.

That was where we left it. I don't know. I mean, I understand why Susan would want to do something, to act, but I have this sense that everything is futile. And I don't want them in our house, our space, again. Poking around while we all fall apart.

'I think that he should simply do his job,' I say to Abigail and Conchur.

Conchur nods. 'Sure when has he ever done his job? He showed the film *Ghostbusters 2* in its entirety to my brother's class when he was in final year. Some parents complained and he had a go at the class over it. Told them if they didn't know the course by now that wasn't his problem.'

'As if he wasn't their actual teacher.' Abigail snorts.

Piotr joins us, holding a protractor. 'I found my protractor!' he exclaims, with a big smile. 'It was on the floor beside my locker.'

'That's great, Piotr,' I say, and look down at my feet. There is a pause.

'Where's Megan?' Conchur asks.

'Oh, they had to go to the shop,' Abigail says. Too quickly.

I catch her eye, and the unspoken will to keep everything smooth and not offend anyone passes between us.

She knows something is up
but not what
it is
exactly.

'Sure, we could have gone with her,' Piotr says. 'I'd love a Club Orange.'

'They wanted to be by themself,' says Abigail, looking at him pointedly.

'Yeah,' he says. 'Do I have to say sorry if they're not here?'

'Just be sound,' Abigail says. 'It's not a high bar, Piotr.'

It can be.

'Were they okay?' Conchur asks.

They need to be alone.

I smooth my uniform skirt down and take a packet of crisps from my school bag.

'Anyone want some?'

Everyone does and I regret offering because I'm actually starving. I nibble the remaining crisp sadly, feeling like a martyr.

'We could get you another pack in the shop.' Piotr adjusts his school bag a little, and grins. 'They say they want to be by themself, but friends might help with that.'

'Better,' Conchur says.

Piotr smiles.

He still thinks
they're a girl.
The girl
he wants.

I swallow back a scowl.

'I feel like maybe we should just listen to Megan though,' Abigail says. 'Give them some space.'

I nod.

'But if we do it Piotr's way, we get more crisps,' Conchur says.

'My house is haunted again. Remember I just told ye?' I tilt my head to one side and try to look like it's no big deal. They stop their shuffling and listen. Being haunted is the ultimate distraction tactic. I tell them a bit about the Ouija board, the shattered glass. The mould. I keep my voice casual, make it sound as though it's all much lighter than it is.

'Maybe Susan's right,' Abigail says. 'I mean, like, it feels like someone should do something.'

'He was no help the last time though,' Piotr says. 'They're still, like, fully haunted.'

Conchur nods.

'I just feel like there is no situation that will be made more comfortable by inviting your geography teacher into your house, you know? Plus, Mr Q is will probably bring poor Oz along again. He, like, carts him around from ghost to ghost. Mortified for him.' I widen my eyes.

'And I'm mortified for me too,' a voice says, and I know it's Oz because this is the kind of thing that happens when you bitch about people in a place where they also are.

I smile. 'It's going to be excruciating,' I tell him. 'Like the last time but more. This time there is a broken shot glass. Interesting mould. Mice that aren't mice.'

'Mice that aren't mice are pretty common,' Oz tells us, 'but

223

do you know what? They're actually usually mice in the end. Mice are small.'

Abigail, Conchur and Piotr stare at us. I suppose it's one way to take their minds off Megan.

I scratch the back of my head and look at my feet. I'm tall, but I am not as tall as Oz is. He's strapping. You'd put a uniform on him and send him off to old-timey war.

'You haven't been responding to my messages,' he says, and I see Abigail turn to Conchur. Ugh, they're going to be asking me things and insinuating things and all sorts of nonsense.

'I'm sorry,' I say. 'It's the reason that you'd think it would be.'

'Ah, you've decided you despise me.'

> He doesn't think that.
> But he cares what you think of him.
> And Nina.
> He is worried about Nina.
> What if she tells everyone
> what happened.

I shake my head like a dog who just hopped out of a lake. I wish I were a dog who just hopped out of a lake. Life would be muddy, yes, but simpler. I don't think dogs get haunted.

'Are there like, ghosts of dogs?' I ask him.

He shrugs. 'I don't know. I'll let you in on a little secret. Most of Dad's ghost-hunting is him going around explaining EMF meters to people, and then telling them how wrong they are. Probably why he likes it.'

I smirk. 'If there was any justice in the world, he'd be behind you right now.'

'Oh, Dad knows exactly what I think of him,' Oz says, and his voice isn't hard to read.

'He showed *Ghostbusters 2* to my brother's class,' Conchur offers.

Neither of us responds.

Piotr is eating a ham-and-cheese roll.

I feel a bit rude. Like I'm having a conversation in front of my friends and they're not . . . invited to it, somehow?

'Look, we should talk properly before my dad and me just show up at your house,' Oz says, shrugging his jacket more over his shoulders. 'And I'm sorry about *Ghostbusters 2*, Conchur.'

'That's okay,' Conchur says. 'It isn't your fault.'

Oz walks away, presumably to the Belgian front.

'HE LIKES YOU,' Abigail mouths.

'He does not,' I say, but there's a little grin there. 'It's just he has to hang out in my haunted house and might as well be friendly, like.'

'Is that what you call it?' Piotr grins.

'It is,' I say. 'What of it?' See, Piotr says sexual things like that sometimes, but because I know to my bones that he doesn't fancy me they're not, like, charged or anything. I like it that way, that little bit of distance. Even with Megan. I mean, even though I like them, it's not that simple, with me. The way I am. I think it'll take time, with him and Megan. Time and a little bit of cop-on from him. Maybe I could say something if I got him on his own in the right mood. You can't really have hard conversations this way, when it is all of us together.

Maybe that's why I like the group. Huh.

225

Conchur touches me on the elbow.

His father's cancer's back.
He doesn't know.

Oh fuck.

a change

I am standing in front of the seam of mould in Susan's room again. I run my fingers over the paint. It's still warm, a little papery to the touch. Like the skin of something very old.

'It doesn't feel like paint, does it?' says Susan.

And I jump.

'I'm sorry to be in here.'

She's wearing her work-clothes, tailored trousers and a dove-grey shirt, a thick green necklace.

'Don't be, Daisy. It's a strange thing, and of course you would be curious. I'm curious myself. I wish there was an answer, you know?'

We both stand looking at the mould as though it were a painting in a museum. Something that we're straining to understand.

'Did . . . ? Did anything like that ever happen before?' I ask. 'Like back when I was little.'

There is a pause.

'I don't know,' Susan says. 'Therese didn't like visitors that weren't paying.'

'Susan?' I say. And I want to tell her that I'm hearing the

creatures again. That there is something making me know things I don't want to know. Attaching itself to me and the people that I touch.

She's waiting for this to be your fault.

I gasp.

'What?' she asks.

'I just got a sort of jolt,' I say.

She can't help it.
You look so like her.

I put my hand to my face.

'We'll get it sorted, Daisy. We will. It's just this year has had so many difficult things already.'

'I think Conchur's dad is sick again,' I tell her, without thinking.

'Oh, that's awful,' she says. 'I must ring Laura.'

'No,' I say. 'He didn't say it to me. It's just a feeling that I got. From how he was.'

There is a pause before Susan responds. Her voice is low, and she moves her head, working to meet my eyes.

'Are you getting lots of feelings lately, Daisy?'

'It's not like that,' I say, pushing my toes deep into the carpet, wanting to be anywhere but here. 'Where's Nina?'

'In her room again. Tidying it after me. She says my stuff's all over the place.'

'You could have my room instead,' I offer.

'And you'd go in with Nina? I don't know, pet. That would be a lot on you.'

She'd do it if she wasn't scared of you.
She doesn't want to be, Daisy.

228

But she is.
She always was.

'Are we going to Dad on Saturday again?'

'If we've time. But, Daisy – let's not tell him about any of this. It would just confuse him. Bring up old things that have been laid to rest.'

I nod.

'We don't exactly have heart-to-hearts, Susan. You know that.'

'I know, pet.' Her hand on my shoulder, without asking, and she squeezes and it's not a harsh touch really but I flinch. 'I hope . . .' she says. 'I hope this doesn't escalate. I don't know what we'd do.'

She's asking you to stop, Daisy.
As if you could.
As if you have a choice.

stains

The mould on the walls is spreading, vein after vein popping up all over. Trailing one into the other. After Granny Maude died, her house began to decay. They do that if there aren't people in them. The ivy winding up the front began to creep inside the walls, the attic. They had to kill it, carve it off in chunks. Pull up the roots. Myself and Nina helped. We were little kids, and I remember the sap all on my hands, and filling bucket after bucket with leaves and stems rough with little roots. Afterwards, the front of the house looked so unfamiliar and so ugly. Stained and cracked with all it had been through. Susan looked at it, and her mouth was set.

'It isn't coming back,' she said.

We nodded, but Nina cried because of how different things were now, and how she missed the ivy and Granny Maude. I missed them too, but I didn't cry. I'd learned the value of making something go away by then. There were parts of me I couldn't touch. Because if I did, They would know and They would reach for me.

It's hard to get rid of an invasive species. And we didn't visit very much after that, so I don't know if the ivy came back. I bet that in some way it wanted to. Plants don't think the same way that we do, but they're alive, and part of that is wanting, needing things. Sunlight, food . . .

A home.

We're trying our best to keep the mould in check, spraying it with bleach and water, scrubbing, but it twists and clings. The scent still lingers, even through the bleach or washing hands in scalding soapy water. It's on me all the time. I don't feel clean.

Nina is worried about Susan. She says she isn't sleeping.

'She just lies there, Daisy, eyes looking at the ceiling, and after a couple of hours she goes downstairs and cleans the kitchen or something. And this morning I found a scissors in her pillowcase.'

I look at her. I don't know what to say.

To notice that . . . she can't be sleeping either.

All my fault.

We're babysitting for the Mahons tonight, which will give Susan some space. Though the house isn't exactly a cosy haven where she could eat pizza and drink a big glass of wine in her slippers.

'It could be my trying to get to sleep clashes with her trying to get to sleep . . .' Nina says, tying her hair up. Babies *love* Nina's hair, but Nina does not love getting the head pulled off her. '. . . And the scissors is probably for something practical.'

'Like stabbing ghosts?' I raise an eyebrow. 'Wish it worked that way. It's tough on her, Nina.'

She doesn't want to hurt me.

She will hurt you.

'She'll get through it,' Nina says 'She's strong. And we're all together. It hasn't killed us.'

231

The thick marks on her arms.
The thing that isn't me inside her room.

I swallow. I can't let myself think like that. There has to be a way.

There is a way.

'Daisy?' Nina asks. 'Are you okay?'

'Oh. Sorry,' I say. 'I just spaced out for a minute. Did I tell you Oz Quigley came to talk to us the last day?'

'Us?' Nina says. 'Was it the group he talked to or just you?'

'Mostly me. He wants to have a word before they come back to investigate.'

'Oh, I'm dreading that.' She rolls her eyes. 'It's just going to be more giving out.'

'Well, this time they might get some use out of all their tech. And, like, whatever this is might stop?' I try to smile. It doesn't work exactly.

'Do you really think that?' Nina wrinkles her forehead. The lines in it look like what Susan has all of the time.

They're proper family.

'You seemed to, before?' My voice is thin, uncertain.

You don't belong here.

'That was different. Daisy, this is real. And it's tied to you.'

Ruining everything.

For everyone.

I startle.

'What do you mean by that?'

'I've been . . . seeing *you* again.' Nina's mouth twists awkwardly.

'Seeing me?'

'Yeah, like with the sleepover? Remember when you watched me sleep that time?'

'That wasn't me, Nina.' I close my eyes and try to clear my head of mirror-smiles.

Tap

Tap

Daisy.

'Oh, I know that. But, it looked like you. That's what I mean.'

'Can we not call it me though? I mean, it isn't me.'

'I know. But . . .'

'What?'

Nina puts her wallet and keys into her backpack and zips it shut. 'It didn't just look like you, Daisy. It felt like you. It even smelled like you.'

'How do I smell?'

'I don't know how to describe it . . .' She leans her head over and takes a big whiff of me. I push her away.

'I can't believe you just did that.'

'It was research. Ugh, I can't describe exactly how you smell, like those big long marshmallows you like, and soap and skin and something. It's a nice smell.'

Part

of

you.

'Has Susan seen it too? I ask. 'Is that why scissors?'

233

Does she want to hurt me
like
a
mother?

Nina shrugs. 'I just know that she's scared.'

'Of me?'

'I don't know,' Nina says again. 'But . . . is there a way to stop this, Daisy? I mean . . . is it the same sort of thing as when we were small or is it something else?'

I close my eyes.

'I don't know.'

I don't know anything.

Except that this is all my fault.

I am open, take me.

I said that. She didn't hold me down this time. It was all me.

You didn't mean it,
Daisy.
Not enough.

I hoped when I started listening to Them again that there would be a clearer sort of path.

I imagine my reflection creeping out of Nina's room, and back to me, and shudder.

'Have you seen me recently?' I ask. 'Like the not-me me.'

Nina squints. 'Not in a few days. Maybe all their energy is going into the creepy mould or something.'

The mould that isn't mould.

She has to tell you.

'Nina . . .' I begin.

But Susan calls us down, it's time to go.

but this is something else

Liam Mahon is nine months old. The first time we babysat for him he was six weeks old, brand new. He is still very much a baby, but also so much bigger than he was.

He reaches out his arms for me with a big smile.

Liam likes me. I'm his favourite. It's nice to be the favourite. He's got little tufts of blond hair like his mom and big brown eyes. He has four teeth, three on the bottom, one on the top.

'Look at his lovely new smile!' I say to Claudia.

She's putting on her earrings in the mirror. I look at her reflection and not mine.

The Mahons' house is like ours, but warmer and with no ghosts. The walls are painted different colours, there's art and photographs up everywhere. It feels like a family home, not a stopping point or a compromise.

Claudia offers us tea and tells us that there are pizzas in the freezer, and snacks in the press. I love her.

'Does he need a bath?' Nina asks. Liam loves baths. He is a splashy man.

'No, not tonight. Give him a snack, there's one made up in the fridge, and then bottle, story time and bed. He's been up and down a lot with the new teeth, so you might be busy.'

'It'll be fine,' I say. 'There's two of us.'

'You're so good, girls. Thanks a million!' She looks at her phone. 'My cab is nearly here. I'll see ye soon.'

She gives Liam a big kiss on top of his little duckling head.

'Love you, Liamy.'

'Lauauauauaulalallalala!'

'He's got a great little voice,' Nina says.

'Yeah,' she says. 'And he knows how to use it. Thanks again, girls, it shouldn't be too much of a late one.'

She always says that, and it bears absolutely no relation to how late of a one it will be.

She closes the door behind her and Liam starts to cry, like he always does when she goes. It only takes a minute to settle him. He likes to hold my two fingers and kind of wobble around, and we do a bit of that, while Nina sets up his snack.

He actually pops off fine after his bottle, which is a relief. We throw him up to bed and lash the baby monitor on.

We snuggle into their big fat cosy sofa and decide what movie to put on.

'I would like a heist,' Nina says. 'I haven't watched a heist in ages.'

'I'm not opposed to a heist,' I tell her. 'But I want there to be at least one woman in a well-tailored velvet suit.'

'You have a film in mind,' she says.

'I do.'

We play it, and it's nice to talk about something that isn't paranormal or intense. It's just calm. I snuggle my head against the arm rest and drift off, until Nina pokes me.

'Hey!' I say, but then I see her face and I stop talking.

236

'Daisy.' She points a finger at the baby monitor.

Liam is lifting his arms up to the air. Asking to be picked up.

'I'll go up,' I say. 'He probably wants his dodie.'

Nina gets up too. 'Just in case.'

'In case of what?'

'In case you need me!' She sounds frustrated.

'It'll be fine,' I say, opening the door of his little bedroom with the nursing chair in the corner.

Liam's wide awake, eyes shining and little tufts all this way and that way from tossing and turning. He's looking into the corner of the room, and turns to us a little bit confused.

'I wish he could talk,' Nina says. 'The air feels very . . . something . . .' She picks him up. 'Hey, Liamín. You okay? You're a very awake baby.'

'Lalala,' Liam says, reaching out for me.

'Lalala, Liam,' I say, taking him from Nina. 'Let's see if you've got a full nappy.'

I put him on the changing mat and unzip his growbag. He must be tired because normally he wriggles an awful lot more.

'Oh, you're soaking, you poor boy,' I say, grabbing a baby wipe and some Sudocrem.

'Lalala.'

'Lalala.'

I get his nappy on and fasten him back up, pick him up. He's so much heavier now than he was when we started minding him. He was so small we were scared he'd break.

'He might need another bottle before he pops off,' I say. 'Nina? What do you think? Nina?'

Nina is standing in the middle of the room, turning around

and around like one of those jewellery-box ballerinas. I used to love those when I was a kid, winding them up whenever I got the chance.

'Nina?' I say again. His hot little head is on my shoulder, and he's beginning to wriggle a bit. I rub his back.

'Daisy,' she says. 'Daisy, look at the walls.'

humiliation

We turn in sync, me pressing Liam into myself, as though I can protect him. Layers of thick stubbly mould coat the walls, from carpet to ceiling.

It smells like home.

I feel the oppressive weight of them in the air, and wonder why I didn't feel it sooner. Of course They're here. They're always here.

It's not the house.
It's not the house.
It's you.

'I feel like we're breathing them in,' Nina says. 'Your creatures. I don't feel safe. How can it do this here?'

'It might be a coincidence, Nina,' I offer weakly. 'Maybe the mould was there already and we missed it?'

'Yeah, I'm sure we missed the thick layers of haunted mould all over the walls of the baby's room, Daisy.'

'It's not like you to be sarcastic,' I say. 'You never were before, Neen.'

She sighs. 'Yeah. I suppose. I think. I think it's like . . . Look at where being gentle got me.'

'Maybe.' I hold Liam tight, the warmth of him feels good

against my chest. He's very here, this baby, so tethered to the world. 'Maybe we just take him downstairs, give him a bottle and don't say anything.'

Keep him safe.

I walk across the landing towards the stairs. Liam, ever the magpie, is grasping for the clasp of my necklace.

'But she'd put him back in here, and it can't be good for his little lungs.' Nina's eyes widen.

Liam whimpers.

'I'm going to put a bottle on for him,' I say. 'You go back in and check the mould again. And maybe take some photographs. It feels like the kind of thing no one will believe.'

'It does, doesn't it?' Nina's voice is flat.

The kind
of thing
that
no one
will
believe.

I have that sickening weight in my stomach. Bearing down.

'We do have to say something, don't we?'

'We do. You're right.'

'He's just a baby.'

'When they came for you, you were just a little girl.' Nina's voice is far away from me.

'Older than him,' I say. I want her to stop talking.

Red hands on my shoulders digging in.

'Not much.' Nina blinks. 'It's just . . . it's sad.'

My voice is sharp. 'Can we not talk about this now?'

240

Or ever.

I give Liam a bottle, and he makes happy gulpy little sounds as he downs it, and then he wants to crawl around for a bit and we play with him, and then eventually he comes up for a hug and snuggles in and looks sleepy.

'Dim the lights,' I say to Nina. 'Claudia'll be happier if he's asleep when she gets back.'

'I'm just going to check on it again,' Nina says.

She runs up the stairs, and I look at the baby monitor, half expecting to see someone else up there, waiting for her.

It's 3 a.m. when Claudia gets home, and she gets the taxi to wait outside for us. It's not that far, but she always does it, all the same.

'Thanks so much, girls,' she says. 'I'm sorry he didn't stay asleep.'

'Claudia,' I say. 'There was something in his room. Like, on the walls. Nina, would you go out and tell the taxi to wait a bit longer so we can show you?'

'Okay,' she says. 'What is it? Is it mice? I hate mice.'

We get up to the nursery, and I switch the lights on. The walls are still dappled with the mould.

'Oh, girls,' she says. 'What's happened? This is rotten.' Her voice is thick with drink, and inconvenience. But there's no fear. Like Liam. No sense of dread. What's ticking through her head seems purely practical.

What's touching us isn't touching her the same way.

'What could have caused it, do you reckon? We've never had anything like that before . . .' She runs her fingers over it, and grimaces at the texture.

Yet.

'It just appeared,' I tell her. 'We're so sorry.'

'It's not your fault,' Claudia says. 'You don't need to be sorry.'

But I do.

'We did a search about mould and babies,' Nina says, 'and decided not to put him down again.'

'I might move the cot,' Claudia muses. 'Would you mind giving me a hand? This will need a level of cleaning I'm not prepared to do after three glasses of wine and a sneaky gin and tonic.'

'Where's Eoin?' I ask.

'I told him to stay out,' Claudia says. 'He needed to blow off some steam.' She smiles. 'He can make it up to me by dealing with . . . whatever this is.'

We shuffle Liam's cot in beside their bed. I notice a crumpled pair of knickers on the floor and I feel embarrassed, like we shouldn't be in here. Like we're encroaching.

You are.

'We should probably go now,' I say. Shuffling my feet a bit. 'The taxi will be waiting.'

'Oh, let me pay ye,' Claudia says, handing over some notes. 'Thanks again, girls. I'll be in touch.'

We smile at her and head out.

Nina turns to me. 'That went well.'

'Yeah, Claudia is sound.'

'I was genuinely worried she was going to go all Salem witch trials on us.'

'Me too,' I say. 'I don't know why.'

'I do,' Nina says. 'People surprise you in bad ways and then you think never again. I never want to feel like this again. But instead of making you stronger, it kind of makes you more frightened.'

'What happened, Nina?' I ask.

'I thought that I was safe,' she said. 'And all of a sudden I woke up. And everything was rotting.'

She –

STOP.

a decision

I sit at the foot of my bed and think about what to do. I think of Liam, how small and fragile he is, and all those little spores in the air going into his baby lungs.

And Susan scared to sleep in her own room.

And Nina –

It's me. Isn't it? It's me it wants. And it would be so easy.

Stop resisting.

When I was little, They felt like part of me.

We were so close.

Her hands on my shoulders and my tears and then . . .

It will be all right.

This sense that something old was watching. But that it wouldn't hurt me. There's this book Susan read to us when we were little. About these kids and they go into a wardrobe and do all kinds of stuff, but there's this lion. And they're friends with him. Even though he's powerful, and has claws and jaws and all the regular lion stuff. And every now and then they have to remind themselves that he is not a tame lion.

Whatever's hunting me is not tame.

But I don't think it means to kill me.

I think that it needs me.

I think . . . I think it's sending me a message. With the mould. With the other me. I have a feeling, if I just gave in, let myself want to live with it . . . then maybe things would be a little better.

For everyone.

I close my eyes, and think back to when I was small.
The fear I felt.
The worry in my stomach.
The creatures weren't anything compared to her.
But I loved her anyway.
I would have done anything.
Anything at all.
And then They killed her.

Tap
Tap
Tap
Tap
Bang

I close my eyes.

245

collective memory

We are six years old and we are ageless. We are in the back seat of the car. One of us is Daisy. Mam is driving. We have been to a big hall where people sat at tables. People got in line to see us. They gave Mam money and Daisy told them things about themselves they already knew, and certain things they didn't.

We are going fast.

Daisy is tired and she wants her chocolate milk. It's in the little cooler in the front seat. Dad is in the passenger seat. She asks him for the milk. He goes to get it, but Mam snaps at him that the child can wait.

Daisy doesn't feel like a child. We are tired, and she is restless, tapping her foot against the seat in front again and again. Until Mam calls her a little bitch. Tells her to stop. We don't want to stop, but Daisy puts her two feet flat on the floor and turns to look out the window. She is trying not to cry. There are burn marks on her arms from the radiator. Mam got angry putting out the socks to dry.

Our brain, Daisy's brain, is fat with people and their stories. It's getting crowded in there, filling up. She flaps her hand in front of her face to try to clear the crowding, clouding thoughts.

Mam says to stop it. She looks silly. Dad says, 'Eyes on the road.'

Daisy starts to cry. She wishes it was over. That Mam would stop. That she could take a break from all of this.

Daisy is ours, one of us.

We listen to her hurt

and give her what she really wants deep down.

A stone against the windshield.

Tap.

Another and another.

Tap.

Tap.

Another one again.

Tap.

The glass begins to crack, lines forming and widening out.

Mam says, 'That's not supposed to happen.'

Dad says to watch the road.

Watch it.

For fuck's sake.

The child.

The child.

The car turns over.

Everything goes black.

And we

are

. . . gone

figment

I was drinking chocolate milk at the side of the road, they said, and there was blood on the little plastic bottle from my hands. There wasn't a scratch on me. And Mam was dead and Dad was crumpled, broken.

I remember being lonely without the creatures at first. After I pushed Them out.

I wasn't used to being so alone inside myself.

But the wall stayed up inside me.

And I got used to it.

The freedom of it.

By then, everyone was telling me They weren't real.

> *I just want my body to be mine.*
> *I just want my life to be mine.*

> > *It can't be.*
> > *It won't be.*
> > *It will be.*

I want so many things.

I want my brain to make sense.

I want to know as much as a regular person would know about things.

I want my mother to have loved me well.

I want my dad to care.

I want to be alone inside my head.

I want Susan to love me as much as she loves Nina and I want Nina to be okay.

an embarrassment

I close my eyes and reach for the creatures. The hum of them is outside of me still. I have to tune in, like the old-timey radio Dad has in his flat. I breathe Them in, and hold my breath, and wait.

It's been a while since Susan took me to him, probably the longest it's ever been. And part of me is grateful for that, but I feel awkward about asking her for anything right now. There's this . . . this distance that has opened up. A little gap that didn't used to be there.

And with each new display of . . . power, I suppose.

That's what They're doing.
Showing off Their power,
I think.
To pull me further from Them.
Towards whatever thing it is They want.

There was a time before,
when you trusted us,
listened to us,
when we were together always.
We kept you safe.
You could be safe again.

I can't engage with them, it will consume me. They will be everything about me again.

Her hands on you.

We saved each other, Daisy.

Light filters through the dust that isn't dust. I close my eyes and reach for the creatures.

I want to go to Dad. But like he was before. Blue scarf. Strong arms. Leaves crunching under our feet. My head against his neck up the stairs to bed. Her hands reaching for me, outstretched. Him stepping away. His voice gentle but definite.

Hasn't she had enough?

Hasn't she had enough of this, Therese?

You need to let her be a little girl.

I felt that night that maybe things would change.

Of course they didn't.

They will.

Very soon.

The house is still humming with whatever the creatures want us to experience. The mould is streaking halfway down the stairs now, winding like ivy, pulsing like blood vessels. I keep reaching out a hand to touch it in spite of myself, feeling a rush of horror, recognition. The gooseflesh on my arms waking up.

Nina tells me what Susan doesn't.

The two of them.

In the bed.

Both watching the not-me walk around the room, clockwise, anticlockwise. Standing at the foot of the bed, head tilted, looking hopeful. It doesn't touch anything except the floor,

251

the walls. No items. Just testing the boundaries of the space in which it finds itself, I suppose. I wonder is it tethered to the house.

Its face in the mirror, fusing into mine.

And everything else is still normal, you know? We're going to school. We're washing up after dinner, watching TV, but all the while this thing is encroaching, weaving through the fabric of our lives, and I can't see a way to rip it out that won't ruin everything.

When we were little we used to play What Time Is It, Mr Wolf? in the yard. And there would be children and a wolf. And we would ask the wolf what time it was and inch our way towards him. But in the space between the question and the answer, there was always this sense of tension. Because it could be dinner time. And you might long to be chased, but no one wants to be eaten up entirely. And the more steps you have taken, the closer you are getting.

To a wolf.

Susan loves me.

I know that Susan loves me.

But I don't want to get too close to the limits of that love, you know?

Something big and old is stalking us, and it sometimes looks like me. And it's my fault. I want to say I can't help it. And I couldn't when I was a child.

But.

I chose this.

Stood in front of the mirror and called the bad thing home.

I splash water on my face. My skin feels tight, like there's not enough of it to stretch over my skull. I walk the edges of the bathroom, touching the walls. The shower door. In our old house we had a corner bath. We never used it. Part of me would love a bath right now.

To dip my head under the surface.

Close my eyes.

And wait.

a wall between you and other people

I can't think clearly.

It's getting harder to decide which thoughts are mine.

I'm tired.

I'm very tired.

School is weighing on me, and today I took my lunch up to that lab, sat underneath a bench and ate alone. It's getting louder, being around people. They're crowding in, wanting to tell me things. And then at home.

I'm always cold, and Susan and Nina are on eggshells. Watching me, and thinking of my double pacing round. Before we were haunted, I felt more sure of my place in the family. I'd almost forgotten to be afraid of ruining everything. And that was nice. A gift.

My phone buzzes.

It's Megan.

I missed you at lunch today

I'm sorry pal
The world's a lot
I couldn't

It's okay
you know I deeply get that

how are you feeling about Piotr?
I mean is that still going on?

I swallow. Maybe I shouldn't have asked, or phrased it better.
They're typing and then it stops and then it starts again.

I feel exhausted to be honest
But also like it will be fine
You know

That's good
I really hope so

I just think there's part of him that's really
hoping I will change my mind
Or something

About being with him?

About being myself

Oh Megan.

I mean we were so close
And it's like if we can't have this one
specific kind of closeness he gets weird

and like none of it's in words it's just a
vibe and if I said anything he'd just deny
it but I feel it

like a ghost

a bit like that maybe
how is your ghost?

oh, awful
mould everywhere
Susan thinks it's my fault

Haha

I type *I'm serious* and then delete it.

I don't want them to know. I don't want the creatures
anywhere near them.

Your hand upon their skin.
You let Them see them.

It'll be grand.
Sure Mr Q'll have them out in five minutes

What does he do?

Well, last time nothing
But this time I expect him to like punch them in
the face or something

Will Oz be there?

Yeah

They're typing again, but then it disappears, and I don't respond because I don't know what to say. Oz is difficult to put into words. How I feel about him. Or anything.

It isn't safe.

I hope it goes okay

Thanks Megan
You're a good friend

Thanks friend
Love you too
Ghosts and all

I look at that message for a long time. I think about how I didn't say I love you but they heard it anyway. About how I would say it to Mam, over and over and over again in the voices I heard on TV shows, willing her to mean it back at me, how I would say it to Susan, because I wanted her to keep me here. About how I say it to Nina, because I would do anything for her. Anything at all.

I'm not a person.

Not at all.

Not really.

I think about how sometimes it feels like the world is turning round and round without me in it . How I'm trapped in this space

257

where the edges of what's real are shifting constantly. And how my friends are all coping with their own things and I'm avoiding them and how a normal conversation, awkwardly trying to support a friend, can feel like a gold coin inside my hand. A savepoint.

Even with my walls
I am still a person people reach for.

But they shouldn't.

I open up my bag. I have science homework to do, three experiments to write up and illustrate, so I start doing that, making my writing as neat as possible. I kind of like writing up experiments, there's a structure and a sense to it and you get to also draw pictures on the paper with all the little squares which feels a bit primary school. In a good way. I'm not good at drawing but it's always felt a bit comforting to me. I put in my headphones and turn on a study playlist that's basically just soothing alpha waves, try to zone out, focus on the task.

They don't love me.
They don't even know me.

There's something nice about drifting away, but the time passes too quickly. I'm done. I close up everything, and check my phone again.

Still nothing.

No one does.
Not all of me
but Them.

I turn the music off, and hear the hum of Nina's voice and Susan's through the walls. I sit for a long time, wondering if I should leave my room and join them.

Or if a part of me already has.

rearranging everything

On the way to maths Oz Quigley grabs me and pulls me into the music room. Well, he doesn't grab me, so much as put his hand on my elbow and kind of steer me. But I feel grabbed.

I rub my arm and glare at him. 'How dare you, and I don't mean that in a cute way.'

'I have to talk to you,' he says, and there's panic in his voice. 'You keep being with your friends and it's not really a "with your friends" conversation so I decided to –'

'Manhandle me?'

'Man-oeuvre you.' He shrugs helplessly. 'It's not my style, you know that. But we have to have a conversation if she's at it again.'

'*At* it?' I stare at him. I will despise him if he's not careful. He's giving me plenty of cause.

'Okay. Not the best word choice. She's not the Brits. BUT. We're going back this weekend. Dad and me. To you.'

'We've discussed this already.'

'In that we mentioned it was happening. But, like, Daisy, this isn't real. Like, what's haunting your sister . . . it isn't.'

He holds his hand out. 'And it's not a good idea for us to come around yours.'

'Because of you and Nina?'

He sighs.

'Are we still doing that? Yeah, because of *me and Nina*.'

He doesn't do air quotes but his voice basically drips with them. I've never seen him like this. His shirt is creased and his hair is all askew. One strand is sticking straight up.

'Oz, don't take this the wrong way.' I reach a hand up and straighten it. 'Your hair was annoying me.'

'My hair is annoying me,' he says. 'I play with it when I'm stressed and then it gets all greasy but also somehow . . . fluffy? It's unconscionable. Follow me.'

'I don't know if I feel like going with you to a second location.' But I stop leaning against the wall, straighten up.

'There's a class timetabled here in fifteen minutes. If we go out the fire door, which is disconnected from the alarms because Ms Dunphy likes to smoke here, and up the fire escape, we can be in one of the old labs and have more time to, like, unpack this.'

'I don't know how much there is to unpack, Oz,' I say. 'Like, it is what it is. I probably shouldn't even be talking to you, you know?'

His voice is panicked, low. 'But it's my family.'

'No, Oz. It's you and your dad hopping into *my* family. And our mess. I get that it's frustrating, but it has very little to do with you.'

'You don't know,' he says.

We walk up the fire escape and into the science lab, the entrance to which is held open by an empty can of Fanta.

He wants to tell you.

260

'Know what?'

'About Nina.' He turns to me, just before we pass through the door. 'I mean, I don't even really fully know. But . . . you're close to her. Basically her sister. I assumed she'd . . .'

Basically.

'We are close,' I say, joining him underneath one of the big wooden workstations.

'I thought she might have. There were times.' He sighs. 'Look, it both is and isn't my business. But you know me a little, right?'

I nod.

'Ugh. Okay. I can't be completely honest with you without letting someone down, but I think you should ask Nina to stop doing whatever it is she's doing. It's going to blow up in her face, and it won't solve anything.'

I squint at him. 'I'm missing maths class for you to, what . . . talk shit about my cousin, tell me I'm in a bad situation, which I know, actually, and that you can't give me information that might make your worry more understandable.'

It's Nina.

'IT ISN'T NINA!' My voice comes out much louder than I mean it to.

He flinches, looks at me. 'I didn't say anything.'

'You've said plenty,' I tell him. 'And look, I'd love to help you, Oz. I'd love if this were something that could be . . . like . . . called off. Or something. But. It's different from last time. Because it's me. It's my fault this is happening.'

'I don't believe you,' he says, and obviously he's wrong, but it's nice to hear all the same.

'I don't lie, Oz.'

'I just don't see how it could be your fault.'

'I . . . called something. When you were over last. To help Nina, I think. I thought that maybe your dad would be nicer to her if there was something real.'

'But, Daisy. I mean, don't tell my dad but . . . Ghosts aren't real.' He widens his eyes. 'I mean, I've been on a fair few investigations with him now, and I like to think I'm open-minded, but . . . they're just not.'

I sigh. 'I know. I told myself that too. For years. But I don't know I ever quite believed me.'

'You're fifteen, Daisy.'

'And you're what, seventeen?'

'Yeah.'

'A lot can happen, in a life. So, like I told your dad when you were over, when I was little, I was earning money for my mother. And I would hear these . . . things . . . They would be telling me secrets about people . . . and then she died.'

'I'm sorry.'

'You didn't kill her,' I say. 'People always say they're sorry when they hear I'm bereaved, but not every mother is a mother-mother, you know? After she died, I stopped hearing the voices, and Susan kind of convinced me that it was all my . . . trauma . . . I suppose.'

'Okay . . .'

'So, when I called it, I didn't know what to expect. But they're here, there's mould everywhere. Susan's sleeping in with Nina, there are noises at night, everyone is seeing versions of me that aren't me just kind of hanging around, and I'm not, like, *hearing* the same way, but I'm remembering more, and I can kind of tune in to it. Whatever it is.'

'And you think it's real.'

I look at my watch. 'It's almost lunchtime. Want to come see my mouldy house?'

This is such a bad idea, Daisy.

'I have history.'

'Don't we all,' I say. 'Don't make me manoeuvre you. We'll hop on the bus. Susan's at work. We'll be there and back by the end of the day.'

'Um . . .' he says. And I can see a lot of different things flickering across his face, but I'm not sure what any of them are.

'You don't believe me.'

He meets my eyes.

'I'm not calling you a liar, Daisy. But this . . . this doesn't feel like a very truthy truth.'

'Then gather evidence.'

I run my fingers through my hair. If anyone knew I was here with Oz Quigley, they would assume that we were getting with each other like normal people. Not, like, debating ghosts. His mouth is very straight. Thin-lipped, almost stern. Barely a mouth at all really. Like when you're a kid and you draw men and women, and the women all have a lipstick mouth and the men all have a line. I wish something as simple as a kiss could fix this. I wish I was the kind of girl who had love stories instead of ghost stories. That he would just reach out and hold my hand. His fingers are long and his nails are very perfect. Not like mine, all bitten to the quick.

'Please,' I say.

He nods. Okay. 'Okay, friend.'

I don't correct him this time.

someone else's eyes

It's weird having Oz come to the house this way. At my invitation. It's the kind of quiet where little sounds are big sounds. Our feet crunch on the gravel. My key scrapes in the lock. As we cross the threshold I feel a sense of dread wash over me. You know when you go on holidays to a warmer country and when you get off the plane there's like this wall of hot air that envelops you. And it should be nice, because who doesn't like being warm, but it also reminds you that you need to change your clothes, to put on sunscreen, that you are something new here, something foreign, needing to adapt. *Oppressive*, Caroline used to say. *This heat is oppressive.* I look up at Oz. I feel a bit oppressed.

'Do you want a cup of tea or just to see the ghost stuff?'

'Um, tea, I suppose.' He shuffles. 'There's definitely a vibe here. But there was a vibe before as well. Like something hostile, so I can't tell if it's different.'

'Excuse me. We are all extremely lovely. Did I not just offer you a cup of tea?'

'Yeah, but you were glaring.'

'I'm always glaring. It's just the way my face is.'

I click the kettle on and take out two mugs.

265

'I'll show you the mould stuff while the kettle boils.'

'Daisy?' he says.

'Yes, Oz.'

'You know when I grabbed you earlier?'

'Yeah.'

'Were you *really* annoyed? Like, should I not have touched you?'

'I'm not big on hugs and things,' I say. 'Because of . . .'

Her.

'. . . it doesn't matter why. But I don't think it was, like, a creepy way to touch me or anything like that.'

'Okay,' he says. 'I'm sorry. That you feel that way about hugs and things. Hugs are nice.'

'Puppies are nice. Hugs are optional.'

The kettle clicks off.

'I'd just. I'd hate to be, like . . .'

Him.

'. . . like anyone who would treat someone like they're a thing, you know, exploit people.'

I pour the water and pop the teabags in.

'I don't think you have to worry about that. I mean, I'm not . . . normal.' I force a smile. 'Other people have less worry about being touched. But asking first is good, I think, in general. Do you take milk?'

'A drop,' he says. 'Can I put it in myself?'

I nod.

He puts a literal drop of milk into his tea. It's no way to live. I should ask him to leave.

'Thanks,' he says, swirling it clockwise with a spoon. 'And

you might not feel normal, but I'm not sure that anyone does. That's not to minimise whatever you went through.'

Her hands on the back of my neck. Nails on collarbones.

I cannot breathe.

He isn't safe.

'You can go if you want to,' I say. 'You don't have to stay and see all the ghost stuff. It was probably a bad idea to bring you here.'

He takes a sip of tea.

'No, we're here now. Might as well. And it could help me to prepare for the weekend.'

I look at him.

'I don't know if there's anything in the world that can prepare you for a weekend of looking at mould with your dad and being party to the tensions in my family.'

'It's hard, eh?'

I swallow, and put my tea down. 'It's fine. Susan and Nina are great. I'm just sorry for putting them through this.'

'It's not your fault.'

It is.

And you can stop it.

I scoff.

'No, Daisy. Even if it's *because* of you, I can see how much you hate what's happening. I don't think you would have done this on purpose.'

A step ahead, Oz fumbles his tea but doesn't spill it. Luckily, as we'd both be scalded.

'Yeah, well. It's happening. And if I weren't in this house, it wouldn't be.'

I point to the mould on the stairs as we go up. It curls around the mirror and thick veins of it run through the door of Susan's room.

'It started there, in Susan's room, we think, and it's spread through the hall and down the stairs. It's not in Nina's or my room yet.'

'It's not like normal mould,' he says. 'The patterns.'

'The texture's weird as well,' I say, making as if to rub it with my fingers. 'It's more tactile, I think, than normal mould. I've not had experience with huge clumps of mould in the past to be fair, but it's always looked a bit more . . . powdery . . . I guess.'

'It permeates the air.' He swallows. 'But this does too. I think that's what I felt. When I came in. That sense of breathing in something that's . . . wrong.'

'Hmmm.'

I'm still holding his hand, I realise. I let it go.

He reaches out with one hand to stroke the mould. And freezes.

'Oz?' I say, then louder, 'Oz. Oz!'

The tea falls to the floor, it soaks the carpet. His eyes stare off beyond me, into nothing. His lips are bluish, and there's a shadow of something trailing down the side of his face, as though the mould had grown there too.

I touch his wrist.

He is so frightened
that his parents will split up
and when they do
that it will be

because of him
Because of what
he knows.

'Daisy.' His voice is higher and quieter than normal. A frightened child awakened in the night.

'Yeah?'

'Could you hold my hand again? Please?'

I reach out and grab his hand. The cold burns through me.

Cold
cold cold
Daisy.
I . . .

He's so cold. I reach out my other hand, wrap it around him. Press my warm body against his, until he feels more person-temperature.

He takes a breath. Another breath. They come, faster and faster, higher and higher.

'I don't,' he says. 'I don't.'

I rub his back. 'It's okay.'

His tea has spilled all over the carpet. It has gone through my shoes. It soaks the ground. I put my hand on it. He's still making those sounds. It's like Nina, I think. Nina when she has a panic attack. That's what this is. I rub his back.

'I don't know . . .

'I don't . . .'

'It's okay,' I say again. 'I'm here. You'll be okay.'

I sit him on the top step, rub my hand up and down the length of his spine.

'I've got you. Okay?'

I avoid looking at the mirror. I don't want to see what the me in there is doing.

'We need to get you a glass of water.'

'Don't leave me.'

'I'll just fill your mug in the bathroom,' I say. 'It's literally two steps away. And I'll talk to you the whole time.'

'Okay,' he says. 'Water would be nice. Even from a bathroom tap.'

'Kind of disgusting, eh?' I say, running the tap.

His breathing is still shaky, but evening out.

'Don't tell anyone.'

I smile, and hand him the mug. He gulps it down so quickly. I get him another.

'It tastes like air,' he says. 'You know when you're underwater and you realise you can't breathe and then you come up and the air doesn't taste like air. It tastes like life.'

'You want another mug of life there, pal?' I ask.

'Nah, you're good,' he says. 'Probably lived long enough at this stage. If I could go out before I have to come back here and watch my dad torn between excitement and power-tripping by making Nina feel small, that would be absolutely fine with me.'

'If I've to be here, you've to be here too,' I say.

We smirk. He stands up to his full height. There's a lot of it. He kind of unrolls. Like a fancy carpet.

There are thick dark circles under his eyes, the panic attack clearly took it out of him. He shouldn't be in this place any longer, I think. Get him out. Put him somewhere safe.

'I think that you should go,' I say.

'I think that I should too. Are you going to come back to school?'

I shake my head. 'I might as well stay here.'

His face is panicked, pained.

'It's not . . . safe here . . . Daisy.'

I shake my head. 'It's home though. So I'm used to it, or something.'

We're back in the kitchen, and I'm washing the cups and putting them back in the press. Oz waits around. He stands very tall and very straight.

'You have great posture,' I tell him.

He smiles. 'I get that a lot. I can't help it. People kind of assume when you stand like that that you're confident or something.'

'You are confident though,' I say. 'You seem so sure of who you are.'

He shrugs, and I can see the residue of what happened upstairs in the strain of his bones, the shadows under eyes.

This is what I do to people.

'I don't feel that way. I worry all the time that I'm not a good person. Especially since Nina.'

'What did you do to her, Oz?' I ask.

He swallows. 'I let her down. I feel like I'm still letting her down, Daisy. I always thought that I'd be the person who'd do the right thing. No matter the cost.'

'Sometimes there's not an obvious right thing.'

'This isn't one of those times. She's hurt and she's right to be hurt. You know?'

'I don't know,' I say. 'I'm waiting for her to tell me, but she's

271

all closed up like a shell. And I could . . . I mean, the thing that put the mould where it is, it could tell me, but I won't do that to her. It feels like it would be a betrayal to hear it from someone else. Does that make sense?'

'Not exactly,' he says. 'I mean, I get it. But what if the information meant that you could help her?'

I scratch my neck. 'You have a point but I just have this sense that I'm not supposed to know yet.'

'Sometimes information hits you at a terrible time,' Oz says, 'and all you can do is react. I wish . . .' He sighs. 'I don't know if I'd live it again differently. I don't know if I could. I just wish I was better.'

I reach out and touch the crook of his elbow. My fingers brush against the rough polyester of his school jumper but it's *his*. His arm. It feels like something.

> *Nina on a screen.*
> *Her face.*
> *Her breasts.*
> *Shock.*
> *Horror.*
> *Closing windows quickly.*
> *Wanting to vomit.*

I look at him. He looks back at me.

'What did you see?' he asks.

I'm reeling, trying to make sense of what I've seen. It doesn't make any. That nauseous feeling. If he asked her to send them to him, why would he be so shocked? And anyway . . . I mean, we all know what bodies look like. They're fairly easy to find.

I scan my brain.

'You like Salt and Vinegar Tayto,' I say. 'They say that you should have a bag.'

He narrows his eyes at me.

'What?' I say. 'Sometimes they're just a bit . . . sound. It makes them even creepier.'

He looks at the clock. 'I should go,' he says.

'You keep saying that,' I say. 'And here you are.'

'It feels wrong, leaving you here,' he says.

'You're not a bad person, Oz,' I say. 'I was convinced you were one, then I got to know you. Imagine my disappointment.'

'Thanks, pal.' He smiles.

'Now go.' I push him towards the door.

He walks away, and closes it behind him. I watch him growing smaller out the window. It does make me a bit, not sad, but aware of my aloneness here. In this haunted house. But I suppose I'm the haunted one. I look down at my phone and there are all these messages from Abigail.

> Where are you
> You're going to be in trouble
> I think they're ringing Susan
> I got your science homework
> She says you need to do it again
> Are you okay
> Daisy
> I opened your notebook and

She sends me a photo.

It's my book, but instead of the painstaking notes and diagrams, it's just nonsense. Scribbles. Repeated glyphs and shapes in harsh blue lines, so fiercely scribbled that sometimes there are holes carved through the page.

I look at them. They suddenly take shape. Not glyphs at all but the familiar letters.

W
H
A
T
A
R
E
Y
O
U
D
O
I
N
G
T
O
M
E
DAISY
YES
NO
GOODBYE
HELLO

HELLO
HELLO

'Hello,' I say. 'Hello.'

Hello

My voice feels very strange in all this silence.
Then the hum of something at my neck.
A large cat chirping at a little bird.
This won't end well.

Daisy
Are u ok
Daisy?

the thing about ghosts is

They can touch you you can't touch them
They can touch you you can't touch them
They can touch you you can't touch them
They can touch you you can't touch them
They can touch you you can't touch them
They can touch you you can't touch them
They can touch you you can't touch them
    They can touch you you can't touch them
They can touch you you can't touch them
They can touch you you can't touch them
They can touch you you can't touch them
They can touch you you can't touch them
They can touch you you can't touch them
They can touch you you can't touch them
They can touch you you can't touch them
     They can touch you you can't touch them
They can touch you you can't touch them
They can touch you you can't touch them
They can touch you you can't touch them
They can touch you you can't touch them
They can touch you you can't touch them

They can touch you you can't touch them
They can touch you you can't touch them
          They can touch you you can't touch them
They can touch you you can't touch them
They can touch you you can't touch them
They can touch you you can't touch them
They can touch you you can't touch them
They can touch you you can't touch them
They can touch you you can't touch them
They can touch you you can't touch them
          They can touch you you can't touch them
They can touch you you can't touch them
They can touch you you can't touch them
They can touch you you can't touch them
They can touch you you can't touch them
They can touch you you can't touch them
They can touch you you can't touch them
They can touch you you can't touch them
          They can touch you you can't touch them
They can touch you you can't touch them
They can touch you you can't touch them
They can touch you you can't touch them
They can touch you you can't touch them
They can touch you you can't touch them
They can touch you you can't touch them
They can touch you you can't touch them
          They can touch you you can't touch them

Unless they want you to.

someone you can blame

I wait at the kitchen table, my hands flat against the wood, unmoving. The world is happening around me. Mould leaking out and marking up the walls, red hands, blue swirls on curtains. I wonder how much more damage I will do before this stops. Something is burrowing its way into my brain, and maybe it was always there, inside me. Oz was so cold against me on the landing. I feel the sting of it inside my bones, and something else as well. The way he makes me feel. I don't like that I can feel that way about someone that Nina doesn't like. Someone who hurt her. I wish that I knew how, but it's not my place to ferret it out. Nina will tell me herself when it is time. I don't want to go behind her back, to betray her.

Susan informed us of your particular history.
In case it was pertinent.

The air smells faintly of hot chocolate and I can taste the fear when Susan gets home, worrying. It ripples off her, and when she sees me it turns into anger. I am safe, so this can be my fault. She pulls off her scarf and throws it at a chair. It hits the floor.

'The school called,' she says. 'I had to leave work early. I was worried.'

278

I try to smile.

IloveyouIloveyouIloveyouIloveyouIloveyou

'I came home,' I say, getting up and folding her scarf carefully. 'It felt important. But I don't know why. I've just been here, like, sitting and thinking.'

'Daisy, you can't be doing that,' she says, her voice softening.

'I know,' I say. 'I'm sorry about school.'

'No.' She swallows. 'I mean, mitching is not the best idea, but a day here and there isn't going to kill you. But I don't think that you should be alone here. It's heavier where there are fewer of us.'

I nod, but I am floating far away. She doesn't get that it is me. It's me. She carries on.

'That night you babysat . . . it was intense.'

Mould on the walls of Liam's little room.

And Susan frightened.

I meet her eyes and tell her that I'm sorry, but I am floating somewhere far away.

'It's not your fault,' she says. 'It isn't you.'

'But it's me it wants,' I say. 'It takes my shape.' My voice is flat.

She walks to the kettle, clicks it on, then takes a chair beside me.

'I don't know what to do,' she says. 'And I'm frightened, Daisy. It makes me feel the way your mother did. Sick to my stomach, powerless to act.'

She could have helped you.

'I'm scared too,' I say. 'I'm glad . . . not that she's dead but that I live with you and Nina now.'

279

She squeezes my hand. 'I'm glad too. But I wish that I could be a better mother to you. You deserve one. When you were small I knew what I was doing, more or less. Like, when everything happened with Fiachra, I knew he had to leave. And so I sorted it. But this isn't that. It scares me more.'

Because it's hurting
Nina.

'It's like the bigger you get, the smaller I get.' She shakes her head. 'I shouldn't be talking about any of this with you. It's just I had this idea, that the older I got, the more together my life would be.'

'Wait,' I say. 'That's not how it works?' I slap a hand against my cheek. She smiles. 'You're doing fine, Susan,' I say. 'You've been through a lot.'

'Not compared to you, love.' She swallows. 'Hopefully Mr Quigley will get rid of this for us.'

'I don't think he will,' I say.

Her face goes pale.

'What?' I ask her. 'What?'

'Is that you talking – or them?'

I look down at the table. The pattern of the wood.

If you cut a tree open you can tell how old it is
by counting
rings inside the trunk.

She knows.

Her question hangs in the air for what seems like an age while I search for any sort of answer, knowing all the while that there is nothing I can say to make this not be true. Or stop it happening.

'Me,' I say. 'I have to work to hear Them. Or be touching someone else's skin. It doesn't take whatever They are, Susan, for me to know that this won't help at all. Our geography teacher is not going to fix this.'

'Last time it went away . . .'

'And then got worse,' I say. 'Before, it wasn't Them. It wasn't me.' I find a loose thread on the knee of my tights and pull it tight and wind it round my finger. Cut off the blood, and wait for Susan's words.

> *She said,*
> *You are a rope*
> *around*
> *my*
> *neck.*

'And it's like it was when you were young?' she asks. 'The same as that . . . the creatures?'

Her eyes dart round the table, to the salt and pepper, the sugar bowl, to anywhere but mine. The top of my index finger pulses red and swollen, like a tick, and she's still saying things, avoiding eyes.

'I want the truth.'

> *She doesn't want this truth.*

'No,' I tell her, finally. 'I'm pushing Them away now, trying not to hear. Might be why They're angry. Back then I didn't know how not to hear Them, and I wasn't as scared of what They meant. Mam was what haunted me.' My throat is very dry. I swallow. Twice.

Susan meets my eyes. 'She haunts you still.'

Now it's me who wants to look away. I nod.

'You know, you read for me once,' she says. 'We came over for lunch and she kept pushing. I was out back then, but not to her.'

I shrug. 'I don't remember.'

'You were so young. Only two or three. You could barely talk at all when you wanted to express yourself, and I think part of me wanted to see what it was you did. I didn't believe it. And she was holding Nina and I saw those two hands wrapped around my baby and I grabbed her back and held her while you spoke. You were a baby too, but there was no one there to keep you safe, my Daisy. And I'm sorry.'

> *There are trees called healing trees*
> *and people hammer nails into them*
> *to release their pain.*

'What did I say?'

> *But really they're just hurting something else,*
> *another life.*

'I thought you had been coached,' Susan said. 'I mean, I knew from Nina that it was unlikely that a child could even learn to say those things . . . but it seemed less unlikely than . . . supernatural stuff, you know?'

'What did I say to you?'

'A few things. Some that had already come to pass. And some that hadn't.'

> *I don't want to hammer nails*
> *inside her.*

'But it was accurate?'

'I didn't know. For a long time I didn't know.' She closes her eyes. 'I assumed Therese would have known what to say

282

to me from Fiachra. To upset me. And you were so small. Your little hand, here.'

She gestures to her forearm.

I cannot feel my fingertip but I focus on it, chase the numbness.

She will leave you

it will break her heart

is

what

we

told

her.

'You were so small, with your two big eyes all wide like you were asking me for a treat or something. And her eyes burning at me from across the room. I could see the tendons in her neck and I remember thinking, *Oh. She hates me. Or maybe I hate her. Do I hate her?* I didn't know then how bad things had gotten for you. Or maybe I wasn't looking properly. She was good at putting on a front. I felt like I was rude to not feel right around her. And Fiachra didn't seem worried.'

She's looking far away past me, as though she's searching for him, how he was.

'Do you think that the thing was haunting her too?' I ask. 'And that it maybe changed her?'

No.

'Maybe,' Susan says. 'Maybe not. I know if anything was hurting Nina, I would do whatever I could. Whatever I could to stop it.'

I look at her.

Say me. Say me as well.

She smiles.

'And you too, Daisy. But I suppose I started out with Therese, comparing the way she was with you to the way I was with Nina.'

'I get it,' I say, standing up to make a cup of tea.

'Could you make me a chamomile?' Susan asks. 'I need to calm down.'

'I'll make two.' I smile at her, get up.

'Daisy,' Susan says to me at last, 'I understand that it is hard on you. That this year has been hard on all of us, but you and Nina especially. And I've . . . not been myself. Since the split. There's just been so much to cope with, you know, thing after thing . . . and you're not the one who should be holding us together.'

'I miss her,' I say. 'Caroline.'

'I know you do,' Susan tells me. 'I do too. So much. But I fucked that one up. A bit like now. I feel like another person would have this under control, you know?'

'Susan, it's ghosts,' I say. 'You can't control ghosts.'

'Increasingly I can't control anything.'

'Would you like to get back together with her?' I ask.

She sighs. 'It's complicated. I think there was a time when I would have given anything for that. Anything at all. An arm. A leg. But now, with time and space . . . It wasn't working.'

She won't forgive her.

I peel the string from round my finger joint. Watch the blood flow back in. I do not feel it.

'Okay,' I say. As though I get it. And I feel like maybe I do get it, on some level. I feel very jaded by today and very old. 'It's a whole lot. All of this.'

'It is.' She sighs. 'It's been a while since we talked like this, eh, Daisy?'

'It has,' I say. 'I liked our chats.'

'Me too. I suppose Nina is always there, and she's had so much going on, and then there's been the hauntings, One and Two. I don't know. I'm chasing my tail.'

'Susan?' I venture. 'I want to ask you something, but it's a hard one.'

'Ask me, pet. The worst I can say is no.'

'Have you seen the thing that looks like me?'

She reaches out to me, her gaze tender.

'That is you, pet.'

It hits me like a slap.

'No, it's not,' I say. 'It isn't me.'

Susan sighs. 'I haven't brought it up with you because it's a lot for you to be dealing with, Daisy, but it's you. It's you.'

'But the night of the slumber party, Nina saw . . .' I start.

'The night of the slumber party Nina had a nightmare,' Susan says. 'It's a separate thing to these other incidents.'

'Other incidents . . . ? What does it do?' I ask. 'I mean, what do I do? When I go into your room?'

'Not much,' Susan says. 'You look at things. You smile. You walk around the edges of the room sometimes, like you're mapping them out, over and over.'

Scissors under her pillow.
Just in case
of
you.

'It's not . . . it's not that you're doing anything threatening,

Daisy. But when you're there, we can't take our eyes off you for a second. There's this feeling that something bad will happen if we do.'

I swallow. What do you say to that?

I look at the woodgrain of the table, dark honey on pale honey.

'Why haven't you been telling me this stuff?' My voice comes out a whine, like she's not letting me go to the cinema or something, instead of withholding vital information. 'I mean, it's me. Even if it's not me, you know?'

'It scares me, Daisy,' Susan says. 'And I'm trying to work out what to do about it. Because it can't continue. And I know you don't have any control over it. But we shouldn't have to lock our bedroom doors at night.'

'You lock your bedroom door?'

'You get in anyway.'

'But doesn't that prove it's not me?' I say. 'I really don't think it is. Could we, like, maybe get a baby monitor or put a phone camera in my room or something just to check?'

'I don't see what difference it would make,' Susan says. 'It's not about proving or disproving. It's about coping with the situation we're in.'

We aren't coping though.

'I think it would make me feel better though,' I say. More sure. 'And aren't these situations about evidence? Like, if it's me, it's what, a mental-health thing? Possession?'

'It might be,' Susan says. 'You've always had those dreams. That . . . sleep paralysis . . . If you would like to talk to someone, Daisy, we could do that. No harm in it.'

286

Mould on the walls.
Mould down my throat,
inside me.

My voice comes out so shrill: 'It isn't ME. It's Them. You need to listen.'

Her expression is blanker now, removed. The kettle clicks. I look down at my hand. I could hold it over the sink. Pour the water on. It wouldn't hurt me. I'm not really here. Not all of me. I can feel my face twist into a scowl. I think of the reflection in the mirror, imagine it walking closer, closer, like a crab. Smiling at me. Did I give it the car keys to my body somehow? I think of the pages of my science book. My hands did those. I thought that I was doing everything right, and instead it's all a mess I can't control. I put my head in my hands and bite my lip. If I were Nina, I would be crying right now. It's like it's all blocked up.

Stop your fucking whining.

My hands on my face feel dry. Chapped. The wrong shape somehow. I gasp and push them down onto the counter. Look at them stretched flat. Thank God. They're normal.

'Sorry, Susan,' I say. 'I'm really sorry.'

'Look.' Susan sighs. 'We'll get you the support you need if it comes to that, but that's a conversation – maybe this weekend will help, you know? It did before. It did stop for a while. And I know it's not your fault, Daisy. We love you.'

I nod. 'We could visit Dad, maybe this weekend?' I say.

She pushes her hair back from her face and sighs. 'Maybe, love. If we feel up to it.'

He's told her that he

287

doesn't want

to see you

I try not to react, but that knowledge scrapes my insides. Leaves them raw.

It has been years since he has been anything like a father.

I shouldn't care.

I should have learned by now.

'I need to start my homework,' I say.

'Would you like me to bring you up another cup of tea?' Susan asks, and it's kind of her but also a message that I should go up to my room to do it. That this – the talking, sharing-feelings bit – is over.

'If the school asks, tell them I grounded you or something,' Susan says. 'I mean, I could, but the way things are is punishment enough.'

For all of us.

I nod and make a small appreciative sound. My head is racing. The chamomile tea is cold by now and it kind of just tastes like dishwater. I am not calmed, or soothed.

I stand up, and my legs remind me of how long we've been sitting down.

'Where's Nina?' I ask.

'Oh, she's babysitting at the Mahons' tonight. Claudia asked for only her this time. She went from school.'

Scared of you.

My hands ball into fists. My eyes sting angry. It's so unfair. It's all just so fucking, fucking, fucking unfair. I didn't ask for any of this.

'I suppose I'll head up so.'

288

'See you, pet.'

I stamp up the stairs. Slam the door of my room and rip an entire new copybook to shreds, page by page. I can't believe Nina didn't tell me. I can't believe I had to ask Susan about this. Why are people so bad at being people. Why can't I just be normal, not rich or smarter or better-looking or talented, but just regular? Not haunted. In control of what my body does. And why can't people just tell me things? They used to be more open.

It reminds me of just before Dad went away.

The pauses. The looks. The weight in the air.

They spend their nights in fear of something like me.

I gingerly pick up every single page. Put them in a clear ziplock bag left over from a sandwich and stuff it in my school bag so I can bin it there.

I don't want any evidence.

hungry memory

You are two years old.
She is screaming at you.
You have been playing with her bottles of spices.
Lining them up.
One has spilled and it is all over the carpet.
It is red, so red.
You feel the sting of it in your eyes, your nose.
YOU, she says.
YOU.
Her voice lowers.
You make everything worse.

(You don't, my darling.
We are so grateful for you.)

You are a rope around my neck.
She has the hoover and she pulls the cord of it tight around
her throat.
Her eyes are bulging.
This is you.
This is what you do to me.

Every single day.
Over
and over.
You look at her.
You cannot move.
She pulls the hoover towards you.
You want to move but you cannot.
She calls you a mistake.
Her worst mistake.
A little freak.
Her hands yanking at the tubing.
Rolling the machine over your small foot.
Snapping you from one pain to another.
You scream.
She grabs your foot and squeezes it.
You're fine.
Don't be so dramatic.

(A small bone in your foot has cracked.
Oh, Daisy.)

You push your hands in front of your face and you are still crying, you don't know how to stop crying, you are in your body and it hurts.

The hoover whirrs. It's loud. You do not like it.
It's always something with you, isn't it?
One thing after another.
I can't.

291

I just cannot.
Her face crumples too.
I hate this.
Oh.
I hate this.
I hate.
This.
You will be the death of me.
It's true.
She sweeps a hand through the air between you, as though
tracing the edge of a cord.
You have rubbed something horrid in your eyes.
It stings.
It's stinging and you scream and scream and scream.
And she is screaming too over and over.
Two open throats are keening through the air.

(We see an opening in her.
We take it.)

She lifts you up, hauls you to the bathroom.
Holds your eyes under the cold tap.
Hold still.
Hold still.
You struggle.
I am trying to help you, she says. This is what help looks like.
Help isn't always nice.

(We are journeying to you, my darling.)

But Mammy knows.
We have to make sure it's all gone.
Weren't you silly to rub your eyes with that stuff on your
hands?
Silly Daisy.
You're lucky I was here.
You wet yourself.
Oh.
I try my level best with you. And every time.
And
Every.
Single.
Time.

(Soon.)

my mouth my hands my throat

I wake in darkness. Everything is wrong. I can't make out the time. I can't move, but I wonder if I'm moving and just don't know it yet. Could I be here and also somewhere else, crawling the walls of someone else's room? I focus on the edges of my body, the dryness of the sheets rough on my skin, abrasive. I see the outlines of the windowsill, my desk. My school bag propped beside it. My wardrobe door is open a crack and the gap looks like an inky mouth. A chasm.

I think very hard about my ankles, and try to convince them to move just a little.

Like when you have pins and needles, and shaking yourself feels like the hardest thing in the world but it's necessary.

I think. If I could crook my ankle just a little, then maybe the movement would come back. It's not that I am numb.

The feeling's there. It's just I can't connect to my body. I'm trying, but the usual way doesn't seem to be working and the more I think about it the more I amn't sure how people move. How did I do it up till now? What did it look like?

The saliva's pooling in my mouth.

And I am looking at that gap in the wardrobe.

And I am thinking, Something's watching me.

It is.

We are.

I imagine it yawning, wide as a mouth, and a pair of such familiar hands spindling out towards me. Holding me close. Too close. Too tight. And pressing. Pressing. Pressing.

At my throat.

My
Throat
Starts
To
Ache
A
Small
Insistent
Itch
At
First
And then
It's stopped by something.
I can't breathe.
My body flops.
A fresh caught fish.
Involuntary gasping, and suddenly my mouth is full of mould
A gritty paste
It tastes like earth
Like milk
Like skin
And something rotten.

It forces its way out of me and out of me and out of me and
underneath the door and up the walls and everything is ruined
I have ruined it I always do I ruin things
My fault.
My fault.
I reach my hand out to touch it.
It squeezes through my fingers horrid, cold.
I sit in my stained sheets looking at the ruin of my walls and
wanting to . . . what?
Not to die exactly
But maybe not to be coping with any of this
Maybe not to be anything at all
To surrender
Give up
Let it take me

Yes

I have been so focused on the threat outside me.
But I cannot ignore the threat within.
I called it home.
I hear a voice scream
DAISY
DAISY STOP IT
I startle.
Drink the air into my lungs.
Susan's voice splits through me.
DAISY DAISYDAISYDAISY

Tap
Tap

My ankles work, I push myself out of bed and run towards
her voice.

'DAISYDAISYDAISY'

She sounds a way I've never heard before.
I push and pull at her bedroom door but it's locked.
I scream outside:
I'm coming.
Let me in.
I'm here.

What do you need?

A scream. A scream that carries on. That severs the air around
us. And then a ragged cough, a gasp a cough.
My heart.
'SUSAN, LET ME IN. NINA? NINA, ARE YOU OKAY?
NINA? NINA?'
The door is there. Thin pale wood. Brass handle. I knock again.
Again. Bang it with the flat of my hand on every panel.
I can hear them moving.
Murmuring.
They can hear me, can't they? They can hear me.
'Susan.' I tap. I try again.
'Susan.
Susan.
Nina.'
A voice that keens, that screeches, 'Oh my baby. My baby.

My baby baby, oh my baby . . .'

'Susan, do you need me to call someone? The ambulance? Police?'

It's like she doesn't hear me.

The door still resolutely shut.

I bang on it again, again again. Until my hands are sore. Until it opens.

Susan looks me up and down. 'Go back to bed. I think you've done enough.'

I push past her to Nina, who is sitting up, rubbing her throat. Susan is fierce – something in her voice I've never heard screams at me, 'You get away from her!'

She grabs my arm and pulls me back, tries her best to shove me out the door. I ground my feet and grip out at the wall. I won't go though. I can't. I need to know my sister is all right.

She's not your sister.

Nina is sitting on the bed with her two hands cradling her throat. 'I'm grand,' she says. 'I'm grand now, Mom. It was a dream.'

'It wasn't a dream.'

'Or a hallucination. She was outside the door.'

'The door was locked,' Susan says slowly. She's looking beyond me, not at me.

'The door was locked, Mom. It was the thing. Not her. Like I've been telling you.'

'I saw her,' Susan says. 'I saw her do it.'

'What?' I ask.

'It wasn't her,' says Nina.

'What wasn't me?' I ask. 'What happened to you, Nina?'

298

Susan turns to me. 'I can't look at you. And I can't leave you alone with her. You need to get out, Daisy.'

'Just tell me what happened.' I'm on the brink of angry tears. I swallow them back and do a rant instead. 'Remember before this house when we used to fucking talk to each other?'

Susan glares at me.

'I love you, Daisy, but leave it. Leave it.'

Nina gets up. Her hands are still cradling her throat, like she has made a collar of them.

'I was watching but my eyes were really heavy and I must have fallen asleep, because I remember you in that quilted dressing gown again – and then you had your hands around my throat. But it wasn't just a dream. Mom woke up and had to pull you off me. Or not you. Them. The creatures.'

Susan sighs. She's staring out the window.

'Jesus Christ, Nina. I'm sorry.'

'It wasn't you.' She moves close to me. 'I know it wasn't you.'

'She thinks it was.' I point over at Susan, who turns to me, her eyes glittering with something I can't read.

I feel nauseous. I put my hand on my stomach, bend a little.

'I'm fine now, Daisy,' Nina says. 'Daisy. It's okay.'

'Take your hands off your neck, Nina.' Susan's voice cuts through the fear, confusion.

'Fine,' Nina says. She wiggles, and her face changes. 'I . . . I can't . . .'

The mice that aren't mice start moving, chiming. A bloom of mould spreads slowly up the wall.

I put my hands over Nina's, try to peel her fingers back. They won't budge.

'Stop it, Daisy. Squeezing. Hurting me.'

Susan startles and I move my hands away. Hold them up like Susan was the police. I want her to see I amn't hurting Nina.

> *But you are.*
>
> *And you can make it stop.*

Susan has moved closer too, and she rubs at Nina's fingers. Nina grimaces. 'Back off, Mom. It's squeezing me. It's hurting.' Susan moves away, and Nina nods. 'It was, like, the closer either of you got, the more it was pushing me to hurt myself.' She waggles her elbows. 'I know it looks ridiculous. But I'm okay.'

'Nina, this is so far from okay.' Susan's voice raw with panic.

> *Try again.*

I lift my gaze up to the mirror. I know that who I'm seeing isn't me.

'Nina.' I swallow. 'I think it will let me help now. If you're okay with that.'

She nods. I move close, place my hands over her hands.

'Try to move your fingers now.'

I feel them flutter tentatively.

'Okay,' she says. 'Okay.'

She lifts her hands.

Thick, indented handprints caked in mould coat her neck.

Susan gasps. She reaches out her hand, to touch her daughter, but the mould crumbles off, littering the bed. The indented fingermarks swell and fill again, until Nina's neck is just a normal neck. As though none of it happened.

I look at my own hands. If the creatures are a part of me, and They can look like me, and They can hurt her, isn't that the same as me hurting her, more or less? My presence here's a dangerous thing, a trap.

When I look up, Susan is staring at me.

'We can't go on like this.' There is a little tremor to her voice that breaks my heart. 'We cannot do it.'

She looks at me like I could make it stop.

You can.

For them.

'Mom, we're haunted,' Nina says, rubbing at her neck. 'It's not going to just go away. And it's not Daisy's fault. *I* started this. Daisy's done nothing but support me since the beginning of this, and it's been hard.'

Her face crumples. 'I haven't . . . There have been times this year I haven't wanted . . . to be in the world at all. I just . . .'

Susan moves to wrap her arms around her.

She knows what that is like.

She's felt it too.

'Oh, my little girl. My baby. Nina. I'm here.'

I look at her. I want to hug her too, but I still feel the sting of Susan's eyes.

'I love you, Nina,' I say. 'And I'm so sorry for what you went though.'

'I'm not . . .' Her voice is halting, cracking. 'I'm not strong like you . . . I'm not resilient. You have a wall in you to keep stuff out. Contained. Mine keeps crumbling, wanting to spill over.'

'You could just tell us, Neen,' I say. 'You could.'

'I CAN'T!' she says. 'My mouth wants to make the words but I just *can't*. You know?' She swallows back another sob. 'Mom,' she says, 'I'd love a glass of water.'

Susan sighs. 'We'll all have to go down then, love. Because I'm not leaving you alone with *that*.'

301

'Mom!'

'Sorry, Nina. With her.'

She turns to me. Her eyes glint fierce. 'Sorry, Daisy.'

She isn't sorry.

Something changed tonight.

'It's okay, Susan,' I say. My voice is small.

There is nothing I can do.

If I just . . . gave in. Opened up. Tuned in all the time. Would it stop hurting people that I love?

Would that be enough to make it stop? Would anything?

'I'll go down and get a glass of water for Nina,' I say to Susan.

I walk down the stairs and to the sink in the kitchen, and I feel as though the house is somehow cramped and vast. I'm far away from things that make me feel safe, and everything I'm scared of is inching closer. I have the sense that out of my field of vision there are mirrors. On the ceiling above, the floor below.

Snatches of movement out of the corner of my eye.

I close my eyes as I pass the mirror in the hall, feel a shudder over my skin, a film of ice.

When I get back upstairs, the door is locked again.

A voice.

'Just leave it.'

'Mom!'

I put the glass down and go back to my bedroom.

I shut the wardrobe door, but the gap is still there, gaping. Mould thick on the walls. Mice in the pipes. It wants me to tune in. To hear it. It wants to nuzzle closer into me.

Inside my life, my skin.

Where it's so warm.

full of you

Can I call you?

It's Abigail.

OK

I am looking at myself in the mirror in the hall, and feeling sick to my stomach.

I picture mould coating the inside of my ribcage, furring it thicker and thicker.

Susan has bought dehumidifiers for every room. They're whirring all the time.

The mould is spreading.

Nina wore long sleeves again today.

I couldn't bring myself to ask her why.

Because it's me.

All my fault.

I'm worried Susan doesn't love me any more. I could be wrong. She's pushing me away, but there's still dinner. She still asks how my day was at school. It's this wariness in her eyes, like I'm about to bare my teeth, to bite her.

'Why do you want Mr Quigley to come back?' Nina asked her yesterday. 'After what he did before?'

Her mouth crooked sideways. 'We've been through this, love,

there's no one else,' she said. 'No one. When I talk about this to Tricia, or Owen, or even Caroline, they can't understand it. They keep giving me real-world solutions. Get someone in to do X, Y and Z. But I've done *everything* and there is nothing left.'

Nina nodded. 'I get it.'

Susan put her hand on her, and said 'I know you do.'

The phone buzzes and I am jolted back to where I am.

This house.

These stairs.

This moment.

I close my eyes and try to keep the creatures far away while Abigail is speaking. She hates the phone, it's weird for her to call.

She needs
a friend.

Her voice is funny, dipping in and out.

'Mom and Dad are fighting again,' she says. 'I'm holding the phone up to the wall so you can hear a bit of it.'

'Oh,' I say, and listen for the rise and fall of their voices.

She will grab his arm
so tightly that he
will have five
small bruises tomorrow.
She can't let go.
She can't lose him again.

'Have you gone in to check on them?' I ask.

'No!' she scoffs. 'Let them at it. It's not like they're going to *fight*-fight like, it's just horrible, horrible words all back and forth.'

'Do you ever think that they'd be better off apart?' I ask her.

304

'What kind of a question is that? You're supposed to be making me feel better, Daisy.'

'Oh,' I say. 'Okay. I can do that.'

I rub my eyes.

'Do you have somewhere to be?' Abigail asks.

I swallow. She needs me.

'It's just a bit strange at home at the minute,' I say. 'With everything.'

'Is there ghost stuff happening?' she asks. 'Has Mr Q been over yet?'

'Tomorrow,' I tell her. 'But it's boring. I mean, it's freaky but it's not as important as what you're going through. What started the row?'

'Dad being Dad. He was late picking me up again, and I didn't mind but it's like not a great area, where I do French grinds, and there were some men in a car who said some horrible racist things to me and I got upset.'

'That's absolutely fucked. Are you okay?' I ask.

'Yeah, yeah, it's fine. But I wish they'd ask me that instead of going at each other about whose fault it was.'

Her voice cracks. 'I don't want them to split up again, but this isn't right either. Why is it so hard?'

I sigh. 'I don't know, Abi. I think it's hard for everyone right now. Like, not to take away your specific hard, but I don't know . . .'

There is a pause. I hear her take a breath.

'Yeah,' she says. 'The Megan thing is weird. What did we do, like?'

'I don't think *we* did anything. Like, I think they just need space from certain people.'

'I just feel bad for Piotr. It's hard when you think someone likes you and they don't, or they do but decide not to be with you for whatever reason.'

She says reason like a reason is the most ridiculous thing in the world.

She wanted it to be Megan and
Piotr and her and Conchur.

I squint my eyes to try and get it away from me, but at the same time that feels like a truth.

'Is Conchur okay?' I ask. 'With his dad and everything?'

'He told you about that?' Her voice is sharp and I realise he didn't. They did. Oh no. I decide to bluff through.

'What, is he sick again? I just meant, like, getting over it.'

'It was years ago, Daisy,' she says. 'Are you sure he didn't tell you?'

'We don't really talk on our own,' I say. 'I mean, we message every now and then, but not like you two do.'

I rub my face and sit down on the top step of the stairs. I should go in my room, but I don't want to. My stomach is unsettled, there's a sweet taste in the back of my throat.

'Oh,' she says. 'Okay. Maybe I should go. They've kind of stopped.'

'Abigail?' I say. I don't really know what I want to ask her though.

'Yeah?'

'Are we . . . good?'

'I'm ringing you when I'm upset, Daisy,' she says. 'Of course we're good. You're my friend.'

She wanted more from you.

You let her down
Again.

She sounds so tired.

But
she is not surprised.
This always happens.
And it is exhausting.

I feel this weight, this sadness, as we say goodbye, end the call. Like it's a bigger goodbye than intended. I wanted more from me as well, I think.

My ear feels funny, when I rub it my hand comes away black. My phone screen's covered in mould, thick and soft and horrid.

I bring my fingers to my nose and smell it, and without knowing why I put one finger in my mouth and suck.

My friends are not my friends.
My family is not my family.
Everything is rotting, turning wrong.

Tap
Tap
Tap
Tap
Tap

I vomit old hot chocolate onto my hands. It drips through my fingers and stains the carpet, dark brown like dried-up blood.

repetition

The door of my room opening wakes me. I startle, but it's Nina. She clambers under the covers beside me.

I look at my clock. It's four in the morning.

'Why are you here?' I ask.

'I couldn't sleep. I'm scared of tomorrow. Isn't that weird? More than ghosts. I don't want them in our space again.'

'It'll be okay.'

'See, I don't think it will. I have this feeling. And Mom. She's changing.'

'You've noticed that too?' I ask.

Nina curls towards me in the bed. I can't make out her face, too close, too dark. 'It's like something is making her forget how much she loves you. And she does love you, Daisy.'

'I feel like everyone is mad at me or something,' I say. 'Abigail rang earlier and her parents were rowing and she was just off, you know? I felt like I couldn't say the right thing.'

And Megan.

I should message.

Tell them I've fucked up.

'There is no right thing, Daisy,' Nina tells me. 'And if she could see what our house is like, she'd be thanking God she didn't live here.'

'What do you need me to do tomorrow?' I ask.

'Don't leave me alone with him,' Nina says.

'Oz?' I ask.

'No,' she says. 'No. Austin . . . Mr Quigley.'

She holds her arm out for me to touch.

I close my eyes.

Everything was going wrong.

Everything.

It felt like the world was tilting and she couldn't find her feet.

She was losing her grip on stuff.

Falling behind.

The only time she felt like she could get anything right was debating.

People looked at her like her words held weight and it was a rush.

He would tell her what to say. Suggest approaches. Give tips.

He lent her a book. And there was a phone number written in the back.

She messaged it.

Just Hi and a smiley face.

He rang. He said he was hoping that she'd call. That she seemed sad and he knows it's probably not the proper thing but he wanted her to have someone to talk to.

She talked to him.

About her mom, and Caroline.

About how scared she felt. Worried that she had done something.

That if she wasn't there. If her mother didn't have her and Daisy to mind then maybe things would have been different.

He didn't tell her she was ridiculous.

. He just listened and made noises like agreement in his throat. Like he was really listening.

He told her she had a good understanding of people, better than a lot of adults.

And that was it.

For ages they messaged back and forth, and he would ring and they would talk.

She couldn't tell anyone about it.

Because it wasn't the kind of thing a teacher was supposed to do.

Not that we're doing anything inappropriate, he told her. I'm just your friend.

Your good friend, I like to think.

Definitely my good friend, she told him.

After a while he told her things as well. About his paranormal research. Houses he had visited. The stories behind the ghosts.

She thought he was so brave.

He laughed.

My wife doesn't think so. She thinks I'm an eejit.

He laughed again but she could hear the hurt inside his voice.

He didn't talk about his wife again for ages.

He listened to her.

Made her laugh.

She touched his arm once during debate team practice and he was really brusque with her.

Didn't call her for a few days.

She felt terrible.

Sick.

Like she'd broken something precious.

She rang him eventually and apologised.

He said they had to be careful.

That they were playing with fire.

That it couldn't happen again.

And that

he couldn't stop

thinking about her.

Her breath caught in her throat.

Her knees felt weak.

She hadn't thought he'd feel that way about her.

She needed him.

So much.

And she wanted him too. She did. She was sure she did. This nervous, aching feeling. That's what love is, surely. This sense that if the other person went away then you would break and there would be a void just sucking everything out of you.

She started to tell him how she felt and he stopped her and said that it was wrong. He was exploiting her. They couldn't do this.

She started wearing make-up into school. Wearing her hair in a sweepy ponytail she knew he liked.

And he would message to ask

Why are you doing this to me, Nina?

Making it so hard to forget you.

She didn't want to be forgotten.

One evening he called her back in after class
and gave her a leaflet about a debate competition in Dublin
in the summer
The classroom was empty and he said
I can see your bra strap through your shirt.
Why are you doing this to me Nina?
And she felt so powerful.
A young woman.
He called her
a young woman.
She kept doing things to him
with how she looked.
He would ask her how she was going to wear her hair the
next day.
What shoes she'd wear.
What bra.
Then one night,
did she think she could get out of the house without anyone
noticing?
He had to see her.
She got the bus to a house thirty minutes outside the town.
And went in.
It was an investigation.
The family had gone.
He was by himself.
For a few hours.
I had to see you,
he said.
And then looked at her, and said,

We shouldn't.

And she didn't know what it was they shouldn't do.

But the length of him was pressing her into the wall and his breath hot on her ear and he didn't feel like her friend any more.

What are you doing to me? he said.

He kept on saying.

But he was the one doing things to her.

His mouth on hers and it felt awkward.

But he loved her.

That was why he had to do these things.

Because he loved her.

Love is powerful.

It bends the rules.

She wanted to tell Daisy but he told her she could tell no one.

No one.

It would ruin him, and her as well.

People wouldn't understand.

Even something as innocent as a kiss.

The way he kissed her didn't feel innocent though.

She rubbed her hand over her mouth on the bus home and wondered if this was what growing up felt like.

She wanted to tell Daisy but she couldn't.

And there was a giddiness to getting away with it.

To sneaking around.

Nobody knowing what they were getting up to.

He told her she was beautiful and perfect.

And she felt beautiful.

And she felt perfect.
He wanted things from her
because he loved her.
There were so few ways they could be together.
All in snatched
moments.
She wasn't sure about the pictures.
But he wanted them.
Kept on, not pushing, but mentioning.
Alluding.
Until it felt like it was mean to not.
She locked her door
and got ready.
Sometimes she would feel excited about him.
But other times
it was like
she felt that
she should feel excited.
Like her job was to feel excited by the things he wanted
always.
And it was nice
to wear the matching set of underwear she'd got
in Penneys.
To put on make-up, do the lighting and get the angle right.
He didn't want anything too porny.
Just a photo of her in her underwear
thinking about him.
She wasn't really thinking about him though
not when she took them.

She was focusing on looking
sexy.
She sent them and he replied in all caps
GORGEOUS
THANK YOU.
THANK YOU.
It made her smile.
And she waited for what would come next.
What came next was
nothing.
Blank stares.
A phone number that didn't work any more.
Just nothing.
But it wasn't nothing was it.
It was them.
The two of them together.
Their love.
Their secret, and it made her feel sick, sick, sick.
Invisible.
A ghost.
She tried to write him a letter but she couldn't put it into
words, the things he'd made her feel.
There was a wrongness to it now, her body didn't feel like hers,
it felt like his
She couldn't touch herself without thinking of the empty
house.
The wall.
It would flash through her body and herself and then she
wouldn't want to any more.

315

It was so lonely.
Like she didn't matter.
Like she'd never mattered and she only wanted him to look
at her.
To look at her.
To look at what he'd done.
Because she couldn't forget.
She couldn't sleep.
Or carry on as normal.
There was no normal.
She was haunted.
Haunted.
And she wanted him to see that.
And to know that what they'd had was real.
At least to her.
But when he came the anger on his face made her brain
catch up to her body and she saw things so differently.
He said he was her friend.
He was no friend.
But she couldn't find the words.
Her body and her brain they wouldn't let her.
Something stopped her.
As surely as a hand across a mouth.

My heart is hammering inside my chest.

I want to scream, to kill him.

This isn't about me.

'Oh, Nina, Nina,' I say. 'I'm so sorry. I'm so sorry that this happened. That he did this.'

'It wasn't just him,' she says. '*We* did it. Me and him. We did this to me. Together. And I know that it was just a few . . . I don't even know what to call them, Daisy. Kisses feels wrong.'

'Assaults,' I say. 'You're a child and he's an adult. Assaults.'

'It's not that simple,' she says. 'I wanted it. I went there. I went back. I took those photos. I told him that I loved him. I did love him.'

'Nina,' I say, 'that doesn't excuse what he did, not at all. He's a teacher and you're a student who was going through a lot. It was not your fault. At all.'

'I just didn't know how he could forget me. When I couldn't forget him. And then he was so angry with me. Like I had done something to him. And I . . . this year . . . since everything . . . it's felt like I can't touch the world at all . . . like it's here and I'm in it, and I want to stay here, Daisy. But there are times when I'm not sure I can.'

'You have to, Nina,' I say. 'You have to. I can't. Without you. I know that's the wrong thing to say probably, but I can't. You're my family, and I need you and I love you.'

And I hate him.

Oh, I HATE him.

'I know you do.' Her face is drawn, as though she hasn't slept in weeks. Maybe she hasn't.

Rage thrums through me, hot and thick as blood.

'You saw everything?' she asks, pulling at her sleeve.

I nod.

'I thought you would. They're getting closer to you, Daisy. And I'm so worried about what will happen. And maybe, I mean if he could help . . . He's done stuff to help people like us before.'

317

'Nina,' I say, 'no, he hasn't. He's a liar, and the thing about liars is they lie.'

She turns her back to me. 'I knew you'd judge me.'

'I'm not judging you,' I tell her. 'Not at all. I'm judging him. But you know who I'd like to actually judge him though? A judge.'

'It's not like that,' she says. 'And I don't want anyone to know. You can't tell Mom.'

'You need to tell her,' I say. 'I mean, you can't just keep this bottled up, you need help.'

'I'll be okay,' Nina says. 'I'm not completely broken.'

'Nina,' I say, 'I don't think you're broken, but I think that after something like this, something big, you know? There's definitely healing to be done. You're looking for it, aren't you? With the haunting. For something that would make the world make sense.'

'I don't want to tell Susan. I don't want to tell anyone. I didn't even tell you. I just gave you permission to know.'

'What's the deal with Oz?' I ask.

He knew.

He knew.

They showed me on the stairs.

How could he just know that and do nothing?

'I have no idea,' Nina says. 'I reckon he has to know something though, because he didn't, like, start spreading rumours of what a psycho I was. And I mean, I was faking a haunting to get to his dad at the time. He was not short of material.'

'I don't think he's a spreading-rumours kind of person,' I say.

But what do I know? He almost had me fooled.

318

My stomach churns.

'I didn't think I was a kiss-the-teacher kind of person. I mean, I'm no Laura Fahy.'

Laura Fahy shifted one of the baby teachers at the debs two years ago. He was a chaperone and she was in college at the time, so people said it was probably grand. Laura Fahy had been arrested twice and gotten the best exam results in the country. People spoke about her as if she weren't mortal, but more like Cú-culainn with balayage. Though maybe me and Nina were stories too, now. The haunted girls. This would just be another weird thing that happened to us. Something else for people to sneer about in their fucking groups.

I shudder, and I wonder exactly what Oz knew. I mean, I doubt his father sat him down and told him everything. And would me keeping quiet like Nina wants be friendship or a weird sort of complicity.

They're coming back into our home.
After what they did
to her.

'Tomorrow is going to be horrible.' I pull the covers tight over my shoulders. Nina's breathing has slowed, become more rhythmic. I think that she is sleeping and I don't want to ask her, to check, in case it wakes her. She's wearing a onesie as pyjamas and it covers everything up.

What other hurts has she been keeping silent?
If she'd told me at the time, what would I have done?

His body pressing hers into the wall.
She felt so helpless,
like she'd no one else.

But she had me.

I wasn't good enough.

His voice so sharp, cutting through her piece by fucking piece in our own kitchen.

He needs to stop.

Somebody needs to stop him.

Black mould on the walls and something watching.

Am I cruel for letting this go on?

I think that I could stop Them. The creatures. If I was more brave. Less selfish.

I stare up at the ceiling till morning comes.

Wondering.

They do not speak to me.

They do not have to.

a hopeless heart

Here we are again, and as we eat breakfast I'm turning over in my head the things that I could do to get the pair of them away from Nina. Fake an illness. Set a fire. Scream. Mould coats the door handles and they will be here soon. I sit here, spiralling. I cannot move. I'm useless. Nina doesn't want me to tell anyone what happened, and I won't. It would be cruel, I think, to do that to her.

I hate the thought of him inside this house.
Looking at the mould,
at parts of me that I have kept concealed.
Looking at Nina.

Nina's looking wrecked as well, but she smiles at me across the table and mouths, 'It's fine.'

I mouth back, 'How?'

She laughs.

She's trying to be strong for you.
She shouldn't have to be.

Susan is oblivious, and hopeful. She ruffles my hair and says that we'll get through this. Like the old Susan. The one I could talk to about anything without wondering what the price would be. How can she look at everything that's happened and think that it could all be fixed by a middle-aged predator and his lying son?

Hope is a funny thing.

If I told her about Nina, would she make it my fault, somehow? For not watching out for her enough. I wonder if it is my fault. Should I have been more vigilant, spotted something, ferreted out the truth relentlessly?

She loved him.

And I know in my bones what it is to love someone that hurts you.

Someone who wants more from you than you can give.

Her hands on my shoulders,
opening me.

I take a sip of strong tea, and gag and spit it back into the cup. The milk has curdled.

'Can we have nothing?' I exclaim, picking it back up and spilling it into the sink and rinsing it and leaving it to air-dry on the rack.

'That was the tidiest meltdown I have ever seen,' Nina says, grinning at me. Her eyes are flicking around though, not meeting mine. I wonder if my knowing makes things worse in a way. I wish I was the kind of person who knew the right things you should do or say.

I smile back, as though I'm not spiralling. 'Hate ghosts, love the planet, right?'

Susan barks a laugh. 'I've trained ye well.'

I wish she knew. I wish we could just stop that man from coming into our home.

I wish I could hurt him like he hurt Nina.

You could.

We could.

The thought comes unbidden but it sticks. I would love for Mr Q to suffer. But if there's anything he can do to stop this thing he could maybe do that first, because otherwise it comes back to me ending this myself. Letting it claim me. Because I think that is the only way. To stop it acting out, let everyone else get back to something like normality.

To save my family.

But . . . if I do that they will not be my family any more. Or I would not be theirs. I would be dangerous.

Nina lifts her hair to roll it into a topknot, and I see mould creeping up the nape of her neck.

The creatures – this – could kill them. Her and Susan.

We could.

I close my eyes.

After the crash – with Mam – there was this lull, this moment. When they were tired. Spent. And I could push them out. And if . . . if something like that could happen again. Then maybe.

Something's forming in my brain.

Something I do not like.

But I don't like any of this really.

The doorbell rings. It's them. I bite my lip hard. Try to distract myself from all this hate. To be calm. To act normal.

It isn't about me.

It is.

I go to Nina, squeeze her shoulder.

And there he is again, Oz Quigley in our kitchen. I glare at him. He pales.

323

He knows I know.

I feel sick. He said he was my friend. And all along he knew
what she had been through. The part that he had played. I go
to the sink and fiddle with the dishes. My head is racing and I
can't focus on anything. The world is rushing all around me,
and I'm not inside it any more. They're reaching out for me.
They almost have me. What can I do?

A rabbit in a trap.

Mr Quigley is acting like he's the boss of all of us again.
He doesn't avoid Nina's gaze, even when he says things like:

'Hello, girls, I'm sorry to hear that things haven't cleared
up. Hopefully we can get to the bottom of this.'

He thinks she's doing this to get his attention.
And part of him likes that.

I didn't think that I could hate him more, but there you are.

Susan takes him through the rooms, and I want to follow,
watch him, make sure he doesn't, like, touch anything. His
eyes on us. This is a private thing. This pain that we are going
through. It doesn't belong to him. Yet here he is.

He knew about my mam.
Susan told him.

That stings harder now. I stay with Nina and we listen to him
as though we're hiding, scared to be found. When I was little, one
of my hiding places was behind the curtains. If I hid my feet and
pressed in tight, the bulk of them would shield me. The thing is,
that only works when you're a certain size, and kids get bigger.

We hear him scraping the mould, to take a sample. He agrees
that it looks bad, and asks Susan if we've got a dehumidifier.
As if the whirring of them wasn't obvious.

What is it with everybody and their dehumidifiers, when They are wrapping hands around Nina's throat, killing something bright in Susan's eyes? Filling me with mould and dreams and fears.

She's telling him about the not-mice now. And he's telling her that they are probably mice. Their voices drift upstairs and I hear Oz Quigley say something.

I can't make out the words.

Daisy. I . . .

'I can't believe him, Nina,' I say.

'Which one?' she asks.

'Either of them really. How dare they be in here? How dare they?'

'It's what they do. We invited them in.' She shrugs. 'It's not going to break me. But stay close, please.'

Susan comes down. 'They want us to leave them alone in the house for a bit,' she says. 'Let's go to Tesco. We can stop for something nice on the way home, take our minds off all of this.' She rubs the side of her face. 'I don't think I've been this tired in ages. Maybe not since you first arrived, Daisy, and neither of you were sleeping well, and your dad was still in hospital so I was always on alert, ready for my phone to go, you know?'

She's acting like she doesn't hate me now, like she's not scared.

I know it is a lie.

A smile spread over screams.

I can make it right though. I can fix it.

Nina reaches out and squeezes my hand.

'I'm fine, Neen. And look, I'm supposed to be minding you.'

325

'Why do you need minding, Nina?' Susan asks. 'Or is that a stupid question?'

'Kind of, Mom,' she says. 'I mean, we're haunted, but also I didn't like the way he spoke to me the last time.'

'It was mean,' I say.

'I'll sit in with you if they do that again,' Susan says. And I say, 'I will too,' and she flashes me a look like I'm sitting in her seat or something.

I want to get things right, but I don't know how.

Oz Quigley comes into the room, and asks if I can give him a hand with some of the equipment.

'Dad's tied up with all the mould,' he says.

'You go help him, Daisy,' Susan tells me. 'Myself and Nina can get the shopping done by ourselves.'

Don't leave me alone with them.

Or do.

'But I thought they needed the house?' I can't look at Oz. Can't stomach who he is.

'It's grand,' Oz says. 'I mean, I don't think you're faking, for what it's worth. That's probably unprofessional to say.'

'You're not professionals.' I tell him.

'Daisy!' Susan says, on her way out the door.

'What? It's true.'

She sighs, the door clicks shut.

They've left me here.
They shouldn't have.

'Sorry about that,' Oz says. 'I just . . . I wondered if we should maybe talk?'

'Why?' I ask him. 'What would be the point?'

His eyes meet mine. I can't. I fix my gaze on his forehead, just above his eyebrows. There's a raw red bump over his left one, like an insect bite or coming spot. He tries again, I feel him searching. I put the shutters down behind my eyes.

You knew.

And now I know.

We can't go back.

His body sort of ripples and shrinks in front of me. I see him realise.

'She told you then?'

'More or less,' I say.

He scuffs at the carpet with his feet. It's full of little particles of mould. Thick and black.

He sighs. 'We shouldn't do this here, he's just –' He walks towards the kitchen, and I follow. Shut the door to close the world out.

'You let me think it was you that had hurt her.' My voice is flat, I'm done. I'm done with him.

'She obviously told you that I had,' he said. 'And, I didn't want to make things any harder for her.'

There is a pause. 'Or us. Or my whole family. I don't know, Daisy, what else could I do?' he says helplessly. 'The damage had been done and . . . he's my dad. He promised to break it off with her, and he did, so I kind of hoped. That maybe that would be it.'

The spot above his eyebrow looks so angry and sore. I wish that he could just have been my friend.

Her hands, my shoulders.

Digging.

327

Digging in.
The closer that they get, the worse it is.
His shoulders and his mouth.
His hands.
His eyes.
There's something wrong with me, and I can't fix it.

'I know it was wrong of him, Daisy.'

'What, to groom a vulnerable student?'

He looks down at our filth. And then he nods.

'Yes. And it makes me sick. I hate him for it, Daisy. But I don't want him and my mom to split up. I don't want him to lose his job and not be able to pay the mortgage. I don't want to not be able to go to college because they can't afford it any more.'

'Are these all things he said to you?' I ask him. 'Like, threats?'

Oz looks miserable. I close my eyes.

Her pain.
Her fear.
Remember.

'Look, Daisy, I know it makes me a bad person, the knowing and not at least reaching out to her, seeing what she needed me to do, but I couldn't put it into words. He hurt me too. And I don't know what a good person does in this situation. Like, now you know – how are you going to fix it? Make it right?'

His voice is low and fumbling but I startle. I have no idea. But how dare he?

'It's funny isn't it? How the further away from you someone is, the less their pain matters? Did it take you long to decide that it was something you could simply live with?'

He winces, like I've shocked him. 'I never . . .'

'Never what?' My voice is sharp with rage.

'Never decided that. I just decided to quietly hate him for it.'

'Well, it must have been nice,' I say, 'to be able to decide that for yourself. To have that power. You know it's illegal, what he did to Nina? It's a crime, Oz.'

'It didn't go that far,' he says.

'Is that what he told you? Well, it went far enough for it to be wrong. For her to feel wrong in her skin. To be in pain.' I can't believe he's defending himself. The nerve of him. This isn't his. It's hers. He has no idea what she went through. What they showed me. I was inside her skin. The ache. The hurt.

'Well, she kept quiet too,' he says, like that absolves him.

He wants to find a way
to keep you
as a friend.

There isn't one.

'She doesn't owe anyone her story,' I tell him. 'But you don't get to let her silence enable your own. Did you even offer to help her? Back her up?'

His hands run through his hair and I can feel the breath catching in his throat. He closes his eyes and counts to five and opens them again.

'Daisy, what was I supposed to do? I was doing my homework, and I went on his laptop to type something up and I downloaded a pdf, and there were these images in recent downloads, and I clicked on one. And there she was. I felt sick.'

329

'It is sick. What he did.' My voice a hiss.

'And he told me she had a crush on him, had been acting out, and sent them to him and he was creeped out but wanted to keep them in case they were needed as evidence, if he had to report her to the school for harassing him. Which he didn't want to do, because she was a troubled girl, and needed support, not punishment.'

'How kind of him,' I say. 'You didn't believe him though.'

'The way he puts things, he can be convincing, but no, Daisy. I didn't believe him, not fully. He was working too hard, you know? I could see the desperation there. But it was easier to act as though I did – convince myself. He was making more of an effort with Mom and she was happy, and then Nina was being haunted, and that kind of made some of the things he'd said more plausible – he's a good liar . . . but also I just didn't want to know. I mean. He's my dad, Daisy.'

'Yeah, you said that already.'

He looks so miserable, and I weirdly feel tears stinging at the back of my eyes. And shame and anger at myself for crying, when I never fucking cry, because I thought he was my friend when he was just covering himself, making sure his family would stay intact. I thought he would be better and he wasn't.

He isn't worth my tears.

Your fury though.

'So you were covering yourself?'

He nods. 'A bit at first. It freaked me out, us coming to your house. But then I got to know you. We were friends.'

'You could never be my friend,' I tell him. 'Not now I know.'

He nods, his shoulders curled towards his feet.

And in spite of myself I feel for him. I think about our bodies on the stairs. How scared he was. How cold.

'I wish I could be there for you,' he tells me 'Nina's lucky to have you on her side.'

Hands that look like mine around her neck.

'Look,' I say, 'we didn't know each other a few months ago. And now we just won't know each other.'

He's wearing a T-shirt. I reach out and touch his forearm.

His father sitting at the dinner table.

He cannot eat.

Revulsion.

Sadness.

Fear.

I meet his eyes.

'He told her that he loved her,' I tell Oz. 'He told her that he loved her but he didn't treat her like he loved her. He saw that she needed a friend, and he found in that an opportunity. He would ask her to meet him at times like this. In houses like ours. Haunted ones.

'He asked for pictures too.

'And then one day it stopped. I would say probably around the time you found out.'

'I already hate him, Daisy.' His voice is fit to break.

'But you love him as well. That's parents for you.' I smile. 'The thing is, it isn't over. She is haunted, and there's going to come a time when she's ready to speak out.'

'What should I have done?' he says. 'Reported him? Like, called the guards?'

'I don't know,' I say. 'More.'

'Oz, come quick!' Mr Quigley's voice booms down the stairs. I follow him up, but turn into my room.

My head is spinning. And I don't know what to do.

I want to hurt him.

Mr Q.

I want for him to pay for what he did.

I press my forehead against my palms and focus on my breathing.

It doesn't work.

Mould creeping up the nape of her neck.

Livid marks around her throat.

She might not survive this, Daisy.

Help her.

You're hurting her even more than he did.

Susan too.

I swallow down. My body's full of tension, energy. I need to do something. I need to move.

To act.

To make him feel afraid.

To make him suffer.

tap

When Susan and Dad were growing up on the farm, there were lots of different things that could go wrong with the herd. Impact the yield. I remember Granny Maude telling me about liver fluke, and being so worried that one would get in me. They're these tiny worms that burrow into snails, and then they turn into these little things that cling to grass or water, and cows take them in and they go into the liver and lay eggs. The cows get sicker and sicker, and their dung is filled with more eggs, which go into more snails if they are there. It keeps on going until you stop it. But the liver fluke isn't trying to hurt the cows or snails. It needs them to survive. When I eat chicken, I don't think about what it looked like when it could breathe. When it was a vibrant, feathered thing. I'm just hungry. But my mind could make that leap, I think. If I focused.

There are things that can't.
They eat, they change, they burrow.
And that means they continue to exist.

There are things that people can do, right, drugs and treatments. Watching, waiting, checking, checking, checking. But it's not in any way a battle of wits, because these things, these things that prey on other creatures, they're inevitable. All you can do is cope.

>*Until you can't.*
>
>*And then, maybe you die.*
>
>*There were times she didn't want to live.*
>
>*Nina.*

I hold my head in our hands as the biggest parasite of all tramps through our house. I hear him muttering to Oz, and I don't care what it costs. I want to hurt him.

>*You can.*
>
>*You will.*

I wonder.

>*Tap*
>
>*Tap*
>
>*Tap*

reflections

I am scared.
Scared of her.
She's shouting and I wish that she would stop.
I'm really thirsty, and it is hard to know what parts of me are
me, with so many voices, so many stories swelling up inside
so loud loud loud, but I know I want her to stop and it to stop
and all of that gets mixed up together somehow and then it
happens.
I wish for her to go.
And then she does.
And it is awful, awful.
But it works.

I wonder if there is a way to make it leave again, without
cramming itself inside of me.

If I could feed it somehow.

Mr Q.
Would it want Mr Q?
Want to hurt him?

Yes.

Could I do that to Oz though?

Yes.

I go into the bathroom and splash water on my face. I look at my reflection.

We both smile.

And then I go to find them.

tap

They're in Nina's bedroom.

Nina's bedroom.

Mr Q's sausage fingers are wrapped around a beeping piece of tech, and Oz is holding a thermometer or something. There is a camera on a tripod set up in the corner of the room, and it makes my stomach jolt at the entitlement of him.

'Shouldn't you be gone?' he says. 'I specifically told Susan . . .'

How dare he!

'I know,' I say, swallowing my rage. 'She was just so stressed that she forgot me. And her phone as well. Is there any chance that you could drop me to them?'

I don't lie but today I will do whatever it takes. To get the creatures out of me. To keep them safe.

My family.

Mr Quigley is stern. A serious ghost-man doing serious ghost things. I smile at him politely.

All his fault.
Her pain.
Her grief.
Her ghosts.

He sighs.

'I'm not a taxi driver, Daisy. We're doing this for your guardian out of the goodness of our hearts.'

I raise an eyebrow at Oz. He looks away.

'I'm so sorry to ask,' I say, 'but obviously I can't drive myself. Being an *underage girl*.'

The mould pulses on the wall, and I feel a shudder pass through all of us.

'It's probably the mould, you know,' Mr Q says. 'Mould can do strange things to people's brains.'

'Can it now?' I say.

Mr Q looks at me, and I can read the desire to leave this place on his face, as clear as a line of text.

He hates it here.

Everyone hates it here.

'Come on so,' he says, jangling his keys.

Oz shuffles behind him.

'Oh, Oz can stay behind,' I say.

Oz looks at me. Mr Quigley is looking at the wall, lost in it.

'No,' he says. 'Oz should come. I don't think I want him here alone.'

He loves his boy.

I falter for a second.

'Maybe I could just wait here. It would probably be fine . . .'

'No, no. Look we could all do with a break from this place. I need a decent coffee anyway. There's that place nearby. Come on.'

We traipse downstairs, and they get into the car while I lock up.

Her body crumpled in the driver's seat.

338

'Can I sit there, Oz?' I ask. 'I get nauseous in the back.'

More lies.

I want him to be safer than his dad is.

'Oh. Okay,' he says, nonplussed.

Mr Q rolls his eyes, and I smile blandly. 'Thanks so much.'

The hum of anger in my stomach. I'm trying to be normal. Focus. Chat.

'So . . . you think it's the mould?' I say to Mr Q.

He nods. 'It's textbook. Black mould causes all kinds of hallucinations. Lots of historical hauntings were probably just mouldy old houses. People's brains can play all kinds of tricks on them. Disturbing stuff. I'd warrant that's what this is. If you got rid of the mould, things would clear up.'

'But it isn't normal mould,' I say. 'It's different. Have you touched it?'

Mr Quigley makes a dismissive sound in his throat, which is a lot easier to do the further away we get from the house.

He knows there's something.

He has felt it.

Felt us.

'The first time we were here, Susan had gotten every kind of tradesman under the sun to look at the place and rule out other causes. She hasn't done that this time. Something has put her off-kilter. And this mould is unusual, but I'm no expert. I mean, our house is very clean.'

We live in filth.

In filth and hate.

I hate him.

I adjust my seatbelt, and I think.

339

He is open.

Take him.

Leave me alone and hurt this man instead.

We're coming up to the roundabout and a van speeds past us, almost clipping the wing mirror.

'Jesus Christ,' says Mr Q. 'Some people have no manners.'

'Yeah,' I say.

I close my eyes.

Tune in.

He took something from Nina's bedroom.

When he was there.

A scrunchie.

He put it to his nose.

It smells of her.

That hair . . .

He is open.

TAKE HIM.

TAKE HIM.

TAKE HIM.

I slide my hands down towards my knees. We're in the car park now. It doesn't work that way. I should have known.

And then something hits the windscreen.

Tap

'What was that?' Mr Q's on edge.

'I think it was a ring pull from a can. That's what it looked like.'

'Oh,' Oz says. 'That's weird. Daisy. I . . .'

And then a lorry very deliberately ploughs into the back of the car.

Bang.

And all I think before it fades to black is, there weren't enough taps.

They did it wrong.

And Oz.

Oh no.

Oh, Oz.

stones and bones

Stiff in our coats and shoes at the removal. I shuffle awkwardly towards the back. Nina grips my hand. Susan has an arm around her shoulder. Mr Q is walking with a crutch. His head is bandaged. I think he's still in hospital, just out for this. There's not a scratch on me. The priest says prayers, and Oz is lying there inside a box. We all line up to shake his mother's hand. His father's too, though part of me recoils.

It all feels wrong.

I tell him I am sorry for his loss, he tells me it is not my fault.

It is.

It is.

He says that I wasn't to know. When I swapped seats with Oz that this would happen. His eyes scanning my face for something all the while.

In the car park
Susan had her phone
to call the ambulance.
He thinks about that sometimes.
Shrugs it off.
You're just a kid.

Like Nina is.

342

Like Oz was.

He has said that at least four times now.

'It is not your fault.'

'We'd never blame you.'

I don't need to listen to them to know he's lying.

He is lost.

He wishes it had been you.

Or him.

Instead.

As well.

His boy.

His little boy.

For him it's worse.

Worse than if he'd died.

Removals are harder than funerals, I think. It's the reality of it hitting you. The body of the person who is dead. Their face, their skin. That waxy sheen. Their gone-ness. I didn't think the coffin would be open, but it is.

I see what I have done.

Oz's hands are crossed in the centre of his chest and his hair is arranged to hide the ruin of his skull. His mother's face was kind. She knew who I was.

'It's nice to put a face to a name,' she said. And then she faltered. 'None of this is nice.'

I said, 'I know.' I told her, 'He was kind. He was my friend.'

And he was.

For a while.

Until I killed him.

Susan's hands on my shoulders now, digging in. Just like hers.

I have been here too long.
Just staring at him.

'Daisy, pet?' she says. 'We need to go.'

Her voice is gentle but there's something awful running through it.

> *She can't look at his face.*
> *She can't stop thinking*
> *what it would be like*
> *to lose a child.*
> *To you.*

They have been quiet in me since Oz died. They are still here, but we can sleep at night. In the car, I should have tried to kick them out of me, but he was dying and I couldn't think of anything but that.

> *I am not safe*
> *to be*
> *to be around.*

I try to visualise the wall inside my brain, but when I reach for it, all I see is his face. The way it was when he was on the stairs, so cold, afraid. Everything is pouring into me and I can't stop it.

> 'Daisy. I . . .'

Megan looks at me from across the coffin. Their face is serious, hard to read. I haven't been replying to their messages. I just. Can't.

> *I keep on hurting people.*
> *Over and over.*
> *Everyone I touch.*

I touch Oz's hand, and remember how cold he was on the

344

stairs. That sense of loneliness and dread I felt. That's what he got. The death that he was left with.

Cold.

Alone.

He didn't deserve that.

The lorry driver blacked out for a second, they think. All he can say is he doesn't remember.

And I did that.

To him.

To Oz.

And Oz's mom looked kind.

She looked like him.

I wouldn't want to hurt her either.

The mould is still on the walls but it hasn't grown thicker, hasn't travelled since.

It's dormant.

I fed it, now it's quiet.

And his dead face will never smile at me again. I'm still mad at him. And Nina's been amazing. She rubs my back. I can't believe she's here. She shook his hand and told him she was sorry for his loss, and he said thank you, and his eyes were far away. Somewhere else.

And maybe it did kill him, in a way.

It did.

It will.

I haven't told anyone about what I've done. It's hard to put in words. I think they know. But I don't want to take the doubt away. To put the guilt of that on Nina. For Susan to know what I am capable of.

I killed him and he was my friend. I killed him.

I've felt so cold since then. His face, so wrong without the life inside.

We leave before they close the coffin lid.

And I will never see his face again.

Megan finds me, and asks if I want to go to their house for a bit. I startle.

'We are friends,' they tell me. 'This is big. I'm here.'

I move back slightly.

Oz's face.

His face.

Daisy. I . . .

They shouldn't be anywhere near me. I am poison.

Nina nudges my elbow. 'You should go,' she says.

'You could come as well, Nina,' Megan says, a little awkwardly.

'I'm sorry, Megan,' I murmur. 'I'm just wiped. I can't.'

'That's okay,' they tell me. 'But you need to remember that we're here, okay? We're here for you, and we love you. You don't need to go through this all alone.'

I do.

The only way.

tap

After the funeral, I sit in my room and watch the mould on the walls, trying to decide whether or not it's moving. Not that it matters. Susan brings me up a cup of tea.

'It was a nice mass.' She smiles at me. 'The priest spoke well.'

I nod, I'm numb, keep staring at the mould, until it looks like the surface of a road, a distant planet.

'It's still there,' I say. 'It isn't going away.'

She nods. 'It's not the kind of thing that does.'

I take a sip. It's hot. It burns my tongue.

Susan puts a hand on my shoulder, and I shudder.

'Sorry, love, my mind was somewhere else. I don't want to put anything else on you – but I have to ask . . . Why were they going to Tesco? Did you . . . did it . . . is there anything I should know about?'

She wants to know
if you did this.

I shake my head. 'It's all my fault. All this. I brought this here. And now he's dead.'

I feel the sting of tears behind my eyes. They can't come out of me. They'd never stop.

347

She sits down and gently takes the cup of tea from my hand, leaves it on the windowsill.

'It will leave a ring,' I say. 'I'll get a coaster.'

'That doesn't matter. Daisy.' She passes me a pillow to hold. 'You know I love you.'

Not all the time.

I nod, because that's what she seems to want me to do. I don't trust myself to speak. I'd only get it wrong, kill whatever's left between us now.

'This situation that we're in – it's not something you intended, and it's not fair. But here we are.'

'They might be gone,' I say.

You know that isn't true.
Why are you lying,
Daisy?

I am desperate.

'They aren't gone,' she tells me. 'Look at the walls. And we saw you last night, creeping.'

'It wasn't me,' I say.

She swallows. 'I know. But if you weren't here, they wouldn't be either.'

I feel her words like a punch in my gut.

What does she want of me?

She wants you gone.
You know she wants you gone.

'Daisy,' she says again. She keeps saying my name like it will soothe me. 'When Fiachra was living with us, I tried so hard. But he kept on trying to get to you. Attack you. He'd reach out his hands . . . and I would try to fight him off. With everything I had.'

The table upside down.
Susan pushing hard against the door.
I'm in the corner
with my little saucepan.
Holding tight.

'And there was no support for me. None. I felt really guilty when he had to leave. I never thought I'd do that to my blood. But if he stayed, somebody was going to get seriously hurt. And I couldn't live with that fear, day in, day out. So I did the hard, right thing. Do you understand what that cost me?'

I shake my head. 'I'm sorry.'

'Daisy, you don't need to apologise. I just want you to understand. I loved you like you were my own by then. You know that, don't you?'

I nod again, don't speak. She keeps on going.

'And when you love someone, when you want to protect them, sometimes that means hurting someone else you love.'

'Like me,' I say.

'I don't want Nina to die.' Susan swallows. 'It's that simple.'

'She won't,' I say.

My hands around her neck.
The taste of mould.

'You don't know that.' She touches the pillow that I'm clutching to me, strokes the fabric gently.

'I do.' My voice is coming out so strange, too high, too quick, like I was so much younger. 'Susan, I do. It was a lorry.'

'Daisy, look at me,' she says. 'I know from looking at you what it was.'

I rub my eyes.

There'd be no point.

'Can I hold you, like when you were small?' she asks.

I crumple in to her.

'Shush now. Shush now.' She strokes my hair and holds me like she loves me.

She smells like mothers should. She smells like home.

'The Nina thing,' I say. 'We –'

'It doesn't matter,' Susan tells me. 'It only matters where we are now. And where we are is this. You need to do the hard, right thing, Daisy. Whatever that is, whatever that costs you.'

'I need to leave,' I say. 'To keep you safe.'

There are tears in her eyes. 'I can't ask that of you,' she says. 'I can't.'

> *But she is.*
> *Asking you to leave.*
> *And not come back.*

I look back at the mould.

I can't make it stop for me, and I don't want to hurt anyone else.

> *She looks at you.*
> *And all she*
> *sees is*
> *your fingers tightening on Nina's neck.*
> *Your face intent.*
> *She couldn't make*
> *you stop.*

'I don't want anybody else to die,' I say, my voice about to crack.

'Me neither,' Susan says. 'But I don't know what more we can do, Daisy. I could take you to the doctor, but I don't think it would do much good.'

I shake my head. 'Me neither.'

'I've been racking and racking my brains because I do not want to let you down. I find myself afraid of you and I hate it, love. I hate it. Should we move house again? Contact a priest? I mean, if there is anything that I can do to help you make this stop, I will do it.'

I need to leave.

She knows it.

And I know it.

'Okay,' I say.

There is no other way.

'Do you remember back when you were little, and I would tell you that I loved you from the top of your head to the tips of your toes?' she asks.

I nod. 'Creatures and all.'

'It's still true,' she says. 'I just wish I was better at it, Daisy.'

'You did okay,' I tell her. 'I mean, I'm bigger now. And stronger, right? I'll manage.'

Oz's eyes seeking mine.

His eyebrows.

And the carpet.

'Sometimes there's no right thing,' I say. 'Just lots of wrong ones.' I put my hand upon her wrist and squeeze.

Her eyes scan my face and her mouth twists desperate into something broken. She opens her arms like a question and I nod. She pulls me close, pushing my head hard towards her neck. Warmth of her skin. The rhythm of her sobs. The smell of home. A chasm yawns inside me.

Shutters down.

Feel nothing.

bang

After Susan leaves, I sit alone on the bed. I let my gaze drift to all the eyes underneath the wall. Black and white and bulging. People think that childhood is a simpler time, but that kind of depends on the childhood, doesn't it? I take a deep breath and I close my eyes.

I deserve this.

I rise, and walk to the mirror in the hall. I am there. I stand there, looking at myself until she doesn't look like me any more, or much of anything. Until everything is just a disconnected collection of shapes. I could be anyone. Any sort of thing. I say the words they want to hear.

I am open.

Take me.

I am open.

Take me.

I am open.

Take me.

This time I mean it. I have nothing left.

His dead face.

The shadow on the stairs.

The trail of blood.

They were telling me.
I didn't listen.

That could so easily be Nina. Susan. Megan. Everyone I touch. It isn't safe. My feet hurt from standing, but I keep on going, whispering it fiercely, again, again. I don't want to hurt anyone. I don't want to hurt any more.

I don't want to be alone.
I am open.
Take me.
I am open.
Take me.

Slowly it comes out of Nina's room, and faces me. Our features meld together.

I close my eyes and open them again, and go downstairs and smile that wide, white smile and eat my dinner.

parasites

There isn't time.

I have a bus ticket to Galway, and then Mayo, and the keys to Granny Maude's house. We haven't been there since I was twelve. I have a backpack full of clothes, and a bag of food to keep me going. I have five hundred euro that I took out of the ATM with Susan's card. Her PIN is Nina's birthday. She brought it up in conversation the other day, casually. Met my eye.

She wanted me to know.

A book.

A change of clothes.

My stupid saucepan.

I have a clamour of voices inside me, hurting me.

But I am listening now.

I have no choice.

She took out the tweezers
last night.
Held them to her skin.
She didn't cut.
She doesn't want

to hurt herself
again.

Oh, Nina, Nina.

I hate to think what this is going to do to her.

I left a note. I kept the wording ambiguous. It could be a more final sort of goodbye. And maybe it will be. The creatures are in me now. We're bound together. I don't know what that means. But I am not alone and I'm not safe. I think of Abigail, Conchur, Piotr, Megan. I don't want to see the earth that they are buried under.

Their dead faces. Last night I asked Susan to speak to Nina more. To maybe look up therapists. She said of course she would. And something passed between us. A sort of recognition.

She wants you gone
but
doesn't want to want that.

I think it would be easier if she could just be cold.

Be dead to me.

Maybe she wants to reassure herself that she's a good person.

I will have no one.

How will I stay alive without the world? I mean, I know that there are ways around things. But how will I buy food and all of that? It's about a thirty-minute walk outside of town, but I can't have people see me. I can only stay there for a while, like a few weeks. After that, I'll have to keep on moving.

You will have us.

I shudder, but there is a comfort in it too. They will not let me die. They need me.

356

I just need to make sure they don't hurt Nina, Susan.
The people that I love.
That has to stop.

I ask the taxi to drop me off at Dad's. I want to see him. I'm very aware this will be the last place that I'm seen before I go. And that he has a history of hurting me.

Maybe I deserve to be hurt.

Phil, his carer, greets me at the gate on her way out.

She drank a bottle of wine last night.
Thought about tomorrow,
opened a second.

I shake my head, but I can't really tune Them out any more. It's like the music in a shop, I've no control over it. They're just there, all the time. I don't have to touch, or reach or work to feel Them in my brain and in my blood.

Bubbling.
Hissing.
Humming.

Us together.

with you always

I knock on the door of Dad's little flat. He opens it. He looks well, he's showered, freshly shaven. The buttons are all done up on his shirt. He's wearing the jumper Susan got him for his birthday. She probably put my name on the card.

A lie.

'Daisy.' He rubs his head, the bald spot at the back. 'I knew you'd be here some time soon. Come in.'

I'm not sure that I want to, or why I even came. I move my mouth into a simulacrum of a smile and he smiles back. I wait for him to hate me.

'Hi, Dad,' I say awkwardly. 'How's it going?'

'Ah sure,' he says, gesturing towards the kitchen-cum-living room. 'You know yourself. I . . . I haven't had the easiest week.'

He shrugs, and brushes something I can't see off his stomach.

'Me neither,' I say, following inside.

He shuts the door, and I'm alone with him.

His face all purple.

Susan pushing him away from me.

'I heard about your friend,' he mumbles. His eyes are so bloodshot that the blue of them looks almost neon. I swallow.

Waiting for him to start shouting at me. He's standing between me and the way out.

If he really wants to,
he will hurt me.

I can't read his body or his face.

'I'm sorry,' he says.

'Thanks,' I say, my voice almost a whisper.

'Why is your voice doing that? Are you scared?' he asks. 'Of me?'

I try to shake my head. He looks so sad.

I don't have room for him.
I'm scared of me.
Of us.

'I wouldn't blame you, Daisy.' His voice is coming out faster and less haltingly than normal. And he's telling me that he's sorry, he's so sorry, for what he's done, for everything, for all of it, and I can't even make out the words, they're fading in and out, and I don't understand what he is saying.

'. . . I'm so, so sorry, Daisy. I wanted. I wanted to be able to hold Them off for longer. But I couldn't . . .'

Tears are flowing down his cheeks.

'I know They're in you. I felt Them leave the other night.' He bangs his hands against his head. 'I shouldn't be crying. You're the one in trouble. It's my fault . . .'

He felt Them leave.

'Who do you mean by Them?' I ask.

'*Them,*' he says. 'From me to you.'

His head is in his hands and I don't know what that means. What is he saying?

My voice is a squeak like mice that aren't mice. 'Dad?'

'. . . and I was so angry. I was so angry, Daisy . . .'

He gestures to a hole in the plaster. I look down at his hand, the knuckles grazed.

I brace myself. Look at the door I came in. How far away it is. I haven't been alone with him in years.

Am I safe?

You were never safe.

'I didn't have a choice,' I say. 'I have to –'

'No,' he says. 'I'm not getting it right. I'm not angry with you, I'm angry with *her*.'

'With Susan?'

'Yes,' he says, stabbing his finger in the air. 'Yes. With her. She . . . she was supposed to take care of you. I had to be away from you, you see.'

I'm trying to make sense of what I'm hearing but it doesn't track.

'You kept trying to hurt me, Dad.'

'No. *They* did. They were trying to get to you, always, always. And I couldn't hold them back. Not every time. It was confusing, Daisy. I don't work the way I did before. My brain . . . it's not . . . so it was hard to know sometimes. I thought it was the accident at first. And then I heard Them, saying things to me . . .'

He hangs his head.

'. . . things I don't like to think about. I'm sorry.'

'Wait. Wait. Dad. I still don't understand.'

What is he saying?

He sits up straight again and looks at me.

360

'I'm bad at words. Look.' He puts his hands on his knees. 'When we had the car crash, the thing in you kind of fell out a bit. Away from you. Maybe because Therese died, or maybe from the shock you got. Something happened. And I felt Them go into me. And They still reached for you. But you did something. Didn't let Them back.'

Beside her hospital bed.

I am closed.

Leave me.

'. . . so They went in me, to be beside you, getting stronger and They would keep trying. And the accident, my head. That stuff was real. The hurt. I had to listen to Them, always, always, all the time, and I was tired but I kept Them there inside my head. I found a way to do it because if They got out, They would get to you . . .'

They got to me.

'Because I am the parent and you are the kid, and you'd been through enough. I kept on trying, but I would get angry that I had to and scared for what might happen and it would get mixed up whenever you were there . . . but They didn't get you. For ages They didn't, Daisy. And I was so afraid.'

'Dad?' I don't even know what I'm asking.

'This past while, I didn't want you here because I could feel Them getting stronger. Ready to pounce. And last night . . . I can't hear Them at all now. But you. You can hear Them. The creatures.'

My eyes feel hot. I don't know what to say. I can't. I can't.

'I see it. They are in you.' He pulls his jumper down over his waistband and clicks the kettle on. 'Tea?'

I wish I'd never come here. I don't want to be inside this room. This life.

He didn't want to hurt me.

But he hurt me. Over and over and over again. Didn't he?

'The stuff with Mam, that was real, wasn't it?' I ask. 'That wasn't . . . Them as well?' I swallow.

I don't know what I am hoping for.

He shakes his head.

'Your mother wasn't well, Daisy. I didn't see it until it was too late. I trusted her to know what was best for you, but she was stretched too thin, she wasn't strong enough to be with people. I don't know what came first, the creatures or the way she was with you. Before she died, I was planning to leave her and take you with me. I think she knew. The way that she was driving . . .'

Her knuckles on the wheel.

Her ragged breath.

'I didn't . . .' I don't know what to say. I let it hang.

'I never said it, because you were young and she was gone and I didn't want to tarnish her memory.'

Hands wrapped around a mug.

Eyes fixed on mine,

waiting to hear what I had gotten wrong.

It was something.

Always something with me.

'So you, like, didn't hate me?' It comes out weird, like I'm asking him if he's a wizard or something.

'Never.' He shakes his head. 'I wanted to protect you. And I managed to protect you.' A rueful smile, a flash of who he was before. 'For a time.'

'Nine years, Dad,' I say. 'You did all right.'

He hands me a cup of milky tea. It's perfect.

I say, 'Thank you.'

'What are you going to do?' he asks.

I bite my lip. 'I have to go. It isn't safe. When I'm like this. With them.'

He nods his head. 'I get it.'

'I'll be okay,' I say. 'I don't think they'll let anything bad happen to me. I'm, like, their home. Or something.'

'Does Susan know?' He looks at me, but it's like he's looking out the window, far away.

My voice comes out a whisper, but I tell him. 'She's worried I'll kill Nina. Or not me. Them. The creatures.' I look down at my hands.

His voice is flat. 'And is she right to worry?'

I swallow, whisper, 'Maybe.'

'That's a lot,' he says. 'You're only a kid.'

'I'll be okay,' I say.

He goes over to his shelf and takes an envelope from a pile of old bits of paper and brochures.

'You take this.'

I look. It's full of money.

'To tide you over.'

I hand it back. 'I already . . .'

He closes my fingers around it. 'There are so many times I haven't been there for you, and other times I couldn't be. This is a small way I can be there for you. Now, when you need me.'

'Oh, Dad,' I say. I take the money, stuff it in my pocket.

You will need it.

He takes a gulp of tea. I can see the edge of the bag floating in his cup. He drinks it dreadful.

'What was it like?' I ask. 'With them buzzing all those years?'

He shakes his head. 'Not great. You work out tricks though. Hot cloth on my eyes helped with the headaches. Songs with lyrics helped me to tune Them out, just a bit, but enough to get stuff done. You mother had a lovely voice, Daisy. She used to sing to you, and you would kick your little leggies up and down in the high chair, or jiggle around the floor in your vest and nappy. There was a time . . . before all this, you know, when you were loved the right way. When we were a proper family.'

Her face, her voice
a rope around my neck

I'm not so sure.

'My bus leaves in an hour,' I say. 'I've got to go.'

'You have my number,' he says. 'I'm your father, Daisy. And I want to know that you are safe. I can't do much. But I can care about you.'

'That's enough,' I say.

He shakes his head. 'It isn't. But it will have to be. For now.'

'For now,' I say.

He walks me to the door.

'Goodbye, Dad.'

'You'll catch a cold,' he says. 'Take this.'

He passes me his scarf. It's grey not blue.

He wants to keep me warm.

I screw my eyes shut, throw my arms around him.

'You hate hugs,' he says.

I say, 'I do.'

a presence felt

It's all in fragments now. The bus clamours with everything that people are going through.

Her mother's dying and she wants to make full sure she inherits the house.

I watch the scenery unfold behind me. I rummage for my phone, remember that I binned it in the train station. Just before I did, I got a message from Megan.

Are you okay
What do you need?
I'm here

It made me smile.

I'm doing the right thing.

He didn't delete the video.

There's a part of me that wants to stay tethered to the world. My friends. My life. I need to keep them safe more than I need to keep them with me. Two people are dead. It could be more. And more. They wouldn't care.

She took their phone charger the last time she was babysitting.

It was an accident but she's not going to give it back.
It would be too awkward and having a spare is handy.
I worry about Nina. I'm the only person that she's told. About it all. And she needs people she can trust right now. I'm scared me leaving will be dangerous for her. I didn't leave her, like, a note or anything. I couldn't put it into words

She wants for things to change.
She will tell Susan.

I barely have time to process that before someone else is nudging at my brain.

He likes knowing
she's out there
wondering why.

Leaving was the best thing so, for everyone. But maybe there's a way for me to be in the world without hurting anybody. I mean, They left me once. Why not again?

Never again.
But people will come looking.

And I am strong.

I might not have a future.
But I want one.

And maybe there will come a time when I'm able to break free of Them, when They are weak, or tired, and I can build a wall inside myself to keep Them in, or find the strength to push Them fully out. I mean, eight years. That isn't bad. If I only got half of that again, it would be something.

No wall.
No wall.

She's fairly sure he's hitting her.
But she's not going to say anything.
It's none of her business.

And in the meantime, I can practise pushing everything that's closest to me far away. I press a hand to the windowpane, and the whorls of my fingerprints look like the patterns that frost leaves. There are people who care about me. And I care about them. So much. Too much to want to be near them when I'm like this. This is the way it has to be. For now.

He hasn't told them quite how sick he is.
He doesn't want it to be real just yet.

The sun is setting, and the sky is getting greyer and greyer. It will be night when I arrive there.

Susan used to always say, 'I'll pick you up, if anything happens. Just you call me.'

He'll never find out about it.
She'll take it to her grave.

And now I have to find my way to this place. I haven't been there since I was very small.

What if the keys don't work?

I keep thinking of scenarios where I would need help, and how there is no help, no one to call. What will I do when the money runs out? How will I get food? The electricity and stuff will be fine. Like, I'll manage. There was an honesty box we used to visit a few farms over – if it's still there – and I could get eggs and vegetables and stuff. Milk as well.

I'll work it out.
I've lived through things that other people couldn't.

And They need me to be here. Alive. I roll my fingers against my temples. And wish I had my phone, something on. Distract me from the clamour. Everyone. I amn't even touching them, these people. They're crowding me. They're all inside my head. Too much. Too much.

They need to give him their passwords.
Otherwise how can he even trust them?

I'll find a way I suppose. To manage. People do. Dad did. I did before.

It will be hard. But I have a feeling They won't let me get too badly hurt, if it comes to that.

They need a place to live. A haunted house.

He always fucking does this.
She will kill him.
Literally, kill him.

I wonder if anyone has missed me yet. It would be a bit soon for them to notice. Like, I'm only just gone. It might be a day or two before it trickles into school. Nina might know. I wonder if she'll tell from Susan's face. They'll have to report it.

That I'm the kind of gone that won't come back.

I feel like I'm a ghost. I look down at my hands and imagine them becoming translucent. My skin dissolving, blending into air. They'll speak about me as though I am dead. And in some ways, I am.

I slouch my shoulders, hat pulled low and eyes fixed on my bag.

Maybe it will get easier. With practice.

She wishes she'd never had kids.
She'd be better off.

And so would they.

So many people and their problems. I look out the window at the changing landscape. Sheep in fields. I curl around my bag and close my eyes.

When I open them again I'm in the middle of the bus, having a conversation with a woman who looks to be about Susan's age. I don't know what I've said. Or what I'm saying. The voice. It isn't mine. It sounds like Them.

It's okay,
we tell her.
It's okay.
Give me your pain.
I'll hold it for a while.

She takes my hand and squeezes it. I look at the twist of her face. The wobble of her mouth. Her nose is running. She takes a bracelet from around her wrist. Closes my hand around it. With the other hand, I touch my mouth.

We're smiling.

Back in my seat, I dig my fingers deep against my knees and focus on a day, when I can say,

I am closed.

Leave me.

And be heard. They are in me but They're not me. I was here first. And I will be here longest. I stroke my hand along my own skin and feel a shiver.

Someone else's touch.

When I arrive at Granny Maude's, it's fully dark. The sky is bright with stars. They say there are too many to count, but

369

they're so clearly spaced here, I reckon if I stood still, looking up for long enough, I could make a good go of it anyway.

How much of me is even me right now?

How much is them?

There is a Tesco delivery waiting in the porch, and on the hall table a folder with instructions on how to light the fire, use the oven and the honesty box the next farm over. I flick through them, and I hear Susan's voice.

She's minding me.

I empty the bags. Lots of tins of things, and rice and pasta. I stack them neatly. I worry at first about putting the lights on, but the house can't be seen from the road, so I pull the blinds and just get on with it. It smells different to how it used to smell, of cleaning products. The beds are made, but they feel cold and dusty, so I wrap myself in the biggest duvet I can find and curl up on the couch with the TV on. I eat a bowl of cereal. I know I shouldn't get too comfortable. But there is comfort in a place to hide. To plan next steps.

Together.

The girl is looking directly at you. Her hair is scraped back from her face and she is wearing a soft blue jumper. 'Eight weeks ago my cousin – who was like a sister to me – went missing,' she says. 'It was in the aftermath of the loss of a friend of hers.'

She pauses. There are pictures stuck on her walls of her cousin Daisy. Printed out maps, and little Post-it notes. You cannot read exactly what they say.

'I feel weird talking about him. We never got the chance to get along. And we probably wouldn't be friendly if he were alive, considering . . . the things I've told the school . . . not about him.'

She scratches the back of her head and plays with a pencil on her nightstand.

'There's been a whole lot going on. And Daisy. She would want to be there for me. I think that she might think that going away is being there for me. Showing up by not showing up, or something. My mother isn't telling me everything. I know by her, she's keeping something back. And I don't know if that means that she thinks that Daisy's dead, like everyone else seems to, or if she knows something that we don't know.'

She grins, abashed.

'I want to be there for her the same way that she was for me.' She rubs her hands against her throat. 'Sometimes I can still feel their fingers here. And I wake up choking on the air, like I've forgotten what it is to breathe. I can't relax. And I am frightened, all the time I'm frightened. But I'm here. I'm here. I want to stay. And I want her to stay . . .' Her gaze drifts out the doorway.

'I'm probably telling you all too much. But once I started telling the truth, I kind of got a taste for it, you know? It's satisfying. I was targeted by someone older and more powerful. And it ate me up. I thought I had no choice but to do what he wanted. And maybe at the time I didn't really. But I have more choices now. Or maybe they were always there, and now I'm able to see them or something.'

She swallows.

'And I want more choices for Daisy too. Some people think I'm a terrible person for talking about this when his son's just died. And when Daisy's missing, as though lots of things can't be horrible and true at once. But Daisy would want me to tell the truth, I think. Feel free to get in touch if you disagree, Daisy. I'm rambling, amn't I? Basically, I have no way of contacting you, but I'm trying to find one. And I'm looking for you. And I love you. And I'm not going to stop looking for you. Or loving you. Okay?'

'You believed me before you even knew what you were believing. And I will not accept that you are gone. I just won't. And there are ways to keep you safe. There are. I just haven't found them yet. But I will find them.'

She shows you Daisy's photograph.

'This is Daisy. She was last seen boarding a bus to Galway. We thought she might be in Mayo, but when they went to search, there was no trace. If you've seen her, or think you've seen her, please get in touch. We love her and we miss her very much, even if she's not herself right now, and we're going to keep looking for as long as it takes.'

She smiles, and wipes her eyes.

'There's a link in my bio to more information about Daisy's disappearance, and some photos and videos of her to get a sense of what she looks like moving. Please like and share our posts about Daisy. We want to make sure that as many people as possible recognise her so we can get her home safely to us.'

She reaches towards you, the wall behind her head is very clean.

You check the view count. Twenty-five. But you are one of them. You go back. Pause it.

She is looking for you. And she loves you.

I am closed. Leave me.
I am closed. Leave me.
I am closed. Leave me.
I am closed. Leave me.
I am closed. Leave me.
I am closed. Leave me.
I am closed. Leave me.
I am closed. Leave me.
I am closed. Leave me.
I am closed. Leave me.
I am closed. Leave me.
I am closed. Leave me.
I am closed. Leave me.
I am closed. Leave me.
I am closed. Leave me.
I am closed. Leave me.
I am closed. Leave me.
I am closed. Leave me.
I am closed. Leave me.
I am closed. Leave me.
Leave me.
Leave me.
Leave me.

Acknowledgements

This book would not have been written without my agent, Clare Wallace. I'm so grateful to her, and to Sheila David, Chloe Davis and all at Darley for their support and encouragement. It means the world.

This is the third book I've worked on with Georgia Murray now, and every time her skill and insight astound me and I feel I emerge a better writer. I'm so grateful for that, and to the magnificent Talya Baker, whose keen eye and kind heart have challenged and buoyed me through three novels now. What a joy it is to work with them.

I'd like to thank all at Hot Key, Anna Bowles for 'split' vs. 'spilt' and a whole lot more, Jessica Webb for kind words that got back to me, Isobel Taylor for spooky stories and magic tote bags at YALC, Eleanor Rose for impeccable organisation and compassion, Amber Ivatt and Emma Quick for finding ways to bring my ghosts into the light. I'm always so struck by how hard everyone works and I'm glad my books are your books too.

Huge appreciation is also due to Melanie Conroy and Easypress for speedy and clear-eyed typesetting.

The cover art is from an amazing illustrator called Corey